A WORLD WHERE
WOMEN ARE FEMS.
AND FEMS ARE NOT HUMAN.

DarkDreamer pushed her face against the wet earth.

"Eat," he said.

Alldera bit at the mud, coughed.

"What's the lesson?" he asked.

"The master is always the master, and he does as he pleases according to his will," she mumbled.

But in her heart she knew differently . . . she and the other rebel fems who were planning revenge!

WALK TO THE END OF THE WORLD

Suzy McKee Charnas

"For too long science fiction has been dominated by masculine/sexist writing, but in recent years a group of women writers has been bringing new life and maturity into the field. These women are explicit and committed feminists. We're proud to be among them."

—JOANNA RUSS

—SUZY McKEE CHARNAS

Suzy McKee Charnas

Walk to the End of the World

A BERKLEY BOOK
published by
BERKLEY PUBLISHING CORPORATION

WALK TO THE END OF THE WORLD

A Berkley Book / published by arrangement with
the author

PRINTING HISTORY
Ballantine edition published 1974
Berkley edition / October 1978

For information address: Berkley Publishing Corporation,
200 Madison Avenue, New York, New York 10016.

ISBN: 0-425-04239-1

A BERKLEY BOOK® TM 757,375

PRINTED IN THE UNITED STATES OF AMERICA

To Stephen

The HOLDFAST

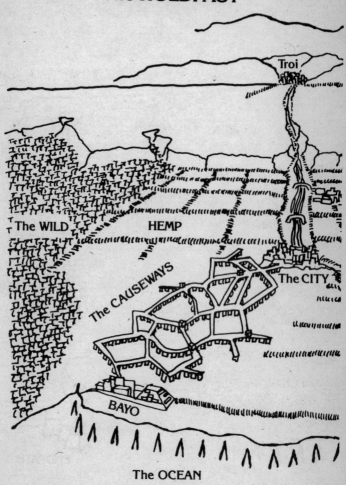

Troi

The WILD

HEMP

The CAUSEWAYS

The CITY

BAYO

The OCEAN

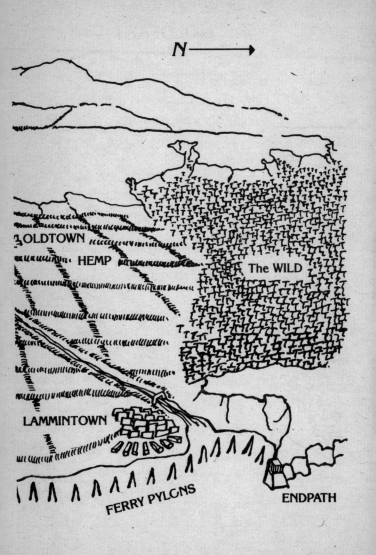

N ⟶

OLDTOWN

HEMP

The WILD

LAMMINTOWN

FERRY PYLONS

ENDPATH

PROLOGUE

The predicted cataclysm, the Wasting, has come and—it seems—gone: pollution, exhaustion and inevitable wars among swollen, impoverished populations have devastated the world, leaving it to the wild weeds. Who has survived?

A handful of high officials had access to shelters established against enemy attack. Some of them thought to bring women with them. Women had not been part of the desperate government of the times; they had resigned or had been pushed out as idealists or hysterics. As the world outside withered and blackened, the men thought they saw reproach in the whitened faces of the women they had saved and thought they heard accusation in the women's voices. Many of these women had lost children in the holocaust.

The men did not notice their own shocked faces and raw voices. They had acted, they thought, responsibly, rightly—and had lost everything. They did not realize they had lost their sanity, too.

They forbade all women to attend meetings and told them to keep their eyes lowered and their mouths shut and to mind their own business, which was reproduction.

Among themselves, most of the women thought as women were taught to think: it would be proper and a relief to think of nothing but babies any more, and while the men were crazy with grief, guilt and helplessness it was support they needed, not antagonism. These women said to one another, let's do what they say for now.

A few objected, saying, no, these men will enslave us if we let them; no one is left to be their slaves except us! They tried to convince the others.

The men heard, and they rejoiced to find an enemy they could conquer at last. One night, as planned, they pulled all the women from sleep, herded them together, and harangued them, saying, remember that you caused the Wasting. It was a Black female's refusal to sit in the back of the bus that sparked the rebellion of the Blacks; female Gooks fought against our troops in the Eastern Wars; female terrorists made bombs side by side with our own rebel sons, whose mothers had brought them up to be half-men; female vermin of all kinds spewed out millions of young to steal our food-supplies and our living space! Females themselves brought on the Wasting of the world!

And the men, armed with staves and straps, reminded them and saw to it that these things were not forgotten again.

It is their male descendants who emerge from the Refuge to find the world scoured of animal life and beggared of resources. They continue the heroic, pioneering tradition of their kind: they kill the few wretched mutants who have persisted outside and clear the spiky brush from a strip of river-valley and seacoast where they establish a new civilization. They call their land the Holdfast, after the anchoring tendril by which seaweed clings to the rocks against the pull of the current.

Seaweed is an important source of nourishment to these new men; so is the hardy hemp plant, a noxious weed to the Ancients but now a staple crop that furnishes fiber, a vision-giving drug, and, because the new men are of necessity ingenious, food. Bricks are made from earth; machine graveyards are mined for metal; a vein of soft and greasy coal yields fuel; wood is brought from the low and thorny forests of the Wild beyond the Holdfast's borders. Nothing is abundant, but men live. They have not completely forgotten technology or culture, and they adapt what they can.

What else do they remember? They remember the evil races whose red skins, brown skins, yellow skins, black skins, skins all the colors of fresh-turned earth marked them as mere treacherous imitations of men, who are white; youths who repudiated their fathers' ways; animals that raided men's crops and waylaid and killed men in the wild places of the world; and most of all the men's own cunning, greedy females. Those were the rebels who caused the downfall of men's righteous rule: men call them "unmen." Of all the unmen, only females and their young remain, still the enemies of men.

CAPTAIN KELMZ

_____

———————— I ————————

In an alley of the silent Pennelton compound in Lammintown, a man waited, his hands tucked into his sleeves against the night's chill. He was a Rover Captain in full uniform under his disguise of blanks. He stood alone in the shadow of a doorway.

Most of the lamps fixed to the corners of the buildings had been smashed. By the light of one that still burned he could discern obscene and insulting figures scratched into the granite walls. The Pennelton Company was assigned away south this five-year, and young men of other Lammintown companies had turned the empty compound into a temporary skidro. He had followed a group of wild lads down here, seekers of illicit pleasures.

The one whose services they had hired tonight was the one he was after: d Layo the DarkDreamer, a young man too, but of no company, no order, and no legitimate use to his fellows.

Heavy-muscled, smooth-moving, a tawny-colored night-slinker, a prowling predator with a broad, blunt-

nosed face and wide-curling mouth, d Layo padded
before his mind's eye. D Layo really did look like that,
though it wasn't manly for the captain to think of even
such a corrupt man as an actual beast.

The Lammintown trumpets brayed, as they did every
quarter-hour. The captain began silently reciting the
Chant Protective, to drive away visions. The chant
opened with a reckoning of the size and reach of the
Holdfast and of all the fellowship of men living in it; not a
great or impressive tally, but it served to remind a man of
his brothers and of what they expected from him.

The Holdfast was a strip of plain bisected by a river. A
good runner could cross the plain north-to-south at its
widest point in three days or run the length of the river
from the coast to 'Troi in seven. The river descended from
'Troi on the high inland plateau. Further east, the City
overlooked the river's fork: the southern branch reached
down over the flats to Bayo; the northern branch emptied
in Lammintown under the pale cliffs. There were the
holdings of men—bastions of order, clear-thinking and
will—to which the rest of the world one day would be
added again.

But not, the captain thought morosely, if the
Reconquest depended on men like himself. He let the
chant drop. It wasn't because he stood alone in the dark
that he saw beast-ghosts, though darkness encouraged
such lapses in the manliest of men. At night the earth
could be felt stretching away on all sides, its vast stillness
stirred only by the currents of wind and water. The mind,
shrinking from such expanses of emptiness, tended to
supply populations of spirits.

However, the captain's personal vice was to envision
other men—even decent, manly men—in beast shapes.
Not many benefits derived from the Wasting that had
turned the world into scrub-desert; the extinction of all
creatures lower than man was one. To think of the beasts
was like willfully calling up the ghosts of dead enemies.

He glanced up at the sky, hoping the DarkDreamer

would come out before moonrise. The moon was the ally of brutes like d Layo. The captain, without his usual complement of Rovers, had no allies.

Trumpets blared; a pot shattered somewhere along the stone-paved streets. D Layo emerged from a narrow passage between two buildings. He was alone and seemed to be in a state of mild dreaming-shock, for he veered as he walked and ran one hand along the wall for guidance. Not many DarkDreamers would venture out still dream-dazed; but d Layo was reputed to be a rash young man.

The captain had the urge to clear his throat of the tightness that commonly afflicted him just before a clash. He waited until d Layo had meandered past. Then he sprang at him, clamping a forearm across the Dark-Dreamer's throat and a leg around his legs to prevent him from kicking, and he threw himself and his captive backward seeking to brace his own shoulders against a wall.

The DarkDreamer plunged like the ocean; he seemed to have no fear at all. He flung himself and the captain headlong across the alley so that both their heads smacked against the opposite wall. The captain grunted and tightened his grip. He scrabbled for a foothold on the cobbles and used his weight to hurl the DarkDreamer down with force. D Layo's head glanced against stone; he made a muffled sound and went slack.

Kneeling on the DarkDreamer's back, the captain glanced quickly around. There was no one. He thought longingly of the knife sheathed on his thigh. It would be gratifying to carry out his original assignment and simply kill this brute.

Instead, he took hold of d Layo's thick hair and pulled his head up. "A Senior wants to talk with you," he said to the blank, handsome face.

D Layo groaned. The groan turned into hiccups. There was the sweet scent of manna, the dreaming-drug, on his breath.

In a harsh whisper, the captain repeated his message.

Then he got up and stepped clear. He felt exhausted. This sort of work was better done in the bright, clean light of the sun, and by younger men.

D Layo sat up. He rubbed at his face and held up his hand to see if there was blood. A thick, compartmented bracelet of metal slid down his lifted arm, glinting. He said, unsteadily, "Are you the cunningcock that's been sniffing after me for the past two months? To give me that message?"

"Until last week, my orders were different," the captain growled.

"You're Captain Helms, aren't you?"

"Rover Captain Kelmz, of Hemaway Company."

"Ah." D Layo got up, making ineffectual brushing-off motions with both hands. There was some blood; in the feeble lamplight, the captain could see the dark line weaving down around the socket of d Layo's eye. "Tell your Senior to meet me on the beach, in the sheds. Only one is in operation; tell him to follow his nose."

"No. You're to come with me to meet him."

"Hell-ums," d Layo crooned, putting an irritating softness into his speech, "be rational. You don't need my cooperation to kill me, but you do need it to talk with me. So we'll do this my way—unless you feel like another round?"

The captain did not feel like another round. He felt worn out and heavy in the hands.

"It's a let-down, I know," the DarkDreamer added, "after you've tagged along behind me all this time hoping for a taste of my blood. Forget it, Hell-ums. You have managed to cause me a good deal of inconvenience recently; settle for that." The dreaming-shock was gone now. D Layo's voice was as the captain had first overheard it months ago: light, lazy, and sweet with malice. "You may have another chance to kill me sometime, cheer up. By the way, which of my many good friends told you where to find me tonight?"

"Go eat femshit."

D Layo laughed.

• • •

Lammintown was a storm-battered, cold-gnawed place, "rock on rock" its men said, boasting of their halls made of blocks hewn from the cliffs. They said that Lammintown men carried the Holdfast on their tough shoulders because no one could survive without the harvests of long kelps, called lammins, from the bay.

There was an edginess in Lammintown these days. For several seasons and more noticeably this past summer the lammin-take had been alarmingly scant. The Lammintown Juniors who had charge of the offshore waters this five-year blamed the moon's influence over the shifting currents of the sea. They claimed that unusually warm water had impeded the maturing of the young kelps. But the Seniors maintained that the young men had mistimed the placing of rocks on the bay floor during the previous autumn, so that the new lammin spores had found no footholds and had died or drifted elsewhere. This crop failure came on top of a long series of economic setbacks in the Holdfast.

Seniors had begun turning up on the work-turfs of the Juniors without warning, hoping to catch them in the act of stealing portions of the scarce harvest for themselves. These Seniors came with escorts of Rovers, often dispensing with the formality of bringing officers to command them. Rovers were powerful defenders of the Seniors and their interests, but they were hard to control, and most Seniors were not skilled in handling them personally.

There had been incidents, and rumors.

The young men of 'Ware Company, whose work-turf that five-year was the whole waterfront complex of lammin-works, had grown more and more restive. Between their resentment and the suspicion of the Seniors, a moonlit night was hardly the time for prudent men to venture into the sheds of Lammintown beach.

To keep the heat under the vats high without tending

all night the wall-mats of the shed had been rolled down and secured. The waiting men were confined with the bitter stink of boiling lammin and the roaring of the furnaces under the two working vats.

A brace of Rovers, under Kelmz' command, flanked the Senior whom they escorted. They were nervous in this strange atmosphere, but they would answer to Kelmz' voice and hands. The Senior himself looked no different here than he looked when at ease in his home-compound in the City. He stood with his stumpy legs planted apart, his hands folded neatly on his belly. Despite the heat, he hadn't even bothered to draw the starched folds of his mantle down from around his neck and shoulders. His round, balding head was tilted back.

High above them, a network of taut, heavy ropes webbed the mouths of the vats. Two young men ran barefoot over the lines, flickering like visions. Now and then one of them would pause for an instant to cast a wide and measuring glance over the heaving surface of the "soup" they tended. The metal hooks they carried swung gleaming from each hand. Their skins were sweat-bright and smudged with smoke. They shaved themselves hairless to keep the soup clean, and they wore only shorts. The hooks, part of their balance, hung as naturally from their hands as fingers from the captain's own. "Lose your footing and lose the soup," warned the work-chants of the sheds.

It was unarguably the dirtiest work men had to do in the Holdfast. Periodically, proposals were made to turn it over to fems instead, but this phase of the processing of a staple of men's diet was considered too important to be entrusted to fems. Besides, attachment to the sheds for a time was a handy punishment for insolent young men. Only one of the pair now running wore the 'Ware Company sign, sewn to the hip of his shorts. The other wore no emblem and was doing time.

Hooks smacked suddenly into the heavily wrapped handle of one of the vat-ladles. The runner's body arced out in a leap from one line to another, by its weight and momentum turning the ladle in the soup. The captain looked hastily away. It made his stomach lurch to see one of those gleaming bodies suspended in the steaming air, like a beast that in Ancient times had leaped in the branches of tall trees . . .

The Rovers stirred uneasily: d Layo had entered the shed. He must have somehow bought himself the freedom of the 'Wares' work-turf, for the runners never even bothered to look down. That was the worst of brutes like d Layo, they corrupted others.

"Servan," said the Senior, projecting his voice above the roar of the furnaces without actually shouting, "where can we talk?"

"Right here, Senior," the DarkDreamer replied. "It's safe. The patrols keep the beach clear at night now, and the lads up there can't hear us." He sat down on the lid of a fuel-box and patted the space beside him.

The Hemaway Senior stood where he was and took a deep, deliberate breath.

"Now, Senior—Bajerman, is it?" d Layo said, before his breath could be expelled in speech. "It's been some time since our last meeting. Oh, please, let's have no apologies over all that, the past is the past. In the interests of brotherly harmony, let's comport ourselves like men newly met. You don't mind the suggestion coming from a younger man, I hope." He beamed amiably. The Senior ignored his impudence, and d Layo went smoothly on, "Now, what can this humble young man do for so great a Senior? Nothing too strenuous, I hope? Your messenger found me at an awkward time; I'm all dreamed out for the moment."

"It's not d Layo the DarkDreamer I've come to see," the Senior said calmly.

"Servan the outlaw, then?"

The Senior said, "You romanticize yourself."

"Which laws do you want broken, Senior?" d Layo smiled. "It must be very important for you Seniors to give up wanting my blood and start negotiating for my services."

"Some laws must be bent, so that they may spring back

into firmer shape than before."

"I hope," d Layo said piously, "that the years will bring me wisdom as great as your own."

Knowing things that were not his business had never brought the captain anything but trouble. He withdrew into his own thoughts, yet kept alert. An officer's eyes were trained to be ceaselessly on the move. His success depended on his ability to notice and counteract any inadvertant cues that might set his Rovers off, especially in unfamiliar surroundings.

D Layo and the Senior could arouse the Rovers themselves with harsh tones or sharp gestures; but they weren't arguing. Far from it. The DarkDreamer teased and mocked with both voice and gestures. The Senior sat back stiffly, resisting; again and again he spoke with the insistence of a man trying to restate the serious core of a wandering discussion. Both men knew this game well and played it with pleasure. They ignored even the rumbling of a ladle rolling in its socket overhead, intent as they were on the levels of their game.

The captain's own game began in his head; he saw the Senior as a large, horn-headed beast. The red-and-black mantle became the burnished hide of a thick-shouldered creature, slow but strong, confident and patient, ready to outlast the subtle prowler opposite him, the tawny hunter d Layo. Come to my teeth and my claws, coaxed d Layo; come to my horns and my hooves, lowed the other. They smiled and played their strategies of menace and attraction.

Kelmz shook his head; but he could no more shake free of these visions than he could shake the roar of the fires out of his ears while he stood within reach of their heat. He hugged his ribs with his elbows, blotting the tickling runnels of sweat on his skin. He was bruised from his struggle with the DarkDreamer. Kelmz was too old for such tussles.

It looked as if Senior Bajerman had gotten what he wanted now. He was winding up the conversation, expounding on the need for the raw strength of young men to be curbed by the wisdom of their elders.

"So true," murmured d Layo. "You'll permit me to take a mature man with me on this journey so that I can have the benefit of his wisdom? A man with experience running Rovers would be most helpful." His dark eyes mocked the captain.

"No!" Kelmz blurted, but he had to pause to calm the Rovers, who reacted to his own agitation. This pause gave him time to steady himself as well. He said, "I mean, Senior, if d Layo means me, I'd rather not."

"D Layo means you," the DarkDreamer said. He rose and arched his back, as if bored with a matter already settled.

"Your are commanded, Captain," the Senior said.

Kelmz bent his head in submission and to hide his angry face. It was clear from the Senior's smug look that he had expected d Layo's request.

The Senior said he would take over direct control of Kelmz' two Rovers for his trip back upriver to the City, adding in a kindly tone, "It should be welcome to you, Captain, to be relieved of your ordinary responsibilities for a time."

Saying nothing, the captain unclasped his bracelet of office and surrendered it to the Senior. In its compartments were the carefully measured doses of manna with which an officer bound his Rovers to him. Kelmz looked at the Rovers, the best of the new squad. He didn't think he would command them or their like again. His arm felt as light as if he had given up its bones.

"Hero!" said the Senior to the Rovers. "I need your escort through danger!"

They stepped forward, speaking passionately and both at once of their prowess as escorts through danger. There was no actual resemblance between them, but the eagerness of their expressions made them look alike. They were very tense; transferring command was always a touchy business. The Senior spoke the traditional calming responses several times; this would serve until he could take time to bind them formally under his control with a manna-dream.

The imagined dangers dream-fixed in the Rovers'

minds made them not only alert and fierce, but
indiscriminately dangerous unless skillfully handled.
Each Rover, in his isolated vision of himself as a hero
constantly on guard, imagined all orders to be for his ears
alone and himself to be the sole subject of all events.
Rover-egotism was considered a sign of healthy, manly
individualism and was encouraged, so that getting even
two to work efficiently together as a brace was difficult.

Kelmz momentarily wished that the Senior wouldn't
be able to hold them; but whatever happened to Senior
Bajerman in that case, the Rovers would have to be
destroyed as rogues, so it was hardly a thought worthy of
an officer.

"Safe journeys," said the Senior. He drew aside his
mantle for a parting salute. The skin of his shoulder was
elaborately patterned with the dark dyes of high rank.

Kelmz and the Rovers all touched their own shoulders
and bowed. But the DarkDreamer smiled.

"Have you forgotten your salutes?" the Senior said,
sharply.

"Have you forgotten that when a man is expelled his
shoulder is stripped? He has no salute to give. It's one of
the charms of being without standing in the companies."

"Do this job, and you'll have standing again."

"Provided the Senior remembers me when the job is
finished."

"I'll remember you," Senior Bajerman said drily. "You
are a memorable young man."

He turned and left them, the Rovers pacing alertly at
his back.

II

"We'll give him time to get off the beach," d Layo said. "We have one stop to make that doesn't concern a person as important as the Senior; and then we're off." Kelmz remained silent. "Don't you want to ask me where we're going? I could see you weren't listening to us just now."

"Nobody was talking to me," Kelmz said.

"I'm talking to you now."

Kelmz discovered painfully that though he was older, he lacked the store of haughty tones and cutting phrases used by mature men to keep their juniors in place. None of that had ever been necessary; he had lived with his Rovers, among whom age meant nothing. Now he found himself unarmed against d Layo's mockery and shaken by what the DarkDreamer had to say. Their mission had to do with Endpath.

Apparently a party of pilgrims had returned from there early that same afternoon with the unprecedented news that Endpath was closed. Now it happened sometimes that pilgrims found the Endpath Rovers standing sentry on the roof of the building and a black flag snapping from the mast. That meant that the Endtendant in service had died and would have to be replaced. Alone with four stone-headed Rovers and a stream of death-bound pilgrims, each Endtendant eventually succumbed to the temptation of mixing an extra cup of death-drink for himself. Some young criminal was always speedily appointed to his place. Being chosen for the job was in fact a death sentence, though merciful; the wrongdoer was given time to purge his wicked soul by service until he himself was ready to die like a man.

Never, however, had pilgrims found the flagmast bare, the doors barred and the parapet deserted. It seemed that the present Endtendant had simply withdrawn, locking the pilgrims out.

The purpose of Endpath was to provide Seniors whose souls were ripe for departure with a simple, painless release and remembrance in the Chants Commemorative. To dream into one's death at Endpath was said to assure the life of one's name among younger generations for as long as the sun shone on the manna-bearing hemps that made all dreaming possible. Closing Endpath to death-seekers was an appalling act.

What d Layo had agreed to do for Senior Bajerman was to go to Endpath and dig the Endtendant out of it—no easy feat, since the place was so constructed that one man could hold it against hundreds. Historically, there had been some attacks on Endpath—by Juniors avenging young friends who had gone there prematurely, driven by shame or by the despair of lost loves. Old men, some said, could maneuver young rivals into death on the Rock instead of meeting them fairly in the Streets of Honor, like men.

"Scared?" d Layo inquired.

Of course Kelmz was scared. He had run Rovers too long and survived too many intercompany skirmishes to retain any fascination with death or any illusions about it. In fact, he had been advised more than once by his age-superiors that his own soul was ripe for release at

Endpath. But Kelmz had no desire to join his peers—not in wearing the mantle of Seniority, not in walking with stately tread to a dignified death on the Rock. Seniors were not officers; it was, in ordinary times, beneath their dignity to run Rovers. So, as Kelmz had declined to take his mantle on turning thirty years and each year thereafter, he had several times declined the pilgrim robe also. He would not give up running Rovers for the privileges of higher rank or for the dreaming-death. Both meant being cut off from the only company that gave him any pleasure, that of his mad-eyed Rovers.

When d Layo judged it was time they walked out under a lattice from which bunches of cooked lammin were hung to drain—like little gray beasts that had once hung in clusters from the walls of caves, Kelmz thought with a shiver. A melancholy dripping sound surrounded them, and an acrid sea-stink had soaked permanently into the sand underfoot.

The moon was up, brightening the beach. Rows of small clay lamps dotted the sand. A few were still alight among the crouching forms of fems who were wringing moisture from the lammins with cord-nets. Young men walked in pairs among them, carrying switches with splayed ends. Occasional snapping sounds, followed by yelps, punctuated the plaintive, blurry singing of the fems. The young men wore their hoods up, being nervous about the moon, which was the mistress of all fems and of the evil in them. Older men outgrew such timidity.

These were hags too worn out for other work. Each squatted with her carry-cloth stretched out from her head and over one extended knee, to make shelter from the wind for her hands and for the flickering lamp-flame by which she worked; each fem's fingers shone darkly with the juices of the lammins.

The sky was wide out here. Kelmz preferred to see the night tamed into neat rectangles between compound rooftops. He searched out the four stars that marked the cross-sign and traced it on his own chest. It signified the opposed wills of Father and Son. Though the old religion

was discredited, the sign had survived as a recognition
and acceptance of its one great truth.

They walked between rows of extinguished lamps. On
the left, the town sloped upward in lamplit tiers. On the
right, the black sea shuffled emptily under the stars.
Kelmz put up his hood. He was glad that Endpath was
beyond sight.

D Layo walked bareheaded, humming to himself. He
said, casually, "Have your Seniors been trying to get rid of
you for long? Well, it's obvious that they must want to. A
man like you with gray hair and nothing but Junior-
stripes on your shoulder must make them nervous,
wondering why you persist in standing out of order, so to
speak. Maybe they feel insulted that you hang back as if
the company of your peers isn't good enough for you."

"I like my work," Kelmz said.

"Too much for your own Seniors' taste; though others
are more appreciative. Did you know that there are men
of the Chester Company here in Lammintown who boast
that their second squad of Rovers was trained by Captain
Kelmz of the Hemaways? You must have earned your
company a fortune in the renting of your services. They
show their gratitude very oddly, I'd say."

Muffled thumping sounds and the drone of fems'
voices came faintly from the shredding-shed ahead of
them. In the moonlight the shed's walls were nearly black
with the stenciled emblems of the companies that had
succeeded one another in charge of it, five-year after
five-year.

"Does Bajerman want to unload you because he's
jealous?" d Layo pursued thoughtfully. "Does our
esteemed Senior have his eye on some young Rover of
yours?"

"Rovers make poor lovers."

"Or have you an admirer outside Rover-ranks whom
Bajerman wants for himself?"

"I haven't the looks for it."

"But the lads love scars," d Layo began, raising his
voice above the growing noise from the shredding-shed.

He stopped. Someone was beckoning to them from the open doorway. "Now what's this? I keep some things of mine in the back here, things we'll need."

He advanced again, warily. Kelmz walked behind him and to one side; he had no intention of catching anything that was meant for d Layo.

The man at the shed door was one of a pair of young 'Wares in charge of the shredding-gang. He peered out of the yellow light and said irritably to d Layo, "Somebody's in back waiting for you."

"What kind of somebody?"

The 'Ware wrinkled his nose. "One of the pilgrims that got turned back from Endpath today, and by the stink of him they should have let him in. He's been sitting in the storage room all afternoon. I hope he hasn't contaminated the place with some famishing disease. See you get him out by morning, and if any of your stuff's missing, don't blame me; he's the only one been back there."

D Layo nodded. "Thanks, Jevv."

"Thanks yourself," the 'Ware muttered. He turned and shouted down the length of the shed, "Pull it in, you bitches! If you make the masters touch you in passing, you'll pay for it!"

He cracked his switch down on the table-end. The fems, working in teams across the narrow surface, pressed their lean bellies against the table's edge. They didn't miss a note of their song. The two-handled shredding-blades jumped without pause between them, chopping and feeding the lammin-fragments steadily back into collecting sacks at the far end.

The storage room smelled strongly of the pickling-tubs along one wall. A pyramid of lammin-packets occupied the center of the floor. Beside the mound a lamp burned, and a man sat straight-backed at the edge of the glow.

"Christ-God-Son!" cursed d Layo. "Shut the door, those bitches have ears and so do the 'Wares."

The sounds of the shredding were reduced to a low, vibrant drumming. D Layo bent and lifted the lamp so that its light fell on the stranger in pilgrim gray. The man's

hair was black, and his face appeared startlingly pale
except for the bruise-blue shadows around his eyes and
the dark stubble on his jaw. It was a young face,
mid-twenties at most, but it was as hard and cold-looking
as a limestone mask.

"How did you know where to find me?" d Layo asked.

"Who is this with you?" The stranger spoke haltingly,
as if out of the habit.

"A man of mine," d Layo said off-handedly, obviously
pleased with the idea. "Captain Kelmz of the Hemaways."

The stranger's mouth turned down. "So the Hemaways
have mixed into this already."

"It was Bajerman who came to see me, remember him?
He used to teach Deportment when we were in the
Boyhouse. Now he claims to speak for the entire Board of
Seniors. Thus is virtue rewarded with advancement."

Kelmz knew, unhappily, who the stranger must be.
During the previous five-year the Hemaways had taught
at the Boyhouse. They had lost control of two boys to the
extent of having had to expel them: one to become
Endtendant at Endpath and the other—d Layo—to his
presumed death in the Wild. Kelmz had been training
Rovers in Lammintown at the time, but the entire
Holdfast had buzzed with the news.

"You've made a deal with Bajerman," the Endtendant
said.

"We dealt together, yes. I'm to get you out of Endpath
and deliver you to him in the City, to be handed over to
the Board's discipline committee for abandoning your
post." The Endtendant made an abrupt, impatient
movement of his head. "If you have other plans," d Layo
added, "you'd better tell me." He settled himself
cross-legged on the floor and with an expansive gesture
invited Kelmz to sit, too.

These were the kind of smart lads Kelmz had never felt
comfortable with. Besides, they had been boys together,
which shut Kelmz out. He remained standing.

D Layo shrugged and turned again to the other,
studying him critically. "Jevv was right," he said,

grimacing. "You do stink. You're not really sick, are you?"

"It's the robe," the Endtendant replied. "I took it from one in the last group of pilgrims to be admitted. The smell of illness discourages curiosity."

"Who knows you're here?"

"No one. A few men know that a pilgrim has been asking for you, that's all. Tell me what the Hemaways have offered for me."

D Layo grinned. "They offer Senior status on the Board! How do you like that? Think what I could do, under a Boardman's immunity! They think they could keep me in hand with their plots and alliances, but with a little imagination and nerve there's no limit to what I might do from a position like that!

"Now tell me how it's all more complicated than I think."

"Simpler. Mishandling of our cases has cost the Hemaways a great deal in standing. They want us both dead, Servan."

D Layo glanced up at Kelmz. "I know they don't like me, but they seem to have found a use for me anyway."

"Yes, to deliver us both into their hands."

"Oh, I can get what I want from them and leave them stumbling over their own feet," d Layo said, carelessly. "I've made a bargain, Eykar. Can you stop me from going through with it?" He coughed delicately behind his hand. "We must consider my manly honor, after all."

The Endtendant gave him a long and chilly stare, and d Layo smirked derisively back at him. Yet some alternative deal hovered in the air between them. They approached that alternative with the easy indirection of men who knew each other well. This was not d Layo baiting Senior Bajerman; these two young men were building on something long established. What they built would have no place in it for Kelmz.

"Come on, Eykar, bribe me," d Layo said. "There must be something you can offer that would make it worth my while to hide you from them."

"I don't want to hide," the Endtendant said. "I only want to stay out of their hands long enough to find my father."

Kelmz looked away uncomfortably. This pale young stranger had been a unique person in the Holdfast long before becoming Endtendant. In a society that took pains to sink the identities of individual fathers and sons into the mass-division of Seniors and Juniors, this man knew his father's name.

In all the Holdfast, no blood-ties were recognized. All men were brothers—that was the Law of Generations— though some were older brothers and some younger. Thus, men avoided the fated enmity of fathers and sons, who once known to each other must cross each other even to the point of mutual destruction. The sons of the Ancients had risen against their fathers and brought down the world; even God's own Son, in the old story, had earned punishment from his Father. Old and young were natural enemies; everyone knew that. To know your father's identity would be to feel, however far off, the chill wind of death.

In a sense, however, the Endtendant was himself the chill wind of death. He did not seem afraid.

D Layo said, "You got tired of waiting for the old man to come to you at Endpath?"

Rubbing at his forehead as if it ached, the Endtendant answered, "I caught myself mixing an extra cup, the last time. For myself." He looked up. "I can't wait for him to come."

"I don't understand why he hasn't," d Layo said. "Knowing your name and where to find you, why hasn't he had you killed to safeguard his own life?"

"That's what I mean to ask him."

Incredulously, d Layo said, "You want to search him out so you can have a polite conversation with him?"

"I'm a man first and his son second," the Endtendant retorted. "The proper approach of one rational being to another is through words, not mindless violence."

"Spare me," pleaded the DarkDreamer, holding up his

hand. "I should have guessed; finding him is just another test you've decided to set yourself—"

"Alone," the Endtendant continued, coldly, "I'll never get to him. I need your help."

Kelmz felt as if he were dreaming this talk of matters never openly spoken of; but the Endtendant was real. Though young, his face was clearly marked by inward struggle, bleached by the effort of discipline even to the icy irises of the eyes. The pallor of the skin was spectral, set off by the brows and close-hugging cap of black hair. Sharp-boned, etched in black and white, it was a fanatic's face, as befitted one bent on smashing the law.

D Layo's voice was tender. "Suddenly, Eykar, it's you who are the tempter, and I the tempted." For him, it would be the danger that attracted: the lure of unformed possibilities as opposed to a settled deal with Bajerman. "To find Raff Maggomas," he went on, naming the Endtendant's father quite casually, "we would have to go south to Bayo and try to pick up his trail there. It's been years since he dropped out of sight—as many as our own years out of the Boyhouse. He may go into hiding, if he hasn't already, when he hears that you're on his track. It won't be easy to find him."

"If that worries you," the Endtendant said, "then those years have changed you a great deal more than they've changed me."

"Eykar," the DarkDreamer said, "they haven't changed you at all." He allowed one beat of silence to mark the existence of agreement between them. Then he pointed at Kelmz with a tilt and thrust of his chin.

"And what about this old Rover-runner here? Now that the plan is changed, it seems to me I owe him for the sleep and the work he's cost me lately, with his cursed snuffling around after me through every dive in town, though I'm sure he's enjoyed himself. Do you have any objection, Eykar, to my settling with him before we start out?"

III

Fickle as a fem, Kelmz thought bitterly, or as devious as one, to plan this all along. Either way, d Layo was wolf enough to take Kelmz on here and now, and never mind official standings or the Streets of Honor.

The Endtendant was looking at Kelmz with a steady, cool regard, though it was to d Layo that he spoke: "So this is the man who won't take his mantle. Did Bajerman send him with you to get rid of him?"

"That's right," d Layo said cheerfully, producing a knife from his sleeve; a thin-bladed, well balanced weapon honed to a bright-edged, satiny finish, Kelmz noted—a professional item. "'Gray head yields to young blade,' as they say."

"Captain Kelmz," the Endtendant said, "if Senior Bajerman were here now, he would insist that you try to enforce the terms of the original bargain. To do that, you must fight Servan here at the outset. In spite of your reputation, I think Servan would kill you. I suggest that you turn your back on those who have turned their backs on you. Come with us. There's no shame in a fighting death, but I would rather have you as an ally than leave you as a corpse on this fem-stinking beach."

"Eykar, you're being reckless," d Layo reproved him. "He'll say yes and turn on us later. Don't you think other men have tried to buy him over from the Hemaways before this? In the end, he'll be loyal to his company, whatever he says now to save his life."

"Treachery is *your* style," the Endtendant snapped. "That's why I need a man like the captain. I'm not such a fool as to travel the Holdfast alone with you, Servan."

The DarkDreamer put on a hurt expression. "I try to help, and what do I get in return? Insults!" He grinned at Kelmz. "Come on, Captain, you can't resist the call of duty: 'Hero, I need your escort through danger!'"

Ignoring him, Kelmz said, "I have a question." He cleared his throat. "What happened to the Endpath Rovers? There have always been four of them, specially trained, with standing orders from the Board to keep the Endtendant safe—inside of Endpath."

"That's correct." The Endtendant stood up. He wasn't tall, and his build was light, but well corded with muscle. Kelmz knew the type: frail-looking and nervy, cable-tough under strain. He held his head back so that he seemed to look at Kelmz levelly, eye to eye. "The Endpath Rovers wouldn't have allowed me to leave, but they were vulnerable. One of their duties was to dispose of the dead. The central chamber at Endpath is a domed circle, where the drink is mixed and dispensed to the pilgrims. Then each man goes apart into an individual cell to dream his death properly, as he would any other dream—in private. My part ends when I've handed the last man his cup and put his name down for inclusion in the Chants Commemorative.

"Later, the Rovers enter and bring the bodies back into the central chamber, where there's a chute leading down to an incinerator under the floor. When the corpses are cleared out, the Rovers leave and seal the chamber behind

them, and I open a sluice-gate from outside. The sea
floods the chamber and scours it out.

"This last time, I locked the Rovers in while they were
still working, and I opened the sluices. They drowned."

"Did you watch?"

"Yes, from the gallery above."

Sometimes an officer had to kill his own Rovers if they
were maimed or went rogue; Kelmz had accepted that
necessity long ago. He felt that any man who would not
look at his own lethal handiwork was no man at all.

"Then you traveled down here alone?" he said,
frowning. It was reckless for a man to risk his mental
balance between the emptiness of sky and land.

"No," the Endtendant said. "I waited outside Endpath
until the next group of pilgrims came. They began milling
around in confusion when they saw that something was
wrong on the Rock. I slipped in among them, dressed like
this, and came back with them on the ferry."

He looked at the captain, waiting. His eyes were
disquietingly clear and steady; Kelmz could not return
their gaze for long. The dull black of the Endtendant's
uniform showed at the breast and cuffs of the pilgrim
gown.

"Are you satisfied?" the Endtendant demanded.

The captain saw a night-plumed being, nervous and
awkward on the ground but in the air a dark and wheeling
grace, lacing the wind with harsh cries.

"Oh, Kelmz is satisfied," d Layo said, sulkily. "Look at
him, he's half in love with you already." He put away his
knife and rose neatly to his feet, yawning. "I'll get together
the things we'll need; you two rest, we don't leave till
morning."

"I've rested enough," the Endtendant said. "Captain,
will you walk outside with me?"

"Of course he will," d Layo leered. "But come back
before sunrise; it's better that no one sees either of you."

The beach was empty; even the shredding-shed was
silent now. The Lammintown horns shouted periodically
over the hissing of the sea. They walked by the water. The

Endtendant held the skirts of the pilgrim robe clear of the wet sand by bunching his fists in the pockets. He looked eastward over the water, as if there were something to see out there.

With the moon up so bright there weren't even any netting-crews out sifting the tides; the plankton that they sought only surfaced on dark nights or if it were roiled up from the bottom by storms. It was too early in the fall for bad weather. Kelmz wondered where he would be when the storms began. He couldn't see his way at all as a companion of these two. He didn't think he would ever be comfortable in the Endtendant's company.

They walked without speaking for some time until, brushing up against the Endtendant's arm by accident, Kelmz felt a tremor in him.

"It's cold," the captain said. "Let's turn back."

"I will; you don't have to."

Kelmz stopped and looked up at the paling sky. "I'm committed to come with you. I won't try to turn you over to Bajerman or to the Board, my word on it. I'm a man, not a boy. You can trust me."

"What choices do I have?" The Endtendant uttered hard cracks of sound not much like laughter. "Of course I must trust you, and Servan, and who knows how many other unlikely types before our journey is over. But I can try to minimize my risks. You must be nearly my father's age; whether you wear a mantle or not, Captain, the years make us enemies."

"The way things stand," Kelmz observed, "you don't have anything but enemies. Even your age-peers would sell you to the Board for extra points, anything to enlarge their share of the lammin-harvest, lean as it is. If you think my age makes me a special risk, why didn't you let d Layo cut my throat just now?"

"I don't like Servan's attitude toward killing," the Endtendant said, drily. "He's too casual. I can manage alone with him if I must."

"Look, I have no place else to go but with you." Kelmz fell abruptly silent, feeling the heat of shame on his cheeks. What a thing to admit to a younger man!

To his relief, the Endtendant merely said, "All right."

Only age-peers shook hands. They gave each other a short nod of assent and turned back down the beach. Already a fem-gang could be heard approaching from the town; the low weave of their plaintive voices made a walking rhythm of intersecting tones.

The Endtendant said, "They shouldn't be allowed to sing. Don't you find their voices disturbing?"

Most men were entirely too preoccupied with the creatures, in Kelmz' opinion. "No."

"I do." The Endtendant put up his hood.

Beyond the silent shredding-shed, the pier reached out over the water. Netters' boats tied to the tall pilings bobbed all along its length. At the far end, where the ferry pylon reared up against the sky, the winch-housing of the coastal ferry was visible. One winch-arm angled darkly up across the dawn.

Some one was standing there, urgently waving: d Layo.

They glanced at each other and stepped up their pace, walking swiftly past the shed. As they cleared it, a man straightened from examining footprints in the sand. He was a high-mantled Senior. At his shout, two other men came charging around the side of the shed: Rovers.

On the run, the captain veered toward the water, shouldering the Endtendant into it. They plunged through the icy tide and clambered into the first of the netting-boats. There was rope coiled in the prow, with a grapnel fixed to one end. Kelmz swung the grapnel and hurled it upward. The cross-arm caught behind the head of a piling above them.

The Endtendant climbed up, the sea-soaked skirts of the robe clinging to his legs. Kelmz followed.

As he had intended, the Rovers had been thrown off by the change of footing. They were pelting around the long way, up the steps onto the pier from the landward end. Kelmz held back a pace, racing down the pier, to cover the Endtendant if he had to, for the Rovers were closing hard. A yard ahead of them, Kelmz and the Endtendant dashed across the gangway onto the deck of the ferry. Someone kicked away the gangway, and gouts of cold water shot up over the rail.

The two Rovers stood panting on the pier, eyeing their trapped quarry. Kelmz' Rovers would have jumped the gap and made the enemy secure. It was a sign of the times that these Rovers did not do so, though Kelmz knew them (by their gear, knives sheathed on the left hip for a slicing cross-draw) to be products of a first-class training officer in 'Ware Company. They were slightly unsure of themselves and should have had an officer in charge of them, not the 'Ware Senior who stood far down the pier talking with another man.

D Layo, ignoring the Rovers and their master, presented the newcomers to a ferryman who leaned stolidly on the railing. This man, bulky in salt-stiff clothing, studied them both from his single eye. The other socket was closed by a discolored veil of skin. He was a young man still, but nearing the top of Junior status by the look of him, nudging the crucial age of thirty years. His name was Hak. A salt-eaten Chester symbol was stitched crookedly to his cap.

He stabbed his thumb in the direction of the two 'Wares, who were striding toward the ferry now: "Friends of yours?"

"Hardly," said d Layo.

The white-haired Senior came emphatically first, though not in haste. Seniors never hurried.

Hak looked Kelmz up and down. "What are you, man, under that blank-coat?"

"Hemaway."

The authoritative voice of the approaching 'Ware Senior rang out: "You, on the ferry!"

"Not Captain Kelmz?" Hak said, with mild interest.

"Yes," Kelmz said.

"Right." The ferryman winked his eye and turned to gaze coolly up at the 'Ware Senior. Apparently what d Layo had said was true: there were Chesters who remembered the work Kelmz had done for them once, to which they owed several recent skirmish-victories against their rival, 'Ware Company. Blandly, Hak said, "Do something for you, Senior?"

"Give me those three men."

Hak looked thoughtfully down into the water. "My gangway got knocked overside, Senior. There it is, floating."

The Senior did not look down. He wore a beard in the fashion of Lammintown Seniors and had singed his eyebrows to make them grow in thick and spiky. Frowning, he looked impressively fierce. "This isn't the first time we've had trouble with you Chesters this five-year. Your superiors will not be pleased."

"Never are," Hak said, sadly.

There was a short pause. The morning wind plucked at the ferry cable that swooped down from the top of the pylon to the deck wheel. Two ferrymen lounged at the winch, looking bored.

The Senior said menacingly, "This is no game, Boyo."

To this insulting term, Hak responded merely by spitting carefully into the water between the ferry and the pier.

The other 'Ware, a Junior, hung unhappily in the background, pretending to be blind and deaf for fear he would have to pay later for having witnessed the scoring-off of the Senior at a Junior's hands. In theory, the Senior should not have entered into any game-point rivalry with the young man, since for anyone over the age of thirty the simple accretion of years measured personal worth on an absolute scale. But informally, fierce competition was the rule among Seniors as well as Juniors, though normally it was confined to verbal games like this one. Older men found in the accumulation of game-points (which they affected to despise) a way of unofficially offsetting the implacable order of the age-scale among themselves.

This 'Ware Senior mastered his anger carefully to avoid further losses in his encounter with the Chester ferryman.

"Listen," he said, "you'd better understand what you're mixing into. There have been reports of unlawful use of my company's work-turf. These are the offenders. They are two unknowns, probably Skidro drifters going home via Bayo with whatever they've lifted in Lammintown, including some packets of prime lammin that are missing from storage. The third one is the DarkDreamer d Layo, who's long overdue for burning. The price on his head is enough points to buy you free of your duties for a five-year."

The ferryman took off his grimy cap and scratched his head. He squinted down the coast toward the next pylon, and the ones beyond that; they marched parallel to the beach in single file as far as the eye could see.

"Who says I don't do my job right?" he demanded suddenly. "What man in the Chesters? Or is it just you 'Wares that say it?"

The Senior's bristling eyebrows rose. "I didn't criticize the way you do your job—"

"Then what's this talk about getting me off my boat? You trying to score me off, Senior? Taking advantage of a rough working lad that's been at sea too long?"

Turning on his subordinate, the Senior curtly ordered him to get the Rovers out of earshot of the discussion. The older man plainly appreciated the difficulties of his position, and he was giving himself time to think. He could hardly send for a Chester Senior, for he would incur enormous humiliation for himself and his company by appealing for help in dealing with an uppity Junior.

The Senior leaned out over the piling and said balefully. "A man who helps a thief is worse than a thief, in these lean times. You might remember that you are no Pennelton, to walk off this boat in Bayo and sleep safe for the rest of the five-year with the whole coast between us. You'll be coming back here on your return run, and when you do, I'll have your standing stripped. You're compounding an injury done my company on its own work-turf, and that's injury to all. It will cost the Chesters a lot to make it good. It will certainly cost them you.

"Think about that, Junior, and consider: who should pay the price of theft, you or the thieves?"

"There's a lot of things lying crooked between the 'Wares and the Chesters, Senior. Maybe it's time it all got put straight. Then we'd find out who owed whom."

Without another word, the Senior turned and stalked off, with his entourage hurrying after him.

"Go stick it up a fem," Hak muttered. Giving Kelmz a sour grin, he stumped off toward the winch deck, shouting at the men standing there. They leaped up onto the winch housing and laid hold of the handles with their gauntleted hands.

D Layo sighed. "Well, Captain," he said, "I suppose I must grant you some usefulness after all."

IV

No Seniors rode the ferries, except occasionally as passengers. Skilled administrators (some were even literate), they were in charge of record-keeping ashore. Aboard the ferries, the older Juniors were responsible for the crew, passengers and cargo between dockings. One-eyed Hak had been crew chief on the coastal run since the beginning of the five-year.

The ferry itself was a converted river craft which had replaced the legendary ocean-goer lost long ago. The story was that a Senior had insisted on taking Rovers on a sea trip with him and that one of them had gone rogue and cut the cable. The ferry had drifted out onto the empty immensity of water and had never been seen again. The largest of the river craft had been altered to take its place, for by that time the building of ships was an art that had vanished with the trees cleared from the Holdfast.

There were tales, of course, of ships of the Ancients which had been driven by fire and by secret and strange

substances that could kill a man on contact. These legends
ranked with stories of craft, carrying human cargo, that
could hurl themselves through the air for great distances.
That had been in the days when the world was so rich in
metal that there was plenty for the fashioning of mighty
machines.

In the Holdfast, requests for metal went through the
company hierarchies to the Board, which might pass them
on to the town of 'Troi. Not many orders were filled; the
furnaces of 'Troi could only turn out so much metal goods
per five-year. Tools, weapons and replacement parts for
the few machines still in use had priority. Extra work-time
and material tended to go into luxury items like jewelry,
which only Seniors could afford.

The ferries were powered by machines. 'Troi engineers
had designed a system of gears by means of which the
strength of men on the winch was amplified and
transferred to rotary blades at the rear of the craft.
Certainty of staying within sight of land was assured by
the long cable which fed down from the pylons through a
wheel fixed to the midships decking. The whole
arrangement was slow and clumsy, but free of the perils of
fast-moving, free-ranging boats. The Holdfast could not
afford to lose another ferry.

All that remained of shipyard skill was the ability to
patch and trim existing vessels with wood won from the
Wild. Each bit of the precious material was polished and
shaped by the hand of every man in a given crew before
being ceremonially installed. The names of the men who
dared the empty lands beyond the borders of the Holdfast
to obtain wood went into special Chants Celebratory
concerning the ferries. Every step of the patching process
was, like most of the things the ferrymen did, part of a
fabric of custom intended to hold ferry-crews together in
manly order, despite their isolation between empty sea
and empty sky.

The huge hold of the coastal ferry was lit by hanging
lamps and stray sunlight that entered the high-set ports.
The air was hot, moist and permanently impregnated with

the reek of sweat, lammins and beer. The noise never stopped.

At the center of the hold was the play-pen, a pit of sand that was the scene of the perpetual contests and games with which ferrymen filled their off-deck hours. Something was always going on in the pen and at the tile gameboards that made up the apron around it. Every match drew its mob of shouting spectators.

Forward, the sweating sloppers tended cook-tubs sunk into the tops of great clay fire-boxes in which fires roared day and night. Aft, past the cargo-space and the rows of crewmen's hammocks, someone was always playing the part of story-box to whatever audience he could keep, bellowing out his tale in order to be heard above the general din. The entire ship reverberated ceaselessly to the growling of winch and propeller blades.

The gleaming skins of the ferrymen, who went about in shorts or nothing at all below decks, reminded Kelmz of insect-armor. Even the interminable activity and racket struck him as mimicry of the meaningless scurryings of those strange, tiny beasts of the Ancients' times.

He had never traveled by water before, except under awnings on the decks of river barges. His journeys had commonly been overland, with a brace or two of Rovers in his charge. There were no Rovers on the ferry; there was nothing familiar or easy. The heat made him dizzy; the stuffiness choked him; the constant rolling cost him several meals. It was impossible to sleep in all the noise, but he didn't need much sleep, having nothing active to do; and he didn't eat a lot.

The food—never enough of it here any more than elsewhere at Juniors' tables—was invariably blue-stew with dollops of the hemp-root starch called taydo in it; thin slices of hempseed bread smeared with plankton jelly; and pale beer to wash it all down. The only relief was the occasional fresh salad made with the lammins that d Layo had turned over to the sloppers on first entering the hold. That gesture had won him friends from the start.

He had built on this beginning by becoming an

enthusiastic participant in the games at the play-pen. As a DarkDreamer and an outlaw he lived outside the company system of work-and game-points, so he took his winnings in cash. This should have made trouble for him since Juniors were always short of cash, their only means of buying any sort of luxury beyond the subsistence distributed to them by the companies. Yet without apparent effort, d Layo shortly became so popular with the young Chesters that he influenced their private status structure.

Officially, work-points determined a company's subsistence portion every five-year, and game-points converted into individual shares of spending cash for the Juniors. But among themselves young men vied for standing on the basis of scars. This system had begun as a defiant glorification of the marks of corporal punishment. By the time the Board had substituted more subtle forms of discipline, the Holdfast Juniors had established an underground hierarchy based not only on verbal contests but on scars gotten in fights. It was rare for a young man not to be marked up, even if he had to inflict wounds on himself.

To Kelmz' surprise, the DarkDreamer had very little to show under his shirt other than the pallid discolorations of an acid-bleached rank-tattoo on his shoulder and a few faded wound-weals that he did nothing to enlarge or freshen up. Smooth skin should have worked against d Layo; but something in his manner and his impressive showing in the ferrymen's games converted it into an asset. Within a few days of leaving Lammintown, it became the fashion on the ferry to modestly cover one's scars with a shirt. The theory was that a man who stood ready to prove his courage in action had no need to show off evidence of past bravery.

Similarly, because d Layo wore no jewelry but his manna-bracelet, the younger ferrymen soon put away their own highly prized ceramic earrings, pendants, anklets and studded belts. D Layo mockingly ascribed these changes to Kelmz' influence, not his own.

By professional habit the captain sported no ornaments. He continued to wear his patched and threadbare suit of blanks, saving his uniform. It was not a Rover's way to display his body like a boastful boy. Kelmz was hoping the anonymity of blanks would help him spend the voyage in quiet obscurity.

However, on the first morning out he woke from a fretful doze to find a ribby, freckle-skinned lad, ostentatiously scarred on chest and arms, waiting silently by his hammock. This Junior politely requested that Captain Kelmz come join a group at the story-box. Once Kelmz accepted out of courtesy, he found himself trapped into a pattern that repeated itself daily, to his intense embarrassment.

The young men would begin complimenting him. By reputation, it seemed, Kelmz was strong, skillful, efficient, loyal, brave, honest, and on and on until he couldn't tell whether they were describing some mythical paragon of the manly virtues or trying to make a fool of him. He would sit among them with a flush in his seamed cheeks and his big hands clenched, until he could bear no more of their bright-faced praise. When he finally started to rise and leave them, someone would say, "Will the Captain tell about the time two Rovers went rogue on him on the river-road near Oldtown?" Or about the skirmish with Birj Company at the City breweries, or a fight in a Lammintown Street of Honor, or even the time he had carried his friend Danzer, fatally injured, five miles on his own back?

These lads knew Kelmz' life better than he did himself, and they pressed him unabashedly about events that he would have preferred to forget. By convention, a man could not refuse to tell a story that he knew or to come back next time and finish one that had been interrupted. Kelmz' stories were always interrupted.

D Layo claimed that some of the regular Chester story-boxers were angry because Kelmz was stealing their audience. Kelmz said he didn't understand how the young men knew so much about him.

The DarkDreamer laughed at that. "Kelmz, you are an innocent. Haven't you ever looked past your Rover-brutes at anything? Man, you're a walking legend, and for once there are no Seniors around to check the lads' demonstration of their feelings. How would you expect youngsters to regard a famous fighting man who sticks by his Junior status and his dream-doped Rovers in spite of all custom and pressure?"

"They don't know anything about it," Kelmz muttered and refused to discuss the matter further. He felt as if he had won the young Chesters' respect falsely.

The situation grew serious when the freckled lad turned up one morning with a gold-glazed earring which he pressed on the captain as a gift; then he asked for a story that was part of a courting-series. Kelmz didn't care about the jealousy of the lad's prior friend, an older Junior chiefly noticeable these days for his sullen looks; but he felt he had no right to divert the young Chester from companionship within his own company and age-group. Though Kelmz was not an officially mantled Senior, by any biological reckoning the freckled lad was on the Junior side of the age-line. The appropriate attitude of an older man toward a younger was wary concern, not lust. A man could hardly have a relationship of equals with one less mature than himself. Kelmz had no intention of descending to the vice of boy-stealing. Besides, after the years with Danzer, Kelmz had formed the habit of avoiding close bonds with other men.

He retreated; he went up on deck, where he found the Endtendant standing at the rail.

The Endtendant spent daylight hours alone there, with all that bleak sky overhead and fathoms of water below and nothing but the line of the land, gliding past, to look at. He even kept his back turned to the chanting ferrymen on the winch, as if he actually enjoyed solitude in the open. He was slightly tanned by sun and wind. His eyes were the same pale windows on the chilly place behind the mask.

Kelmz nodded a greeting, which was curtly returned,

and leaned on the worn rail a little distance away. He watched the water slide by below. That was a mistake.

The sight of the shifting surface in whose depths nothing lived any more brought horribly to mind all sorts of stories that no decent man should even recall from his Boyhouse lessons, let alone picture in vivid detail: house-sized fish that ate ships, many-legged bladder-beasts skittering along the bottom of the sea to gobble the bodies of drowned men...Kelmz closed his eyes and turned his face up to the cleansing light of the sun.

Fortunately, that afternoon they sighted the tall marshgrass that grew between Bayo and the beach. That was also the day that the Endtendant was recognized.

Thanks to ceaseless prodding by the freckled lad's friend, certain Chesters who were contemporaries of d Layo and the Endtendant had worked out who the DarkDreamer's companion must be. When Kelmz and the Endtendant came below-decks for the evening meal, they found a meeting in progress. Hak was addressing the assembled men with some heat, while those who had precipitated the crisis stood in a group at his right, headed by Sullen-face and the freckled lad.

Hak was saying that he had extended the freedom of the ferry to the strangers on the strength of Kelmz' reputation and because of a natural sympathy for any young men in trouble with Seniors. He had not counted on one of the fugitives turning out to be an outlaw Endtendant.

D Layo got to his feet, brushing sand from his chest and arms. Though his skin was blotched with red marks from a play-pen match, he seemed unruffled and spoke in a tone of light incredulity. "Leaving aside for the moment the question of identities, is it seriously suggested that these young Chesters refuse to help other young men—or maybe even turn them over to the cloth-cocks for cash?"

The listeners guffawed; young men sometimes called Seniors that, meaning that the only thing an old man could still get up was his mantle.

Sullen-face retorted, "If there's a reward, why not? It's

not every day that men have a chance to do their manly duty and get paid well for it besides."

At that point someone noticed the two new arrivals, and a cry was raised: "There's the man!"

Hak called, "Are you Eykar Bek, Endtendant of Endpath?"

And the Endtendant said, "Yes."

"Ah, Christ," Kelmz said, with deep disgust; to throw away their lives so simply was a crime. He set his hand on the hilt of his knife.

"Then something has to be done," Hak declared. "I know who gets blamed by those here when this five-year ends and the work-points and game-points presented by this company are discounted by the Board because we've helped a renegade Endtendant. There won't be plenty to go around to begin with. The Board will be looking for reasons to cut shares where they can."

There were mutterings at this. The Chesters shot sidelong looks at the outsiders or frowned at the floor and avoided looking at them at all.

D Layo smiled. "Brothers," he said, stepping forward with casual grace, "I have a story to tell."

---------------- V ----------------

By these words, he took on the role of story-box, and with it the right to speak.

"When I was some years into my education," he began, "a certain boy was put into my class. Everyone talked about him, not because he was smart and was being moved ahead of his age-peers, but because he was special in another way: he knew his father's name, and his father knew his."

They groaned; he had them. Not one of these young men could fail to recall the fear of his own early years, that somehow his father would identify him and have him destroyed. There were a few well known historical cases of Seniors arranging the deaths of boys whom they suspected to be their own sons. This was the basis of the insecurity that afflicted every boy as soon as he understood the natural enmity between generations. That insecurity was never fully outgrown.

It made sense, after all: sons, fresh from the bellies of fems, were tainted with the destructiveness which characterized their dams. Therefore they were dangerous. It was natural for fathers to protect themselves from their sons' involuntary, irrational aggression by striking first.

On the other hand, the Holdfast needed these sons to live long enough to outgrow the fem-taint and join the world of mature men in their turn. This was the reason for the existence of the Boyhouse and the justification for the strict lives led by its inmates. The rules were harsh, designed not only to wipe out the unmanly streak as soon as possible, but to protect boys from the righteous wrath of their fathers in the meantime.

There had been times when adult men had organized deadly raids on whatever concentrations of boys they could find. This sport had served as a reminder that men would not forget the Freaks, the sons of Ancient men who had turned against their fathers in the Wasting and paid for their treachery with their lives. The raids no longer occurred. The Boyhouse kept the boys, and with them the future, safe; here their souls were beaten into a hardness that would be fitting to the souls of men.

Later, men grew old enough to breed and to search the faces of young boys for likenesses to their own. But no one ever forgot his own time within the Boyhouse walls, hiding in the anonymous mob of his peers.

The young Chesters squirmed in their places, thinking of the boy who had known his father's name and whose father had known his.

"Now, how could this be?" d Layo said. "It goes against the Law of Generations. This man—the father—who was a Tekkan from Lammintown called Raff Maggomas, took a fem from the Tekkan breeding rooms the first night of her heat and kept her with him in a secret place until she had cooled again. He marked her neck, here at the back just under the hair, with blue rank-dye—" The Chesters buzzed with outrage at this. "—and slipped her back into her place. During the time Maggomas kept her for himself, no one noticed that a cold fem had been substituted for her in the breeding-rooms, one fem being very like another. This man Maggomas had put together enough standing and favors-owed to accomplish the deed.

"Next, he arranged to be in the City when that fem was sent to the Hospital to drop her young. Now, what do you think would have happened if the bitch had dropped a fem-cub?"

Laughter; someone called out, "He'd have gone home again a lot faster than he'd come!"

"Since you ask me, I'll tell you," d Layo said. He was good at this, making a play of expression and gesture to wring the full degree of delicious disgust from the unnatural events of which he told. "Maggomas had a confederate at the Hospital, and that man marked the cub with the same blue mark that was on the neck of the fem that had dropped it. So when Maggomas sneaked into the Boyhouse next day, he found the marked cub and read off the name the Teachers had inscribed on its boy-tags.

"But having accomplices means sharing secrets, and you all know how the cloth-cocks talk, sitting with their lumpy old feet up to the hearth-fire day and night. Some years later, word got out.

"By that time, nothing could be proven, and there was always the chance that some youngster had started the rumor as a way of getting at Maggomas for a private reason." Knowing nods from the young Chesters, who were familiar with such private reasons. "Maggomas himself had nothing to say on the subject, though I doubt he was ever asked point blank. He was a Senior himself, and among themselves they are so standing-proud and courteous that they don't even have words to frame such a question. So the fem was burned on suspicion of having witched a man into breaking the Law of Generations, and the Board left it at that.

"Now, think a bit about the son, Eykar Bek. There he was, knowing that something set him apart from his peers and wondering what it was. When the rumors reached him, he heard the name of his father for the first time. Think about living with that: listening for the footfalls of a murderer at night, studying the faces of the Teachers for one who had been paid to strike for Maggomas...

"Well, if such plans were made, they never came to completion. What did happen was that an unfortunate friendship was permitted to develop between Eykar Bek and another boy—a bad boy, a boy of clearly corrupt character, a boy who was in fact destined to become a DarkDreamer."

D Layo bowed facetiously, and some of the Chesters applauded.

"Now, what do you think came of this attachment? Why, trouble came of it, as any fool could have foreseen. The bad boy's curiosity led him to explore the art of the DarkDream. He involved Eykar Bek in his activities; they were caught; they were punished. One of the boys was dumped into the Wild to die. The other—Raff Maggomas' son, as it happened—was exiled to Endpath to become Endtendant, even though he was not yet invested as a Junior."

Suddenly d Layo shot out a pointing hand: "And there he is. While he's here among you, you might ask him why he abandoned his assigned work-turf. Ask him why he turned away a mob of sick-stinking whiteheads (with perhaps a few broken-spirited lads mixed in among them) and left the death-manna for someone else—or no one else—to brew. Ask him where he's going and who he's looking for and what he means to do when he finds him!"

The sullen-faced man gnawed at his thumbnail, saying nothing. No one spoke. They all looked at the Endtendant.

Kelmz heard Bek's voice rattle rustily in his throat a moment, before the words came out: "I have a question for Raff Maggomas."

"Only one question?" a Chester shouted. It wasn't a joke; nobody laughed.

Another cried, "Why hasn't he had you killed?"

"Have you any real, blood brothers that you know of?"

"My question," the Endtendant said, over their excited murmuring, "is this: I want to know why I was singled out from among those who otherwise would have been my peers. I want to know the reason for blackening my whole life with the shadow of another man, of another generation."

A Junior stood up and said, "I have a question I'd like asked too, as long as you're going to be asking questions. This Maggomas must be an old man now, maybe he'll know the answer. I'd like to know how come Seniors live on limitless credit for doing nothing while working men have to get by on the pitiful rations they give us. That's what I'd like to know." He sat down again.

Other questions followed. The Chester Juniors asked what they would never have dared to ask any Senior to his face: how was it that the cloth-cocks took the most powerful manna to dream themselves into fitting strength of mind and virtue, but still acted with spite and self-indulgence when awake? How was it that they said one thing and did another, all the time cursing the Juniors for famishing deceitfulness? Enforced the age-line except where it cut them off from the objects of their own lusts? Would hear no petition from younger men unless in the presence of the Boardmen, whose power over young men's lives was utterly intimidating? Ruled that a young man had to carry all his life a name picked from a list drawn out of the Boardmen's dreams, though he might wish to call himself after some friend or hero in respectful memory?

Their voices raw with fury, the Chesters gave the Endtendant no chance to speak. He stood silent, ice-eyed, like a personification of the cold heart of their rage.

When the excitement began to die down, Hak made one last try: "How do we know that this DarkDreamer has told us the truth?"

"Ask one you trust," d Layo rejoined. He nodded at Kelmz. "What does the first fighter in the Holdfast, the man who won't take his mantle, have to say?"

Kelmz cleared his throat and said he thought truth had been spoken.

The Chesters set up a roar and a storm of clapping. Hak bowed to it; he promised on behalf of the whole company to do what was needed to speed the Endtendant on his way. Immediately, d Layo outlined what he wanted.

"When the rumors of his having claimed a son got out, Maggomas left the Tekkans and went off to Bayo, and we haven't heard of him since. We can't go to the Board and ask them where he is, and the men at Bayo are Penneltons assigned there this five-year, so they won't know anything. Some of the older Bayo fems might remember, though, and anything they know we can get out of them—if we can reach them and deal with them privately. We need you lads to see to it that we won't be disturbed in Bayo.

"Set us down on the coast a little way north, and you go on upriver and dock at Bayo as usual. We'll make our way there through the marshes and try to enter the fems' quarters after dark. All you have to do is to make dinner in Bayo such a drunken, enjoyable affair that no Penneltons come wandering outside while we're looking for a way into the fems' section.

"After that, we're on our own—but the longer you can keep our visit among you secret, the better for us and for you."

"Done," said Hak, promptly, before any more could be asked. "Done!" shouted the Chester Juniors. Someone added, "And a DarkDream to seal it," a cry which others took up.

Ferrymen were only permitted to dream between runs, under the auspices of their Seniors. Now they were daring in their excitement. Learning that d Layo had only enough manna to serve a few, they quickly put together a group of eight to represent the complicity of them all in the fugitives' lawlessness. Sullen-face and the freckled lad were both included.

For the others, Hak had kegs of beer broken out to go with the scanty evening meal. Supplies were apt to run short at the end of the coastal run, and the only ferrymen to escape the grip of hunger tonight would be those lucky enough to be caught up in a dream. Some of the more

talented chanters performed around the play-pen, improvising lyrics and obscene pantomines, a welcome
distraction to the others.

Hak was a good chief; he knew how to pull his people
together. Kelmz was ashamed of d Layo's blatant
theatrics, and he hoped that the one-eyed ferryman
wouldn't suffer for all this in the end. For a man who bore
no responsibility himself, d Layo was adept at maneuvering those who did.

The dreaming-group went back to the story-box area
and hung mats from the ceiling for privacy. A ferryman
brought a pitcher of beer and some mismatched mugs on
a tray; another supplied a mixing-whisk of straws bound
with cord. D Layo squatted by a brazier and heated the
beer, not bothering with the Chants Preparatory. The
others, seated in a circle around him, began to murmur
the Chant Thankful, which extolled the virtues of the
hemp: it provided fiber to clothe men's bodies, food for
their nourishment, and manna for the dreaming of their
souls. Sullen-face sweated a lot, and stuttered every time
he chanted the refrain.

It was, Kelmz thought, going to be one sorry excuse for
any kind of a dreaming.

D Layo used the doubled-over hem of his shirt to pad
the hot handle of the pitcher. A sweet scent rose as he
shook powder from the compartments in his bracelet into
the steaming liquid. He whipped the mixture in the cups
before taking the ceremonial first sip from each one.

A man could grow attached to the rituals, especially if
(like Kelmz) he was accustomed to being dream-giver to
Rovers who were utterly dependent on him in that role.
The Chants Commanding, which went with Rover-
dreaming, kept running through Kelmz' mind. He
glanced at the Endtendant, whose angular face showed
nothing at all.

It was absurd to impute nostaligia to him, of course.
The dream he had given had always been death. He could
hardly have put off his own bracelet of office with any
feeling but relief.

D Layo began handing out the cups. Bek refused with a wordless shake of his head, and no one made anything of it; but when Kelmz hesitated, he noticed that several of the ferrymen were watching him anxiously. Perhaps they had never DarkDreamed before. They trusted Kelmz' judgment and were waiting for him to drink.

This wouldn't be the first time Kelmz had Dark-Dreamed. He had indulged once or twice to no great effect, with fellow officers. That had been before he had started seeing beasts, a thing that had come upon him suddenly, soon after Danzer had died with his throat torn out by a rogue Rover. Kelmz had not DarkDreamed since then. His waking visions were DarkDream enough.

Now he looked into the cup, warming his hands on the glazed surface, and thought why not? He was an outlaw among outlaws, his legitimate life was over. He drank.

The manna-beer tasted gluey; d Layo hadn't taken time to mix it properly, the slovenly brute.

The others drank too. They hunched closer together and listened to d Layo, who had begun a low, singing-chant.

A man was supposed to be an individual. He was supposed to go apart and strengthen his soul with a dream from among those taught in the Boyhouse, which were all on the same heroic themes: dreams of victorious battles against monsters, dreams of power and wealth bent to the good of lesser men, dreams of manly love and lifelong loyalties, dreams of endurance and achievement—an endless selection of patterns keynoted to the manly virtues. In this way the soul could be schooled independently of the drowsing flesh. Each man, in command of his own dreaming, chose the proper dream for his own needs and weaknesses.

D Layo told them to forget all that and give him control. He would show them how to free their souls for the delight of knowing what they were, not what they ought to be. It was seditious nonsense that undermined manly self-discipline and integrity, but he made it attractive.

"Let me teach you," d Layo murmured, "to relax your mind and soul, to open the dark core of yourself and free what lives there. Every soul is equal before a Dark-Dreamer, and every soul is unique; what is your soul?"

The insidious lure of DarkDreaming lay partly in this deliberate abolition of hierarchy. D Layo led them into the void of their hidden selves, where any mad chaos was possible. He was skillful, nothing like the fumbling fools Kelmz had encountered before. Gently, the Dark-Dreamer touched Sullen-face, drawing out the hesitant movements of his limbs and his slow-curling fingers. The man's mouth simpered open, his hands began to stroke downward on his own chest and thighs. He cringed, he melted, he was a fem.

Revolted, Kelmz looked away. For himself, he realized, he had hoped to see beasts—real beasts, hot-hided, pungently scented alien beings—not the pathetic perversions of other men.

Now d Layo was working on Hak. One-eyed Hak, chief of the crew on the coastal run, tumbled over and rolled on the floor, shielding himself from invisible kicks and blows, yammering. The DarkDreamer seemed to dance over and around him, perfecting the ferryman's performance with a touch, a whisper, a tug at the sleeve.

Kelmz began to shake.

He couldn't understand the meaning of the upright-walking being that came toward him, sniffed at him, put its hot, smooth touch on him. Panicky, he reared back to escape, but there were barriers. He struck out. The tall-walker evaded him and withdrew. Alone, penned in, he squeezed his eyes half shut and swung his head away from the bright, flaring heat and burning smell. Deep tremors of fear shuddered through him. He swayed from side to side, nosing the air for a familiar scent. There was none.

A sound found its way out of his throat, a whimper. He rocked his weight from shoulder to shoulder and moaned out his despair and isolation; but there came no answering voice.

• • •

It was day. Close by, a man slept all asprawl, snoring. Another had burrowed his way under a pile of woven mats so that only his haunches stuck out, collapsed sideways over his bent legs.

"Stand up, Captain," the Endtendant commanded.

He was right to give that order, though he was only a Junior. Kelmz stood, blinking.

"Sun's fire!" he croaked; "I was a beast!"

D Layo was laughing. "Look at him, he's upset because his secret is out. What a secret! He should know as many men as I do who dream themselves a coat of fur or feathers when they get the chance!"

SERVAN D LAYO

_____

VI

Servan was high as a flag. Each go-round with manna was
a gamble for him; his tolerance for it was undependable.
When it left him exalted he was the victor. He shook the
empty bracelet along his arm as he walked. He would
have to see about getting hold of some more good stuff,
now that he'd used up his supply on that pack of
ferry-punks.

The ferrymen had let them off at midday. The three
men made their way through the marshes in the still,
warm afternoon. The hike gave them time to emerge from
the after-effects of the dreaming. Kelmz, in particular,
needed that. He was in a black, bewildered mood and
walked apart from the others.

As for Servan, he held onto his euphoria; he was
practiced in keeping alert enough to function well in spite
of his intoxication. That their destination was the
fem-center of the entire Holdfast increased his good
humor. He had always intended to visit Bayo, in order to
fill a gap in his professional background—as he explained

several times to his companions, between snatches of
song. Inside his head an on-running paean of praise to his
own good luck rippled along, woven of scraps of songs he
had wrung from various fems who had passed through his
hands. Completely unable to produce a true note of his
own, he had spent a period of his life pursuing others'
music. That craze was over now, but he had learned a lot
and still liked to sing, however tonelessly. Besides, one
thing he still had a craze for was needling Eykar, and he
knew perfectly well that his singing needled Eykar.

There was no one to hear him but themselves. The
grass of the marshes was allowed to grow undisturbed to
head height, curing in the salty mud. The Bayo fems were
sent to harvest it as needed for weaving, and you could
always hear them coming a mile off, singing their
work-chants. The scattered stands and thickets were
deserted now.

The footing was soggy, but Servan liked the hiss and
rustle of their passage through the tall, yellow stems.
Stripes of gold and shadow glided over their skins and
clothing, giving a fantastic, underwater motion effect.
The sunlight struck obliquely toward them between the
ribbons of grass; they must have been slogging along like
this for some time. He'd hardly noticed.

Soon there came the piping of the flutes of Bayo, which
were said to skirl as ceaselessly as the horns blew in
Lammintown. There was a song that said the flutists'
indrawn breath sucked up the spirits of dead fems and
that it was these ghost-voices which sang so sadly from the
instruments. An interesting conceit. Servan was eager to
see fems on what must be considered their homeground.

Bayo had begun as nothing more than a crude outpost
of the City, which lay forty miles inland. The flats between
the City and the southern mouth of the river were
perfectly suited to the growing of lavers. These freshwater
weeds, both tasty and nutritious, grew best in nutrient-
rich, shallow waters. So the south channel of the river had
been dammed into ponds, into which the City's sewage
was fed. Then stone causeways had been built bestriding

the ponds and linking Bayo with the City. Lastly, the structures of Bayo itself had gone up, to house a permanent fem labor force and whatever company of men was assigned to supervise them.

Surrounded on the seaward side by the golden grass, the thick crescent of Bayo buildings crouched, compact and unadorned, between the southern margins of the ponds and the river's mouth where the ferry docked. Bayo's walls were of mud-brick, fired to withstand the summer rains. All the structures had been erected on a ramp of similar brick that sloped noticeably upward from the dockside warehouses to the farther horn of the crescent, where the pyramidal men's compound reared up overlooking everything. The quarters of the fems comprised the curved center.

This evening, from the bright-windowed men's compound came cheerful rills of flute notes and a drum beat reinforced by the stamp of dancing feet. The Penneltons' greeting-feast for the ferrymen was in full swing. Hopefully, the Chesters would maintain the secret of their complicity with the fugitives outside for some hours yet.

The three of them squatted in the high grass, weary and coated to the knees in marsh mud. An unpleasant odor hung in the air, penetrating even the dank salt-smell of the marshes. Probably the odor was connected with the cloudy emissions from the chimneys clustered on the rooftops of buildings adjoining the warehouses. Those would be the workrooms, a good place to enter, if they could get past the guards.

Three pairs of Rovers patrolled the lighted gallery which ran along the inside curve of the crescent. Servan considered Rovers to be highly overrated as fighting men. Once you figured out that they worked on the principle of the pre-emptive strike, it was easy to deal with them. Acting out of fear themselves, they interpreted others' fear of them as a presage of aggression and responded by attacking first. Seen in this way, theirs was a reasonable sort of behavior. Servan had a theory that the famous "mature" composure of Senior men was primarily

protective, to prevent the unintended triggering of Rovers
against the Seniors themselves. Servan had adopted the
show of serenity in his own contact with Rovers quite
successfully.

A man like Kelmz, however, was not to be wasted in a
situation like this. Servan waited while Kelmz sized up
their position independently and came, naturally, to the
same conclusion. The captain made a stay-put sign and
moved off silently toward the warehouses. For a big man,
he could travel very neatly when he chose to.

Servan sat back to wait, turning his mind firmly from
considerations of food. They had eaten nothing since
morning, and now that the manna-high had worn off, he
was hungry. He hummed part of a song concerning
"Rovers, red-handed, mad-eyed warders, dreadful and
deadly to fems."

The two Rovers guarding the work-room and
warehouse end of the crescent came swinging down the
gallery in step, bald-headed and thick-bodied like two
rough clay men made from the same mold. That their
features could not be discerned in the shadows of the
thatch overhead seemed only fitting; their anonymous
madness was their most formidable aspect. Servan knew
from experience that they were so nearly soulless, like the
mechanical men of Ancient legend, that they were a
disappointment to kill unless fully aroused—something
that at present was to be avoided.

He thought he knew what Kelmz had in mind. If
successful, it would save Servan some trouble. If not, he
would do what was called for. He never liked to plan too
tightly for the future.

The Rovers wheeled and marched back the way they
had come. A shadow rose from the darkness behind them,
and Kelmz fell silently into step at their backs. They
stiffened visibly, but didn't turn or break stride. Kelmz
would be matching their tread so exactly that each of
them would hear only his own steps amplified by his
companion's in a manner that he had been taught not to

fear, so that he could work as a member of a brace or squad.

Servan would have to tell Kelmz later what an artist he was. His praise would certainly irritate the captain—art was a famishing untrustworthy attribute—and at the same time it would have the virtue of being true. Kelmz had an artist's luck, too: the Chesters were doing their part well, for no one stepped outside the men's compound to piss or settle a bet. There was no break in the pounding rhythm of the Penneltons' dancing.

Smoothly, the captain moved up and put his hands on the Rovers' shoulders. He wheeled with them and they came back down the gallery, secured by his authoritative touch. If he had hesitated, they would have turned and cut him down. By the time Servan and Eykar gained the gallery themselves, Kelmz and the Rovers were again at the far end of their patrol, backs turned.

The doors to the work-buildings were not locked, for no fem would try to get past a Rover-watch. The two men simply walked in, entering a huge room full of hot, sour air.

The cement floor was cluttered with machines, bins, tables, and chutes. At the far end, layers of stuffed hempen sacks mounted toward the ceiling, presumably containing some of the finished product. Most of the equipment seemed to be idle. A few fems were present, wearing sweat-rags bound around their heads and stained aprons that reached from armpit to knee. Three of them stood nearby, fixing a piece of wire mesh over the opening of a pipe that stuck out of the wall. The pipe and the trough under it seemed to be the prime source of the pervasive sour stink. From this group and others came the murmur of voices; that was surprising. Though normally fems sang at work, the majority of them were held to be incapable of any but the most limited fem-to-master type of speech.

There were no men about at all. This was the first time Servan had ever seen any number of fems together without at least one pair of Juniors overseeing their activities. It made his hair prickle.

Some signal must have been given; suddenly every fem in the place acquired a slight stoop or cringe. The faces of the nearest ones went slack and foolish before his eyes. Witchery? He almost laughed. He had seen a dormful of boys change in just such a way when a Teacher walked in on them unexpectedly in the Boyhouse.

One of the fems tending to the pipe came toward the intruders, her calloused feet rasping on the concrete floor. She knelt to kiss the ground in front of them. There were scars on her lean back. Nobody bothered about pretty appearances in the work-rooms of Bayo, it seemed. She had wide shoulders for a fem and a strong neck, and she was almost the size of a fair-grown boy.

Servan addressed her close-cropped head. "Where are your masters?"

"This fem feels that they are all in the men's compound, please-you-master," she whined, slurring her words in the manner of fems. She sat back on her heels, so that now that he had acknowledged her presence, he might see her face if he wished to. "Is there something this fem might offer these masters?"

A trickle of white fluid ran off the lip of the pipe into the trough, setting off a to-do of shouting and wall-rapping from the fems working with the mesh.

"She can offer her full attention," Servan snapped to the one before him. She kissed the ground again in apology. "Is there some fem here who's been in Bayo for the past three five-years?"

"This fem can try to take the masters to one such," she said, using the proper formula that avoided any suggestion of actual competence on her part. She arose at his gesture to guide them.

Then the outer door opened and Kelmz walked in. The two Rovers strode ahead of him, heads up and nostrils flaring.

Every fem in the room froze.

"Christ," Servan groaned, "and his unfortunate father!"

Close up, the Rovers were impressive. Their heavy torsos gleamed, and the short capes they wore strained across their shoulders. They stood with their legs bent in an aggressive crouch. Each Rover had a knife in his right hand, and his defensively gloved left hand tensed before his belly, ready to lash out with a metal-studded blow or to turn the slash of an enemy's weapon.

"Kelmz, you're moon-mad to bring them in here!" Servan said.

"I can hold them," said the captain.

Eykar said sharply, "Will they be missed?"

Kelmz shook his head. "They're fresh, probably just on duty an hour or so. Nobody will check them for a while. I think they're worth the risk to us. You want to keep these bitches shivering when you have to go among them."

His hands rested lightly on the Rovers' shoulders; he stroked them a little, calming them. But he had an odd, abstracted air, as if he touched them from a great distance.

VII

In his time Kelmz had done enough guard duty among workgangs of fems to be unfazed by them now. He attended to the Rovers, who padded warily along rolling their eyes and quivering under their scarred hides. To them, fems were drug-distorted demons.

Servan watched Eykar as they all proceeded through the fems' quarters. Eykar's eyes, that Servan knew to be remarkably keen and untiring, missed nothing; but his face remained austerely uncommunicative. Probably he was holding in his disgust. What he had been taught about fems in the Boyhouse (as Servan knew, having had the same lessons and having had opportunities since to prove them against reality) was not enough and not even particularly accurate. It was one thing to be told that fems were smelly, misshapen and alien-minded. It was another to be surrounded by them.

No fems ever went to Endpath. They had no souls, only inner cores of animating darkness shaped from the void beyond the stars. Their deaths had no significance. Some men believed that the same shadows returned again and again in successive fem-bodies in order to contest for the world with the souls of men, which came from light.

It was hard to connect these crude mud walls and their stunted inhabitants with the great witch-fems who had overthrown the Ancients' mighty civilization. The Chants Historical told the tale: at the peak of their power, the men of Ancient times had been so fascinated with their own technical prowess that they had neglected the supervision of their treacherous fems. Technics had seemed to offer the promise of overcoming the sullen chaos of the void itself by the extension of manly will from the face of the earth out among the stars. The Ancients had concentrated first on attacking the moon, through which the forces of the void were focussed on the world.

The Moonwitch had not been destroyed by the missiles the Ancients had hurled; she had fought back through her minions, the fems. With her magic the fems had inspired the natural inferiors of the Ancients to join in a coalition to overthrow the rule of order and manly reason. There was some question as to the exact apportionment of blame for the rebellion of the Wasting among the various kinds of lesser beings (collectively known as the unmen). Each kind had a proper place, after all, under the authority of men: the beasts of all elements furnished men with raw materials; labor could be forced from the lazy, savage Dirties; even the fems had certain minor skills to offer their masters in addition to giving them sons.

To the logical mind, however, the answer was obvious: there had been beast-fems, and fems among the Dirties, and the sons of men had turned Freak under the tutelage of their dams. The common denominator of corruption and rebellion among all the unmen had been fems.

Even at the time, there had been names for fems indicating some understanding of the danger they represented. One Ancient book used in the Boyhouse mentioned fems as "bra-burners." Since "bra" was a word in an old language meaning "weapon," clearly "bra-burner" meant a fem who stole and destroyed the weapons of her masters.

The weapon of the fems was witchery, and that could only be destroyed by burning the witches themselves. The Ancients had begun by burning other kinds of rebellious unmen, out of a reluctance to recognize the power that the fems had accumulated. By the time the fems' primary responsibility for the wars of the Wasting had been openly acknowledged by the Ancients, the world had already begun to slip from the grasp of men.

Yet it never fell into the hands of their enemies. The fems' witchery was by nature irrational, utilizing epidemics, uprisings of crazed Dirties, destructive storms (to which the Ancients properly gave fem-type names), and poisons released into air, earth and water. These weapons were so virulent and undiscriminating that they also killed the unmen themselves. That anyone survived at all was due to the foresight and tough-mindedness of a handful of ruling men.

Shelters had been prepared earlier against the aggressiveness of the most powerful of the Dirties: Reds and Chings across the ocean and Blacks at home. Seeing at last that the light of manly reason was doomed to be overwhelmed by the forces of chaos, the wisest leaders of men withdrew to these shelters, taking a handful of fems with them for breeding purposes.

Outside of this Refuge, as the area of the shelters was called, men and unmen fell to the plagues and disasters that wasted the world. In helpless horror the men in the Refuge watched (by means of wonderful distance-instruments) the ruin of the civilization they had once commanded but were powerless to save. Some of the refugees went mad, but the strongest among them (many were military men) organized an interim life of discipline and sturdy optimism. They had faith that someday the surface of the earth would be habitable again. Meanwhile, at least the vermin responsible for earth's ruin were dying along with their victims.

The descendants of the refugees (and their properly

tamed fems) emerged eventually to reclaim and make usable the territory now known as the Holdfast. It was the first step in the Reconquest of the whole world in the name of light, reason and order. The descendants of the surviving fems, however, would never again be allowed to become an active danger to the hegemony of their masters. The only type of unmen to have been saved from the Wasting, fems were now closely controlled; modern men were taught never to forget that these beings were by their nature the hereditary and implacable enemies of everything manly, bright and clean.

Servan was disappointed to find no signs of witch-power here in the recesses of Bayo. On occasion he had sensed something secret about certain fems, a holding-back that had challenged him. He had never been able to extract anything from them other than a song or two, and often the fem who sang only half-comprehended the words, which were merely lamentations over hard work and the vagaries of the masters' desires. Though he had considered dosing a fem with manna as an aid to interrogation, when it came down to it he never could bring himself to waste good stuff on them.

In the Holdfast, fems accused of exercising powers inherited from the terrible fems of Ancient times were burned as witches. Here in the dull yellow light of the wall lamps of Bayo, the existence of such powers seemed preposterous. Servan congratulated himself for his own scepticism.

Yet, moving among so many of these bent, dull-eyed figures, he wasn't sorry to have the Rovers along.

Their guide stopped and indicated with a cringing gesture that their goal lay through the doorway to the right. The room beyond was sparsely furnished with clay tables and sitting-blocks. One old fem sat eating curdcake from a chipped bowl. She arose at once and hurried toward them, wiping her mouth and fingers on the hem of her smock so that they wouldn't have to smell fem-food about her. She knelt in front of Servan. So far, all was in order.

"Fossa presents herself, please-you-masters, with important news."

Servan was no kind of fanatic about fems and their proper place, but by addressing them first this old bitch (who should have known better) had committed a serious breach. Kelmz looked ready to break her skinny neck. It was not out of anger but to maintain propriety that Servan slapped her, hard.

She rocked back from the blow, but went right on with the same astonishing forwardness: "Word came from Lammintown. The Pennelton masters watch for you masters. They seldom come to these quarters after sunset. Tonight, they have come twice."

The men looked at each other; Senior Bajerman must have heard about their encounter with the 'Wares and guessed something of their intent and their destination.

Servan said, "Is there a place where the men never come?"

"There is a place where they have never come before, please-you," replied the crone. She was even using hard-edged, manly speech, instead of the slurred soft-speech of fems, so that there would be no misunderstanding.

"Take us there," Servan said.

Fossa was leathery from weather and work; teeth were missing from one side of her mouth so that her cheek had sunk in and her jaw was crooked. She scuttled ahead of them, bowed with age and humility. Yet something in the bearing of other fems toward her as they passed seemed to indicate respect. Servan was intrigued.

They entered a series of low-ceilinged, dimly lit dormitories. Fems slept or reclined in slit-eyed torpor in the beds. Some had small, blanketed bundles lying next to them. Servan was reminded of the brief trip that all boys made to the Hospital adjoining the Boyhouse, to be instructed about the grossly swollen fems due to drop cubs. The lights had been brighter in the Hospital, but the somnolent atmosphere had been much the same.

One of the bundles began kicking, and it raised a thin

cry. The fem next to it hiked up on her elbow, eyes still
shut, and put her hand over the source of the sound. The
kicking continued, but the wailing diminished to small
gasping sounds that were succeeded by quiet. The fem
rolled on her side and went back to sleep.

Fossa gave Servan the cringing, ingratiating smile of a
fem imparting information, so that he should be
reassured that she claimed no credit for knowing
something that he did not. "We teach fem-cubs to be
quiet. It's a good first lesson in obedience."

A number of fems were without cubs. Servan pointed
to one of them and asked why she wasn't back at work,
having dropped her young and apparently lost it.

Apologetically, the old fem said, "There are ways to
continue the flow of milk even when there is no suckling
cub. If a dam's capacity is high, she stays here in the
milkery. Some stay all their lives, for fems have a great
need of this milk now, in their well deserved deprivation."
She was referring to the drastic reduction of the seaweed
ration allotted to the fems, which dated back several
five-years. At that time, successive failures of the laver
harvest had earned a rather freehanded rage from the
men, resulting in fewer fems (and the deaths of the witches
responsible for the blight, since the crops had stabilized
again, though at lower levels). Now the fem population
was built back up in number, but their food supply had
not been expanded. Apparently they were finding their
own sources of sustenance, as Fossa explained.

"The masters entered through the curding room, where
the milk from these fems is made into the curdcake which
fems eat."

Kelmz said grimly, "If I'd known so many of them
could talk I'd have been more careful working around
them. But this old bitch can't even describe what we saw
with our own eyes without lying: that stuff they eat is
brown and gelid, not white."

The old fem responded, after a pause, "Other things are
added, to give fems strength for the tasks set them by the
masters."

An alcove at the far end of the dormitory complex served as an office. Strings of tally-beads hung from pegs in the walls, presumably to keep track of the workings of the milkery. Here they stopped. Servan drew up a worn sitting-block, turning so that he could look back the way they had come. The place fascinated him. It was a DarkDreamer's dream, with its sleep-heavy air, its quiet, the lumpish figures large and small under their coarse, gray covers, the dull light from basket-shaded lamps.

Kelmz used the pause to get better control of the Pennelton Rovers, rubbing them down carefully with his hands as their officer would do, to check for injuries that their inflamed minds would never notice. He kept them facing away from the milkery.

"'The moon's unpredictable daughters,'" Servan quoted softly. "That's from the fems' own songs. And here they are, in full mystery. Eykar, turn your back; you're just a boy where these creatures are concerned; you have no defenses. They might witch you right out of your high purpose."

Eykar stopped pacing and turned his pale gaze on Servan. "In pursuit of which, do you think you might bring yourself to find out what we came to find out?"

Doing so turned out to be simple. Servan asked Fossa about Raff Maggomas, and she told them. He had come; he had stayed with the Quarterback Company assigned here at the time (a hard time, marked by laver failures); he had returned to the City with the Quarterbacks when the five-year was over.

Years later, word had gotten about that Maggomas' son was in trouble in the Boyhouse. The son had been sent to become Endtendant, and Maggomas had vanished. At once, a new scandal had broken. Maggomas had apparently had a lover across the age-line, a Junior Quarterback who was moreover much sought after (however covertly) by an Angelist Company Senior superior to Maggomas; a Boardman, some said. The young man, whose name was Karz Kambl, had also disappeared, presumably to join Maggomas in hiding. Enraged by this turn of events, the Board had passed a resolution barring Maggomas from returning to any company of the City in any capacity.

So far as was known, he had never tried to return and had not been seen or heard of since by any reliable witness. And that had been six years ago. The younger man, now a Senior, was said to be living more or less in hiding in the City.

Aside from one or two breaks (profusely apologized for) when Fossa was called to confer with some fem in the dormitory, the report was a model of concise information, clearly delivered. Servan complimented the old fem on the effectiveness of her intelligence network. She was remarkably well informed. These rumors of an affair had never come to Servan's notice, possibly because he was too closely involved through his connection with Eykar.

He was beginning to be amused by this old fem and was not offended when she went on unbidden: "If the master is pleased with this fem's service, perhaps he will condescend to do a small thing for this fem?"

She didn't say, favor for favor, but she might as well have, the presumptuous hag. Servan burst out into a delighted guffaw. This episode was more entertaining than he could have hoped. He inquired with exaggerated courtesy into the nature of this "small thing."

"Will the master accept a fem to travel with him and serve him?" She was making a gift to a master of another fem! It was marvelous.

Eykar snapped, "Servan, this is too much!"

"It is pretty odd," Servan admitted, "but perhaps this bitch has other help to offer than information—if we cooperate. Besides, think, man: cash is only cash, and we may have to spend high in the City to locate this man Kambl. Like them or not, fems are a form of wealth."

Kelmz objected. "They're also a form of trouble. She could cost us more than she's worth. Fems are stupid and spiteful; you can never even tell just why it is they've betrayed you to your enemies. I know them well. But I have these Rovers on my hands now, so who's to keep an eye on some fem besides?"

"Servan," Eykar said, "since she was offered to him, and if he still thinks it's worth the trouble." Kelmz shrugged reluctant assent, and Eykar turned sharply on the old fem: "What extra aid comes with this gift?"

Fossa kissed the ground to him. "Such poor help as mere fems have to offer," she fawned. "Yet the masters may find it useful."

A bell tinkled somewhere close by. Some of the sleeping fems sat up, reaching for the swaddled cubs beside them or for the clay pitchers kept under their beds. Each of the cubs was put to the breast for a moment only, then handed on to the nearest waking fem who had no cub of her own to start her milk. Some of the fems didn't even open their eyes as they went through the motions of what was obviously a well established routine. The pitchers, now containing fresh milk, were set on the floor to be picked up by fems who pushed carts down the aisles between the beds. Those whose milk-shift had not yet been called slept through it all.

"Let's get on with this," Eykar said, hoarsely.

"Please-you-masters," murmured Fossa, "this fem will go and fetch the one spoken of from another place."

Servan stood up. "We'll go with you." It would hardly be to her advantage to betray them. She would get no reward, for fems were invariably punished for anything found to be out of order. Yet it paid to be wary of their irrationality.

"This fem feels the masters would be happier waiting here," she said.

He laughed. "We're tough enough for anything you or your kind can offer, gray bitch. Lead on."

They crossed a hallway beyond the milkery and stepped between two heavy doors into the embrace of a hot, acrid roil of stench and noise that stopped them in their tracks.

Right at their feet, a hopper was set into the concrete

floor. A huge screw-shaft, bedded in a chute, angled up out of it. The screw-thread was gleaming sharp, and wedged into the hollows of its spiral were fragments of flesh, bone and fat. Above the level of the men's heads, a fem stood on a ladder, carefully scraping this detritus into a bucket. The screw-chute led past her to a row of drums mounted on a platform. The drums turned slowly, driven by a crank shaft at which the fems labored with bent, straining backs. Another fem-crew tended the furnaces under the drums, stepping to and fro with scoops of coal over a gutter in the floor. The gutter flowed with a yellow fluid that drained through a pipe from the drums overhead.

Fossa put her head close to Servan's and said at the top of her voice, "This is the Rendery, please-you-master."

VIII

The Rovers began to shiver and snarl; Kelmz turned and thrust them back out into the corridor. Eykar, who never ran away from anything, followed the old fem to the end of the central structure. Not to be outdone, Servan went too, dizzy with the effort to breathe through his skin or his ears, eyes streaming.

The other side of the machinery featured a broad, sloping table onto which the drums could be emptied. From there, the contents were screw-driven again into an enclosed grinding-mill. On the floor under the mill's outlet was a conical heap of dark, damp-looking particles. A large, tight-woven basket on wheels stood nearby, with ceramic scoops hung from pegs fixed along the rim.

Through the half-open lids of the drums, Servan could see fragments dropping from the fixed blades inside back into the churning material below. The end-drum rotated more slowly and loudly than the others. Its lid had been opened completely and fastened back, so that the contents could be drawn out with long-handled hoes.

Two fems were working the heavier dregs to the lip of the drum, to be tumbled off onto the steaming hill on the table beneath.

Servan's DarkDream-trained mind made the connection between this noxious operation and what the old fem had said about adding other substances to the milk-food, which obviously wouldn't be plentiful enough to go around unless it were stretched; and what more nutritious additive than the flesh of dead fems and of fem-cubs who did not survive the milkery? What was reputedly poisonous to men, the fems had learned to consume safely, having no other choice but starvation.

Some man must have designed the process; it was too beautiful, too efficient to be a product of the fems' own thinking. The concept of making them literally self-sustaining had a certain gruesome sophistication impossible for fems' thinking. He had to admit, though, that a sort of manly hardness was argued by the ability of fems to accept such an arrangement; unless they were not hardened so much as merely too depraved to be horrified.

Fossa tapped on the lowest of the footplates leading up onto the platform. The fems working up there looked down. She shouted something. The nearer of the two fems went to the edge, handed down her hoe to one of the furnace-feeders below and descended. At the bottom of the steps, she untied a filthy rag from the railing and wiped off the greasy fragments that spattered her skin. Then, stepping carefully over and around the scraps lying on the floor, she came toward the men with downcast eyes.

There was no point in trying to speak in these surroundings. When they emerged into the hallway, Kelmz turned from the Rovers and looked the young fem icily up and down, saying with undisguised revulsion, "Must we travel attended by a thing that reeks of its own dead?"

The choice of words was unfortunate. Eykar said in a tight, bitter voice, "You great fool, don't you recognize punishment when you see it?" Imaginative of him, to see a similarity between Endpath and the Rendery.

Still staggered by the impact of the Rendery, the men
were moved smoothly through the fems' washroom—it
was a relief to scrub off the dank muck of the swamps and
the lingering Rendery smell—and out again. They found
themselves surrounded by a dozen fems armed with cloth,
needles and thread, who cut and stitched, outfitting the
men as a party of Hemaways from the City. Using Kelmz'
uniform as a basic pattern, they transformed the
Pennelton Rovers into Hemaways; Kelmz held the brutes
calm in spite of the fems' hands darting about them.

Servan had underestimated the resources at Fossa's
command. The men's clothes, from Kelmz' worn blanks
to Eykar's uniform, were completely reworked or
replaced. The one item that the fems could not supply was
a manna-bracelet. Since a Senior in charge of Rovers
would certainly be wearing one, Servan grudgingly lent
the captain his own.

The work was done in the kitchen, the only place where
the light was good enough and yet not easily noticeable
from the men's compound. From some corner a pack
basket was produced, and food was brought. While the
men ate lightly of leafcurd and beer, fems filled the basket
with supplies for the journey: a white crock of curdcake at
the bottom for the fem who would go with them, two jugs
of beer, a bar of lammin-chew, a square of hempseed
bread wrapped in a damp cloth for freshness, and even a
small box of dry laver-flakes for seasoning—that last a
real luxury these days. There wasn't enough to feed the
men well for the whole trip, but they were all used to going
hungry. What was astonishing was that the fems had
access to any amount of men's food at all.

There was also a razor, some earthenware eating gear,
a mending kit, firestones and tinder, and a pair of spare
sandals that could only be meant—by the size of
them—for Kelmz.

Fossa drew a diagram on the floor with soot from the
cookstoves. The causeways which linked Bayo and the
City were easily navigable in daylight, but at night they

formed a baffling maze. She drilled the men, ever so respectfully, until they could have picked their way in their sleep. Then she scuffed out the drawing with her heel.

The other fem, the young one, returned from washing the stink and grease of the Rendery from her skin and hair. She was introduced as Alldera, the old one's hold-mate, which meant that Fossa's master had at some time owned this young fem as well. Whoever he was, he seemed to have interesting requirements in his personal femhold. Both fems could speak; neither was in any way beautiful, and in addition the young one had been schooled as a messenger.

Alldera had one other unusual, visible, attribute: her legs and buttocks were strongly developed (Fossa lifted the young one's smock to point this out). She had been speed-trained, which was illegal and added to her value. Speed-training was confined to men who specialized in racing competitively for their companies. In any case, no fem should be able to outrun Rovers.

Though as a runner she was more fluidly muscled than most labor fems, her looks were not appealing. The wet hair clinging to her head only emphasized the breadth of her jaw and cheekbones. She had wide-set eyes of an unremarkable pale hazel color, a nose that had been broken and healed flat-bridged, and a heavy-lipped mouth with a sullen turn to the corners. The best that could be said of her face was that the skin was of good quality, though verging on a Dirty coppery cast.

Servan would have preferred a prettier fem, but there were few of those to be had in Bayo. Anyway, as she was she would lend an added touch of authenticity to their group disguise. A fem of no great beauty but specially skilled was just the sort of property that a man like Kelmz might be expected to acquire, once he took his mantle and with it the right to own fems personally.

The four of them were to be Senior-Kelmz-and-party come on one of the unannounced spot-checks of work-turf so common lately in the Holdfast. Kelmz

would play himself, promoted. Any Penneltons they
might encounter closely on the causeways would be
unlikely to know that Kelmz had been more or less
dumped by his company rather than coaxed at last into
Seniorhood. Men assigned to Bayo avoided contact with
the City until the end of their five-year, disliking to be
called "cunt nurses" and such by other City men. The two
younger men were outfitted in simple pants and tunics, to
play the parts of Hemaway Juniors in attendance on their
superior. Filling out the group to a properly impressive
size, there were the two Rovers as an escort and the fem to
serve as pack-bearer.

  She, the ostensible reason for this extraordinary
activity and risk on the fems' part, interested Servan. She
never said a word. Her story, as Fossa told it, was simple
and plausible: a Pennelton, drunk, had gone after her at
her work-bench without noticing the red scarf she had
been wearing at the time. She had refused him, as she was
bound to do in order to protect him from contamination.
But the man's Juniors had witnessed the incident, and he
wanted some redress for his injured standing. Alldera had
been assigned to the Rendery while the Pennelton Seniors
considered whether she should be burned for witching the
man into missing the token of her uncleanness in the first
place. Doing so would restore the drunkard's self-respect,
so it was a likely outcome.

  So Alldera had to be whisked out of Bayo for her life's
sake. The fems in charge of the Rendery would report that
she had bolted into the marshes, where her starved corpse
presumably would be discovered someday as others had
been before.

  It was no news to Servan that some men were excited
by the thought of fucking a fem soiled with her monthly
blood-tribute to the Moonwitch. But somehow the
account rang false to him. The campaign that old Fossa
had mounted was too dangerous to the fems to be
performed merely to save the life of this pie-faced
youngster. How valuable could one fem be to other fems?
It couldn't be simply that the two fems had been owned by

the same master; that was a source of friction rather than closeness among fems. There had to be something else to justify the lengths to which these fems were going to get Alldera out of Bayo. Even the Rovers wouldn't be missed, Fossa promised; that could be managed. They had no guarantee that one of the men would not at some point inform the Board of the organization they had found here in Bayo, with the inevitable result. Yet if these fems were worried by any such possibility, they didn't show it.

Well, then, suppose they were to be reckoned with in some way that was not yet clear. Let them try to trick him and use him in some game of their own. He accepted the challenge. Everybody was an antagonist, after all, at least potentially. The remedy was simply to recognize that this was so, and to try to use the other person before, and better than, he used you.

At last, the preparations were done. The fems picked up every scrap of cloth and thread and put out the lights in the kitchen. Fossa and young Alldera took the men out on the roof of the next building, which connected directly on the west side with the causeways. There, the fugitives found themselves suddenly in the midst of a creaking, droning party of hags whose job was to deploy the laver-carts at various points on the causeways for collection of the next day's harvest. The moon was up, a mere scrap of light not nearly bright enough to show the incongruity of the men's tall forms to any watching sentries. In no time at all, the lighted windows and the music of Bayo fell behind.

Soon the old fems with their rattling carts milled to a stop in the windy darkness. Their mumbling and singing died. The stars sparked cold light from the surfaces of the laver-ponds that stretched away, glimmering, on either side of the causeway.

Fossa, a stick figure in the starlight, stepped forward. She said, "Safe journey, masters."

"Too bad it's not you coming with us, old dam," Servan said. On that note the men and the young fem, canted forward under the pack-basket on her back, departed westward toward the City as fast as they could travel.

The idea was to cover as much ground as they could that night, unobserved, rest all morning in one of the shelters built into all major intersections of the cause-ways, and in the afternoon turn and move as slowly as possible back in the direction of Bayo, as if coming from the City instead of fleeing toward it. It was not unusual for a Senior of one company to inspect, without warning, the work of another company's Juniors. They often did it, in the name of competition and in hopes of shaving a rival company's work-points. A day of slow "inspection," followed by another night of hard running in the opposite direction, should see the travelers to the City walls.

It was the sort of sly plan you might expect from devious creatures like old Fossa. Bajerman would be completely stymied, for he never would descend willingly to thinking like a fem.

They reached the designated shelter just as the sun edged above the horizon behind them. The shelter was unoccupied, as Fossa had said it would be, and they slept behind its curtain while the Penneltons used the causeways to shift fem-gangs from one set of ponds to another for the day's work. Servan kept half-waking at the approach of footsteps and the shrill whistle-signals of the Pennelton drovers.

At midday, the travelers washed and ate and put the lumpy grass-stuffed mattresses they had used back under the benches in the shelter. They rolled up the curtains and stepped out into the brilliant day, facing Bayo again.

Kelmz looked a really splendid Senior in his bright, striped mantle. He seemed to take ironical pleasure in the impression he made, broad and scarred as he was in his finery. Out of an unsuspected vanity, he hated the openwork sandals he had to wear, as if he felt betrayed by the sight of his own splayed and knotted feet. The two Pennelton Rovers strode stiff-backed in front of him, and Servan and Eykar followed at a respectful distance from his heels, intoning the Chant Declamatory in reverent tones.

The fem Alldera trudged along at the rear, her proper place. Servan glanced back: she was just a fem, and an ill-favored one at that. If there were any witchery at Bayo, it was the ability to throw a magnifying and romantic gloss over such a drab.

The artificial, ambling pace required by their plan was tiring to maintain, but at least the afternoon was breezy and bright-skied. Below on either side, the vast spread of the laver-pools lay like a table of mirrors with stubby-legged causeways bestriding it from edge to edge. Diminished by distance, crews of fems turned the long, flexible cables which brought up the lower level growth of laver for its share of sunlight. The notes of the Penneltons' signal pipes sounded piercingly over the glittering flats. The Pennelton Juniors were easily distinguishable by the broad straw hats they wore. Each pair of them would wave and salute when they made out the bulk of Kelmz' mantled shoulders or recognized the Chant Declamatory.

It was funny to see them joyfully gyrating their lean arms, while they must be thinking, where's that Hemaway whitehead sprung from without us being piped a warning by Penneltons closer to the City? And they would snap out sharp notes to get their fems moving faster, ordering them into new positions, anything to indicate active supervision and to avoid being docked work-points.

Kelmz played his part to the hilt. Once they dawdled past a gang lifting loaded laver-carts covered with wet canvas onto the loading lane of the causeway. The hoist squealed hideously. Kelmz glared in passing, as if he really would have liked to stop and lambaste the Penneltons in charge for not taking proper care of the equipment that came with their work-turf. No wonder he was servilely saluted on every hand; he made a convincing pillar of order.

Late in the afternoon, they ducked into another shelter for a light meal and a rest before the night's hard run. Eykar lingered outside, which put off the moment when he would be shut up at close quarters with the fem again.

Kelmz had noticed Eykar's uneasiness about the fem. Sitting between the Rovers and watching her unpack the food, he said to Servan, "You do your friend no favors, keeping that bitch with us. No one would notice if you ordered her to slip in with some gang down there at the ponds."

"She's my property," Servan said. The soporific pace of the afternoon had wearied him, and his throat was dry with chanting. "Tell you what; since she's on your mind, why don't you take her for an hour or so? You've been on a wild-beast chase all your life. Try a fem instead, a little dip into mystery, an adventure for your soul."

"I've done my duty in the breeding rooms," Kelmz said. He slapped down the sandal he had taken off and began rubbing his foot. The Rovers imitated him. "I'm no cunting pervert."

"But you think Eykar is?"

"No." Kelmz studied the fem's bent back. The Rovers, catching his antagonism, stirred and muttered low in their throats. "But he seems to have plenty on his mind without worrying about a famishing bitch too."

"You tend to your Rovers, Captain. I'll tend to my friend."

IX

Servan ate quickly; there was little enough. He took the bowl the fem had prepared for Eykar and the smaller beer jug and went outside. Eykar was standing at the parapet (not leaning, he never held himself slackly) watching the light fade. He took his final portion of food with a nod of thanks, and ate. He had a tired, thoughtful air that Servan remembered well from their Boyhouse days and was always moved to puncture if he could.

"Kelmz is worried," he said, "about you and the fem."

"I'm worried about Kelmz," Eykar said wryly.

"Feeling responsible?" Servan leaned on the weathered stone wall.

"He's with us because I asked him to come."

"As I recall, that was your way of saving his life, wasn't it?"

"Perhaps that was no favor." Eykar swept up laver-flakes neatly on his seedbread. Like all Holdfast men, he was an efficient eater. "I didn't realize the strains he'd be subjected to. In particular, the manna you gave

83

him that night—was it only the night before last?"

"Without him, the others might have ducked out at the last minute, and the whole situation could have gone against us."

"That's why I didn't interfere."

"He's a tough old brute. A little DarkDreaming can't hurt him."

"It already has." A volley of piped notes rose from below. The fem-gangs too far from Bayo to go home and sleep were being herded into lean-to shelters out among the ponds for the night. "I don't think Captain Kelmz of the Hemaways as he used to be would steal Rovers from another company. He knows it can upset their balance to be switched around that way and increases the chances that they'll go rogue and have to be killed."

Servan shrugged. "He's just facing up to the reality of our situation."

"No. I think he's given way to something after a lifetime of fighting it off—a fascination with the idea of the beasts; isn't that what his DarkDream shows? I think Rovers have always stood in his mind for tamed beasts. Now he's looking inward instead. His tie with these Pennelton Rovers is very impersonal, have you noticed?"

"What do you care what happens to that old wolf?" Servan said, kicking idly at the wall. "He's no lover for you, man; remember the age-line."

"Servan, you're a walking prurience, you never change! I just don't want the man to come apart in the middle of all this. You're not still after his blood?"

"No, not right now."

"How long is 'right now?' You used to remember old grudges any time it suited you. Frankly, if anything happened to him I doubt that you or I could take over these Pennelton Rovers the way he did at Bayo."

"Oh? You were impressed? Do I have cause to be jealous?"

"If you had ever run Rovers yourself, you'd have been impressed too."

"I was, actually," Servan said, with sudden generosity. "It was well done."

"Can I count on you not to murder him in a fit of pique?"

Servan threw out his hands in an exasperated shrug. "He caught me off guard in Lammintown; I was annoyed, but I'm not sulking over it. What do you want, a promise? All right, I promise, I won't lay a hand on him. Feel better?"

"That's no promise," Eykar said. "You've always put your hands where you like, and you always will." He bent to rinse out his bowl in the wash bucket beside the shelter wall. "I would not be charmed, Servan, by even your most artful apology for murdering Captain Kelmz."

"You don't trust me," Servan mourned. "Come on, leave that, the fem will do the cleaning up; God's own Freaking Son, what do you think I keep her for, her beauty? Let's walk a bit. I've brought some beer."

They strolled toward Bayo, facing the direction from which pursuit would come if their game had been discovered. Servan had thought several times that afternoon of how it would be to walk right into Bajerman and a pack of Penneltons; while Eykar, no doubt, had been worrying about Kelmz or thinking of the fem.

"Tell me about Endpath," he said.

"It was an uncluttered life," Eykar said. Living there had clearly not affected his reticence.

"You seem to have kept fit." Servan saw, with a flash of heat, Eykar's gaunt frame as he had seen it in the Bayo showers, spare and white and hard as marble. Eykar always had fought what he regarded as the weakness of his body with a self-discipline that would have killed a weak man.

"Endpath duties are light," Eykar said, with a tinge of irony. "I had time to spend."

"How?" Servan pressed.

"Servan, you must create Endpath sometimes for your dream clients. I'm sure you'd do it well. Why cramp your style with reality?"

"Well, let's consider the future, then." Servan swung the jug as he walked, liking the sloshing weight of it. "I must say I think your goal is rather limited. There are big things to be done in the Holdfast by young men who aren't cowed by the cloth-cocks and their Rovers. For instance, you and I could make something of the Juniors' resentments. If we were smart enough and fast enough we could turn the Holdfast upside down to our own profit. You saw how the Chesters took to you back on the ferry."

Eykar said contemptuously, "I saw how easily you maneuvered them, yes. But it was to you and Kelmz that they responded, not to me."

"Oh, they could learn to love you," Servan smiled.

"I'm no leader," Eykar said. "And you—"

"I have potential," Servan protested in a pained tone. "As for yourself, Eykar, you're a weightier man than you give yourself credit for. Look what happened when the Board sent you off to Endpath to kill and die. If I know you at all, you turned the whole thing into an exercise in personal austerity."

"I did my poor best," Eykar replied, "lacking your inventiveness and your talent for being entertained."

Servan sighed. "You think of yourself as weak, but if you were any stronger you would punch holes in the ground with every step you take. What you decide to do, you do; or what in the coldest quarter of the moon am I doing out here with you now, listening to the lavers grow?"

"Amusing yourself, as always," Eykar said, with his rasping laugh. "I did worry about you those first months at Endpath, whether you were amusing yourself, or were able to; needlessly, of course."

"Needlessly! You're extraordinary. Those old Hemaway turds meant to burn me, did you know that?" Servan began to work the stopper free from the neck of the jug.

"I wasn't kept informed," Eykar said caustically. "As soon as I'd put you into their care, the Teachers locked me into iso. Days later, they sent me to Endpath. I had no chance to ask questions."

The stopper came loose. Servan would have put it into the pocket of his shirt, but the Bayo fems had neglected to provide a pocket, they themselves having no pockets and nothing to keep in them. He tossed the stopper in his hand, thinking about those Boyhouse days. They strolled on through the evening without speaking for a while.

In the Boyhouse, Servan had quickly acquired a reputation as a bully, a sly heckler of the Teachers and a thief; in fact, he had been fighting boredom, nothing more. Then Eykar had been placed in his class, and the situation had changed. Servan had grown ambitious. He had begun using his mind, to the astonishment (and discomfiture) of his Teachers. Yet no matter how neatly he could skip and dance around them for the dazzlement of the new boy, Eykar had pressed straight ahead, undistractable.

Eykar had wanted to know everything in those days, but only if it were true. Was it true, for instance, that beyond the borders of the Holdfast there was nothing but the empty scrubland called the Wild? If so, why was the Board committed to the Reconquest of such useless, hostile territory? If they were committed, just where was the Reconquest happening, and what was its timetable? He had gone after information like that along with incredibly picky points of doctrine, as if to him everything was just as important as everything else, and he'd been impossible to divert or even confuse for very long: fascinating, a real challenge.

Eventually, Servan had to meet him on his own ground in order to meet him at all. Subjects that the Teachers refused to discuss, Servan took up with him gladly, if irreverently, and this brought them together. The element of competition between them didn't surface openly until the embarrassing incident of FirstDream.

At the age of thirteen, after years of drill in the proper subjects for dreaming meditation, all the boys in a class were given manna for the first time by supervising Teachers. It was a crucial test. Some boys died under the influence of the drug; it was said of them that they were still their dams' cubs, not men enough to bend the manna to the schooling of their souls. Instead, the manna broke down their feeble counterfeit of manly will, and their souls bled back out into the void. Others could not shake off the phantoms of dreaming-shock after waking, and they were never again free of a craving for the drug. They were turned over to the company officers to be trained as Rovers. Those who were orderly in thought and virtuous in spirit, thanks to their years in the Boyhouse, emerged stronger than before and inspired by the visions they had seen.

Then there were the borderline cases. Eykar struggled with fever and phantoms for days afterward. Servan almost died.

The Teachers pulled Servan back into a lower class, claiming that they meant to overcome his sensitivity to manna in easy stages. Clearly, by degrading him they also intended to punish him for his long history of tricks and insolence.

So he spent several years in the forced company of his age-inferiors. He was put through the ordeal of FirstDream again and again, with no better results. All this he minded less than the endless drilling. The harder they tried to sink him into the morass of solemn virtue that formed the Canon of Dreaming Images, the worse his behavior became out of sheer frustration; meanwhile, Eykar's natural brilliance was beginning to be recognized, however grudgingly. A great future was predicted for Eykar, despite the stigma of his known parentage. He went on seeking out Servan to debate with him, which only underlined the disparity in their situations.

Eventually, in order to alter his apparently fixed status as permanent boy and non-dreamer, and also to get a rise out of the Teachers, Servan suggested that a Teacher go through a dreaming session with him, giving him word- and touch-cues for the proper images, to guide him past the voidish mishmash of fantasy that he was so prone to.

There was an uproar. They thought Servan wanted a Teacher to show him how to DarkDream. They told him twenty different reasons why one did not learn manly self-reliance by submitting to the mental control of others at one's most vulnerable moment—during dreaming. Then they sent him into iso.

Inevitably, sulking hungry and alone in the dark little cage of a room, Servan made up his mind to try DarkDreaming and find out what it was about. On his release, he made secret trips to Skidro, where he located a DarkDreamer who agreed to dream-gift him in exchange for information about certain of the Boyhouse Teachers.

Then Servan asked Eykar along. Naturally, the invitation threw Eykar into a spasm of indecision. In the end, the chance to find out the "truth" of DarkDreaming proved irresistible, and he went with Servan to meet the DarkDreamer—as an observer only.

The DarkDreamer had not been strong enough. Servan had slipped from his mental grip and had begun the descent into manna-madness. Eykar had interrupted the process and forced the DarkDreamer to help him carry Servan back to the Boyhouse and into the care of the Teachers.

"Must have scared you to death," Servan said, "the whole thing. I should have checked that hack out better before putting myself into his hands. How did you know I was in trouble?"

"By your breathing. I don't know what he used, but it was much stronger than anything we'd had in the Boyhouse; Board-quality manna, judging by the effect."

Servan hugged the beer jug to his chest with both arms. "It was a near thing, let me tell you. I was out for two whole days, and when I came to I was ready to be a good boy. They couldn't believe it; those old Hemaway screws kept nagging and bullying until I got fed up and told them a few things about some of their own brothers. I'm sure they knew that some Teachers were DarkDreaming pretty regularly themselves, but they had to put on a show of outrage when I named names. They started shouting about burning me, as a throwback to the Freaks. In the middle of it all, with old Varner roaring away at the top of his lungs and blaming everybody around him for the whole situation, I passed out again.

"The next thing I knew, a bunch of sweaty Rovers came and dragged me out of bed and down into the courtyard. You remember that courtyard, the scene of so

many of our debates? Well, the whole pimply population
of the Boyhouse was turned out to watch those famishing
Rovers truss me up with ropes and sit on me so the
Teachers could cut my shoulder and use acid to obliterate
the boy-mark. Christ, you must have heard me, even in
iso!

"They tied me up in a hammock and ran me to the edge
of the Holdfast and dumped me on the ground. Not a
word, nothing. They left me in the Wild to die. That was
the first I knew that they'd decided not to burn me after
all. I can remember the taste of blood and dust in my
mouth to this moment." He swigged deeply at the beer.
What he remembered best was the silence of the Wild, a
silence towering up into the crown of the sky above him
and spreading under him down into the heart of the earth.

"Varner and others of that time have come to me since
at Endpath," Eykar observed, drily. "The Rovers are
probably long-since killed in Hemaway skirmishes. But
here you still are, Servan, to tell the tale."

Servan laughed. "Eykar, you have a hard heart! Even
you would have been moved, though, if you'd seen me
lumping around in the dust and the thorns, swearing and
roaring and bleeding, until the Scrappers came and got
me. You know, it's not true that Scrappers make their
living salvaging stray bits of metal and such. Their best
source of income is the trade in bondboys. Somebody at
the Boyhouse gets paid to tell them when a promising
lad—like me—is due to be dumped in the Wild. The
Scrappers go and fetch him in, giving rise to all those tales
of demons eating up the bodies.

"What the Scrappers do with the lucky fellow they've
rescued is soften him for sale. It's a manly virtue, after all,
not to waste anything useful that comes to hand."

Eykar stopped. "We'd better turn back, if we don't
want to waste an hour of darkness. Go on; there's more,
surely? Or are you going to tell me that you were sold to
Senior Bajerman, who is waiting for us at the shelter with
a troop of Rovers at this moment?"

"Christ," Servan laughed, "that would be hard on me,

friend! The bondboy business trades on the fact that a lot of rich old Seniors are cunters at heart. That isn't surprising, considering how unappetizing old men can be and the access they have to all the decent-looking fems. They develop an appetite for fems' company, but at the same time they worry about the state of their souls. So a lot of them prefer to turn to some poor young fellow who's been trimmed to the fem-pattern, so to speak— castrated. That's your bond; your cut boy is ashamed to run away, for fear of being found out to be no man by others. The whitehead who keeps a bondboy gets the security of male companionship with a touch of famishing softness thrown in. A neat solution to the problem, don't you think?"

Eykar said, "I was wrong to joke with you about this just now. Bondboys have come to me on the Rock. Do you think you're making up for a gap in my education with this kind of talk? Do you seriously believe that being shut up at Endpath is some sort of shelter from the darker side of Holdfast life? The things you speak of so lightly I've seen stamped in the faces of the pilgrims to the Rock. They talked to me, despite the rule of silence."

In bursts of intensity like this one, Eykar would sometimes speak more of his feelings than he meant to.

"Whatever they say about men choosing to come to Endpath, more are broken and desperate than are 'ripe for release,' whatever that may mean. Cancer drives them, madness drives them, passion drives them; a meager handful are drawn by some feeling of readiness. I'm better informed about the pain of Holdfast life than most men are; so you don't need to enlighten me.

"And it was only in my weakest moments that I've ever thought you might not make your way easily through the worst of it."

"Well," Servan said, "purely as a matter of boring personal history, I slipped away from the Scrappers but kept my eye on them afterwards. Three of them are dead now; one still carries some magnificent scars that he owes to me, and two more are in permanent hiding—unless they've gone to Endpath in their eagerness to avoid meeting me again." He considered elaborating, but decided against it. He slapped the stopper back into the neck of the jug. "I had good luck."

"A fems' notion," Eykar said. "Luck."

"Weren't you lucky to find me when you needed me? Though I always felt that we'd come together again sometime, in the natural course of events. We're as close as smoke and flame. The two of us could put our hearts together and make a blaze that would light the Holdfast from 'Troi to the sea.

"What do you think? Nothing? Or do you think but not speak, being such a true individual, such a very private person?"

"Look!" Eykar said, fiercely, and his hand pointed, dark against the stars. "You can see the glow of the City from here. Do we travel tonight, or do we hang about talking the trifling talk of soft-headed boys, old men and fems?"

There had always been ways of striking sparks from Eykar's flint. Servan was pleased that he hadn't lost the knack; he only wished he could see Eykar's face just now.

Servan rested, crouching loose-limbed against the causeway wall. When he caught his breath and lost the cramps in his gut from running so long, he would slip into the City to bring back blanks for them to wear. Their present disguises were useless on the home ground of the Hemaways.

He could hear Eykar shifting restlessly close by in the darkness. The more you wore Eykar down, the tighter he wound himself, resisting his own exhaustion. He had run well. Now that they had reached their goal—the edge of the City—he couldn't let go and rest, though Servan could hear the trembling in his breathing. There was never any point in worrying about Eykar; he looked frail, yet he generally proved a better stayer than other men.

Eykar whispered, "Strange, to hear the City and smell the City, without being able to see it. That happened sometimes at Endpath in my sleeping-dreams."

Kelmz, who should have known better than to waste rest time in conversation, made some answer or other, and the two of them began talking quietly together. There was no jeering, no point-jockeying, just Kelmz' slow, deep voice and Eykar's edged one.

Head down on his folded arms, Servan listened. Kelmz made some remark about the influence on the City of a large fem population. He got back more than he had expected—Servan smiled to himself—one of Eykar's learned lectures, the sort of thing that had made the Boyhouse Teachers so nervous. Of all things, Eykar was outlining an esoteric theory that the Holy Book of the Ancients had actually been written by clever fems using men's names. Only Eykar would speak of such things in the open at night, and with a fem squatting two feet away!

He laid it out with his usual precision and clarity: the drift of the teachings of that Book could be interpreted as a porridge of unmanly soft-headedness, mushy morals and anti-hierarchical sedition, cloaked in a manly-seeming tale of a Son justly punished for trying to supercede his Father, "God," as lord of men. There was also supposed to have been an older book of much sterner import, which this newer one imitated.

Surprisingly, Kelmz not only did not object to the topic, he showed himself capable of pursuing it.

"But the meaning of the story," he said, after a long moment of thought, "is a manly one: that by challenging his Father's authority—and by the false, famishing mush he taught, as you say—the Son drew down on himself the rightful anger of his Father. Doesn't he accept his punishment, at the end of the story?"

They were off. You couldn't give Eykar an opening like that without a debate. He sounded suddenly wide awake and relaxed in the way Eykar relaxed—by running his brains to exhaustion. Six years virtually alone at Endpath must have sharpened his hunger for theoretical argument. He pointed out that by the time of the Wasting, most of the worshippers of "God" and his Son had been fems and that one of the signs of Freakishness in the sons of the Ancients had been a bent in that direction. Moreover, male functionaries of that religion had been imprisoned for flouting the authority of Ancient leaders.

Kelmz could almost be heard thinking. The standard rejoinder was that the refugees had in fact taken some comfort from that Holy Book. On the other hand, in the end they had rejected the Book and its teachings upon discovery that many of the fems were stricter adherents to its tenets than any of the men.

What the captain came up with was another argument entirely, drawn from his training in military history rather than from any close knowledge of the Book itself. The Book's religion, he said, had once been a fine and manly one, complete with armed battles against unbelievers and the burning of heretics under the auspices of a powerful and strictly organized hierarchy. The entire structure of early Ancient society, with its codes of honor, rigid class divisions, and the subjugation of whole races of the Dirties, had been based on that religion. The problem, he maintained, was that fems had infiltrated and perverted a fine, manly creed—this being ever the stealthy danger that they presented.

"What could be more stealthy," Eykar said, "than to lure men into a net of ostensibly manly doctrine in order to corrupt them with rottenness that only becomes apparent far in the future?"

Kelmz shifted his ground. It seemed unreasonable, he said, to attribute such enormous influence to creatures related to the fem who carried their pack-basket, let alone to suggest that a skill like writing (a matter of organization and efficient presentation of ideas) was something that her low kind could handle effectively.

The old wolf was more clever than Servan had guessed. He must have chosen to engage in this discussion in a fem's presence precisely in order to show up her unimportance in the light of these ancient, weighty matters and at the same time to warn Eykar to beware of her—without insulting him by coming right out and saying that he needed to be warned. Suddenly the conversation was no longer amusing to Servan.

While he had half-dozed, imagining himself back in the

Boyhouse snoozing in the courtyard where boys and Teachers walked and talked under the arcades, Kelmz had been showing a concerned interest in Eykar. Kelmz offered the attraction of an elder willing to meet Eykar on his own ground without pulling age-rank or a pretense of intellectual condescension, and yet able to hold his own.

Well, what of it? If Eykar allowed himself to be lured into an affair across the age-line, Servan could always use guilt against him later. Kelmz was hardly any sort of long-term competition. Yet Eykar was so tense these days, so self-contained, that it was hard to be totally sure of him. Servan shifted uncomfortably and tried to shut out the companionable murmuring of their voices.

When the City's chimes rang, faintly in the fading night, he got up sooner than he had intended.

They fell quiet, hearing him move.

"These disguises are no use to us now," Servan said. He groped for Kelmz' shoulder, rapped it sharply with his fingers. "Give me my manna-bracelet." The weight of the metal, still warm from Kelmz' skin, was placed in his palm. "I'll be back as soon as I can."

Even before he was out of earshot, they were talking again. Servan broke into a trot.

No watch was kept over the City's kiln-yards at night. Nothing could be taken from the sealed, roasting domes, even with the heat damped down to a waver of air over the vents.

Servan strode carelessly over the rubble of old potsherds that surrounded the chambers. He paused to pick up some of the trial bits that had been drawn out through openings in the kilns and laid on a tray so that the supervisors could monitor the progress of the firing. There wasn't enough light for him to make out the colors, but the chips had a lustrous feel, suggesting that they would give to the touch at any instant, like skin. He dropped them, rattling, back into the tray and crossed the yard to let himself into one of the low buildings at the rear. Like the storage-sheds in Lammintown, the City potteries were full of caches of his private gear.

He stood with his back against the door, enveloped in the wet-clay smell, and he inhaled, tasting clay. First light would show him his way. There would be clay figures wrapped in wet rags on the tables, and he didn't want to knock anything down. He waited, not minding. The fine grit underfoot and the powder settling on his lips were welcome to him. Like the City's rippling carillon, this told him he was home.

As a boy he had done a stint in the kiln-yards as part of his skills-training; he had never combed the clay-crumbs out of his hair since. Something about the ability to draw form from a lump of moist earth and to fix it permanently had captured him.

He had begun scheming how to get the company then at work in the potteries to bid on him when he graduated from the Boyhouse; how to stay behind when their five-year was up and they were moved on to another work-turf; how to wangle the privilege of doing free-form work instead of turning out standard figures, utensils, and furniture-blocks. All of which had become irrelevant, of course, upon his expulsion.

Odd that none of this had come up in his talk with Eykar on the causeways. As boys they had often spoken together of the future, though Eykar had always avoided committing himself to any specific direction, saying that he couldn't tell yet. By this he meant that his direction, though still obscure, was fixed by the fact of his identity.

Servan shifted his shoulders against the door. This gnawing on the past was so stupid. He never fell prey to sieges of memory and reflection except when he thought about Eykar. How was it that he couldn't be alone with Eykar for five minutes without giving way to the urge to torment him a bit, to prod and poke him into anger?

The fact was, nothing had changed with time. Eykar still stood in his mind like a rock in deep water, offering nothing, yielding nothing, dividing the current nevertheless. There was no question: Eykar had some power over him. This was a new concept. Servan had never seriously

held the thought "Eykar" and the thought "power" in his
mind at once. All along Servan had thought of himself as
the stronger when it came to matters of any importance.
Now he sensed a pattern that he had missed before—a
pattern of influence that Eykar exercised over him.

Why had Servan put himself constantly in jeopardy in
the Boyhouse, culminating in the DarkDream that had
cost him so much, if not to show off for Eykar? The only
positive result had been Eykar's seclusion in a quiet place
where he could gather his strength and his will, and to
whose advantage was that? Now Eykar wanted to locate
Raff Maggomas; sure enough, Servan set about arranging it.

A shiver roughened Servan's skin. Eykar seemed so
vulnerable in his tension, his slenderness, that you forgot
the impact of his unwavering, translucent gaze.

Lumpish shapes were beginning to emerge in the dusty
half-light. With the light came, as sometimes happened
(though Servan never allowed himself to hope) a
revelation. He recognized, among the draped shapes, the
conventional heroic pose of one figure even beneath its
swathings of damp cloth; it could only be one Zoror or
Zero (depending on the chant), the first of the survivors'
descendants to step out of the Refuge into the world
again, who had found the surface fit for the establishment
of a new civilization.

That was the aura surrounding Eykar's wiry figure in
Servan's mind: the potentiality for mythical action.

Eykar's soul still hid its deepest and darkest dream, and
the potential of that dream made him powerful. The man
who knew his father's name might do anything, might
even make himself immortal with some immense,
transfixing gesture.

That was better; Servan didn't like mysteries. His
pleasure was to bring them to light where they could be
properly appraised and dealt with. Eykar as a compelling
enigma was disturbing, but a man could play with the idea
of Eykar as a legend in the making. Humming, Servan
made his way carefully across the workroom to rummage
in one of the supply boxes against the back wall under the

long wedging-counter.

When he emerged from the kiln-yard, whistling a rude parody of a very serious chant about setting manly examples, his mock-Hemaway clothing had been exchanged for a suit of blanks, and he carried a bundle under his arm. He slipped into the maze of narrow alleys that wound within and between larger blocks of buildings bounded by broad streets and boulevards. The alleys were Servan's true territory; he knew his way through them even dream-blinded. Many Citymen did. There were old-time residents who referred to the alleys as the last stronghold of real freedom. Even the patrolmen hesitated to follow a man into this maze where law and its enforcers were given little respect.

Few other men were abroad at this pale hour. Whichever man saw another first would fade back and detour through another alley, for few men willingly encountered others in the alleys at any hour. Unhindered, Servan navigated the mazeway of crooked strips of paving and hard-tamped earth. He kept automatically alert for surfaces slippery with streams of stinking leakage from the high-windowed buildings on either side and for scattered shards of crockery that could lay open the feet of the unwary.

He would have to arrange a quiet hour or two here in the City with Eykar. Eykar's fastidiousness was a bitch sometimes. He took things so seriously, and his genuine modesty made him a most trying lover. He had been tense and moody during their nights in the crowded confines of the ferry. The City would be the place for the leisurely loving he needed to steady him down; not entirely, of course—part of his charm was the necessity of seducing him all over again, to some degree, each time, defeating him into pleasure.

Thinking along these lines, Servan nearly strode right out into the Street of Honor. He caught the sounds of whips snapping just in time and checked himself in an alley-mouth.

The entire street on which the alley opened was cordoned off with two red ropes. A meager crowd loafed along the sidelines; two bored-looking patrolmen leaned on the corner-posts, and the weapon-lenders were packing up their wares. Inside the ropes, a bout between two overstuffed Seniors was dragging to a close. Sweating and shuffling, the duelists were merely lacing each other's pauches with delicate lines of welts. Servan had seen a man skin and strangle an opponent with one of those thin whips.

These men were apparently settling some minor matter in public to enhance their standings. Each had come with a group of friends—"witnesses" would have been a more accurate term—who looked on with various degrees of embarrassment.

Servan stood still, watching with an educated eye. He didn't intend to give the audience a chance for some better diversion. Even in the innocent course of crossing on his way to somewhere else, any man was fair game to any other's challenge, once "in the red," as they said. The red ropes were moved every night to some unknown new location, so that no man, in anticipation of a challenge, could go look over the ground beforehand for his own advantage. Standings were made and broken by a man's reaction to finding the red rope stretched unexpectedly across his path. Servan had no time for standings this morning, and no desire to be conspicuously framed in red for every curious eye. He would have to make his way around through the alleys.

With a shock, he spotted Senior Bajerman's round, imperturbable face in the audience.

Picturing the Senior's astonishment if suddenly confronted by Servan, he grinned to himself. It would be a surprise for Eykar, too, to be handed over to the Hemaways.

A cart loaded with sand was being drawn down the street by a sweating fem-gang. One of the patrolmen waved them to a halt. The drover, a Hemaway Junior, swore at the sight of the red rope, and began harrying the fems into an about-turn, blasting away on his whistle as if he hoped to deafen the whole street. He would have to take a considerable detour to get that vehicle down to the glass-works at the end of the street where, Servan recalled, the Hemaways were working this five-year. So that was what Bajerman was doing here, up so early; he was taking a break from supervisory work.

And that was what Servan was doing here, too, having chosen this particular short cut without even thinking about it. Confronting Bajerman had been at the back of his mind all the time. It was an example of the bravura style that the City (home, after all, of a sophisticated and appreciative audience) always inspired in him.

In this case, it went dead against his own interests. He had no desire to abort Eykar's grand gesture; he wanted to help bring it about, possibly even help to shape it, and that wasn't a satisfaction to be traded for cheap City thrills. Besides, some easy treachery or other was probably just what Eykar expected from him. Spitting in the eye of expectation kept others baffled and Servan himself flexible.

All of this meant nothing, next to the simple, terrifying fact that he simply could not betray Eykar. The attraction of their boyhood was gone, replaced by something darker and stronger. As a DarkDreamer, what Servan read in the thrust of his own pulse and the tightness of his breathing was that Eykar had him in bondage. He could think of Eykar in any terms he liked, interpret and re-interpret, seduce him, torment him—but he could not knowingly choose to destroy him. The right image came at last: Eykar was a comet, blazing with the effort to hold together through the aching void long enough to win the right of surcease—aware, alone and desperate. Servan was enraptured with Eykar's brightness; to embrace Eykar was to bathe in fire.

I'm dreaming, he thought, licking his dry lips; this is delayed dreaming-shock. He focused his eyes on the duelists who circled each other, shaking sweat out of their eyes to show how hard they were working.

That was reality—the duel, the dancelike struggle against death. But he himself was not free to move, as a man must be free in order to dodge in any direction. Because of Eykar.

EYKAR BEK

XI

Bek listened to the sound of Servan's swift, retreating steps.

Kelmz said quietly, "What are the chances that d Layo will bring Bajerman back with a squad of Rovers?"

"None. He'll do whatever leaves the most interesting possibilities open. Bajerman is a known quantity. Raff Maggomas is not." When Kelmz received this in silence, Bek added, "You disagree? Have you prepared a lecture on the perils of evil companionship?"

"You've known d Layo longer than I have, and better than I'd care to. How can I tell you anything about him?"

"Then you have no advice for me?" Bek prodded. The pleasant effect of their previous conversation was gone, banished by Servan, who wasn't even here. Bek felt hunger grinding away at his weary body; discomfort made him nasty and obtuse, and he knew it and didn't care.

Kelmz said, "No advice."

"My affairs don't interest you enough for you to have

an opinion. Forgive me for asking; I've been alone on the Rock too long; I forgot my age-place."

He heard Kelmz move to ease stiff limbs and sigh. "Is it being so close to the City that turns you into a sniveling, carping boy all of a sudden? If it will make you feel more like a grown man, I do have a question." Stung, Bek said nothing. Kelmz cleared his throat and forged ahead. "A meeting with Maggomas could come sooner than you think, right here in the City. What do you mean to do when you finally face him?"

"Whatever will settle what's between us."

"Have you thought about just walking away from the whole thing?"

"That has occurred to me. It's unacceptable."

"Good."

"You agree?"

"Yes. There's no point pretending not to notice, if there's something riding your mind all the time. You have to stand up to it eventually. But what happens after you find Maggomas?"

"I don't know, I don't see into the future. What sort of career do you think would be open to the ex-official poisoner of the Holdfast?"

"Feeling sorry for yourself?"

"A little."

"Well, I hope it gratifies you; that's all it's good for. Try this instead: suppose you walk up to Maggomas and you lay it out in front of him—all your time, your thinking, your feelings for most of your lifetime—like a sacrifice with his name stamped all over everything. And he says, 'What did you say your name was again? I've had a lot of things on my mind these past years, and I don't exactly remember . . .'"

Bek barked out an incredulous laugh. "You mean you think I'm a conceited idiot."

"No. But when you know there's a skirmish coming up, it's a good idea to consider all the possibilities you can beforehand."

"The answer to your supposition," Bek said, "is that it doesn't matter. I'm going to get some answers, even if it's

just 'I don't know.'" The captain's elbow jostled him;
Kelmz was shrugging out of the mantle he had worn on
the way from Bayo and folding it up. "Captain, there's a
peculiarly valedictory tone to this conversation. Are you
working up to leaving?"

"I want to put these Rovers safe out of the way before d
Layo gets back."

It was a good idea. Rovers were very hard to handle in
the alleys, and Kelmz could hardly walk openly in the City
with them as Senior Kelmz and his escort. He himself and
the affairs of Hemaway Company were too well known
here for him to be able to get away with it. The patrolmen
would challenge him at once.

"Yes," Bek agreed, "they're a hindrance now. Servan's
solution would be to cut their throats and stuff the bodies
into the sewer-pipes, or something equally direct."

"You'll do fine," Kelmz remarked, "as long as you keep
as free of illusions about your friend as that."

"I know him well, as you pointed out," Bck said, drily.
"What will you do with these Penneltons?"

"Give them sleep-commands and leave them in the sick
bay at Hemaway Compound. The officer who'll be
running things in my place doesn't make his rounds till
late in the morning, if it's the man I think it is. D Layo
knows the outlaw business; by then he'll have found a
good place to lie up if need be." Kelmz stood up with a
cracking of his knee-joints. "I won't be coming back here,
so don't wait for me. I have some business of my own to
tend to."

"And if you're needed?"

"Then look for me in the Boyhouse Library."

The Boyhouse Library was famous as the setting for
assignations across the age-line. Startled, Bek said only,
"Oh."

"My soul," Kelmz exclaimed, "he's got you thinking as
foul as he does! Those shuffle-footed Boyhouse cubs
don't interest me. I had a loving friend once. He was a
grown man and knew how to act like one, and he died
acting like one. And that's all."

I've hurt his feelings, Bek thought, taken aback that an

older man would care enough what a younger one thought of him to be hurt—unless they were lovers. What was there for Kelmz in the Boyhouse Library, then, other than boys? Books, of course. Books and pictures concerning the Ancients' times.

"It's the beasts you're after," Bek said.

"That's right." The captain waited, making plenty of room for a burst of scorn or disgust or even good advice.

"A man's entitled to his obsessions," Bek said, aridly mocking them both. "We'll meet you there."

"Only if you can get in without a lot of stupid risk. If not, you let me find you. I know my way around well enough, even without d Layo's wide experience of City low-life. Meantime, keep an eye on your friend—I think he'll sell you on a bet and be sorry later. The other eye you can keep on the fem, there. Now that I've given you some advice after all, I guess I can leave you in good conscience."

Bek restrained an impulse to say something— anything—that would hold the captain back. Servan was more slippery than wet clay and could make his way out of any situation, but Kelmz was the sort of capable and steady man who caught the trouble that Servan's kind avoided.

With a crisp word of command, Kelmz brought the Rovers to their feet. He set them side by side in brace-position, patted them down to check their gear and started them off toward the City before they could get restless.

Kelmz captured by patrolmen, Kelmz brought before the Board for treachery, complicity with a renegade Endtendant and a notorious DarkDreamer—Bek looked up and realized that he must have been dozing. The sky was brightening. He stirred. He was uncomfortable. His body, which he thought of disparagingly as a sort of bestial enemy, had stiffened with hard traveling after the days of inactivity on the ferry. He identified the separate naggings of hunger in his belly, a stitch in his side, and a blistered heel. Every time the fem sniffled or moved so that the pack-basket scraped the causeway stones, the blood jumped in his veins.

He concentrated on watching the City solidify with the predawn light. From what he could see, nothing important had changed. The backs of the outer buildings were haughtily turned on the stinking southern approach, which was dominated by the sewers that fed the laver-ponds. The City stood high on the compacted ruins of previous flood-broken settlements, so that the causeway simply joined the streets without any change in elevation. North and west, the City's thoroughfares sloped down toward the river, which swept past on its way down from 'Troi to Lammintown and Bayo on the coast. Tall levees rose neatly alongside the river. From causeway-height, Bek could see a string of flatboats heading downriver, awnings flapping in the early breeze.

The wind changed, bringing the sound of the City's bells loud and clear over the laver-ponds. There was the flat-noted call of the Blues, the tinkling scale of the Angelists, the rough tocsin of the Quarterbacks with the cracked end-note, and the others in their turns. None of that had changed either.

Someone whistled. Bek squinted and picked out a figure in one of the dim openings between the warehouse walls. It was Servan, in blanks, waiting for him.

Patrolmen should have been watching the cleared perimeter under the outer walls, but they didn't like the smell of the south side and neglected it. Bek could hear the fem's steps at his back as he crossed, a hasty, fearful pattering. No challenge rang down from the rooftops.

The bundle Servan carried was a second suit of blanks, more patches than cloth, two sizes too large and very dusty. At least he'd brought a face-mask and a voice-filter in the old style of truly anonymous dress, so that Bek wouldn't have to risk showing his face openly in the streets. While the fem went off at Servan's command to dispose of the pack-basket down a side alley, Bek changed his clothes.

Servan watched, oddly restless and uneasy. "Where's

the captain and his brutes?" he asked.

Succinctly, Bek told him, wondering if perhaps Servan had sold him out after all.

"And you didn't try to keep him with you?" Servan demanded. "Did you consider the possibility that he might go straight to Bajerman or to the Board?"

Ah, the two of them—Bek was fed up with their suspicions and grudges. "He won't."

"You forget, my friend: you're on one side of the age-line with me, little as you may like the idea—and he's on the other side, with Bajerman."

Distastefully, Bek fingered the frayed inside of the mask. "I notice that you brought no blanks for Kelmz to wear. What did you have in mind for him, Servan? I think he was wise to go off on his own. I only wish I'd thought to ask if he knew people we could approach for information about this man Kambl."

"I know the man to talk to," Servan said, jaunty again, "a client of mine. We'll go right to him. But don't blame me if on the way we bump into Kelmz with Bajerman and a bunch of Hemaway Rovers."

Often during their shared youth Servan had led forays from the Boyhouse during hot summer noons, when the Teachers napped, or in blue-shadowed winter dawns. With him, Eykar had spied on Senior residences, prowled the Market Arc for carelessly fastened shutters and doors, tracked fems on the streets and furtive denizens though the alleys. The familiar landmarks were still there—a patch of broken paving near the brick-yard, a wall that had become a palimpsest of rude intercompany insults, the profiles of certain corners—but an odd, expectant quiet lay over everything.

At the Market Arc, a paved mall under a roof of weathered grass mats, all the stalls were closed. The Arc divided the smoke and noise of the factories from the core of living-quarters on the other side. This morning no streams of work-bound Juniors poured across. Only one group of gaunt-faced young men of the Squires Company was swinging along, and they had the look of all-night carousers on the way home.

The far side of the mall was bounded by the blind, spike-topped walls of the company compounds. The gates, with the company symbols painted brightly on them, were shut.

Beyond the compounds, there lay spacious individual residences to which wealthy Seniors might repair when they had one or two friends with whom they wished to lead private lives. The alleys here were neatly kept footpaths serving the back entries to these homes. The scented air seemed to mute even the chiming of company bells. Low voices and occasional laughter drifted from balconies and sheltered garden corners. Crockery chinked as Seniors took the morning meal in the dignified leisure to which their mature spirits were entitled.

Bek was not as impressed as he had been in his youth. Since then he had seen venerable men shamble into Endpath, weeping into the wide sleeves of their pilgrim robes.

Turning in at a grillwork gate, Servan had a low-toned altercation with the Quarterback who guarded it. This suave young man insisted on scoring him off with insults and disdain before deigning to deal seriously with him. The Quarterback finally took Servan's bracelet to show to the master of the house as identification of the three callers. He returned shortly and dropped it back into Servan's hand as he sulkily motioned them inside. His scowl was a good sign; it meant that he had been rebuked for making a welcome visitor wait. They crossed the rock garden behind the wall and walked under an archway built through the body of the house, to be faced with a curious tableau in the inner courtyard.

Some fifteen fems were ranked silently in rows across the polished flagstones. They wore long hair, indicating that their owner was rich enough to scorn selling their scalps to the fur-weavers. And they were covered with markings that could only be tattoos: stripes, spots, even fine striations like the hair of beast-pelts, as if they were beasts instead of fems. Here was a decadent use of the tattooing craft, the proper purpose of which was to imprint rank-signs on the shoulders of men, not designs on the skins of fems.

Among these creatures moved a stubby man who pulled at his lip and squinted anxiously into the fems' decorated faces. He wore a plain mantle that had been pulled on right over his night shirt, and his brindle hair stood up in sleep-set tufts. He turned toward the visitors, calling,

"Servan, what a pleasure! You've come in time to lend me your good taste. I need to pick the fem that would make the best gift to the dreaming-hosts this afternoon."

Servan's luck was serving them well. With the whole City deep in manna-sleep they could look for Kambl without being observed or interfered with, and the captain would run little risk of being discovered in the Boyhouse Library.

"Not to show up," the Quarterback Senior was saying, "is unthinkable, of course. But to show up empty-handed, for a man of any standing, would be even worse..." The man rattled along like a wheel rolling downhill. Bek glanced back; Alldera, framed in the archway, was balancing on one foot and picking something out of the sole of the other one. The young Quarterback had gone back to the gate. Bek unhitched the mask from his collar and took it off. The Senior, still in full spate, gave him a curious glance but did not pause. "...undervalued because they're obviously pets, and those have uncertain reputations as you know, when ownership changes. But I've invested a lot of time and paid a lot of fine trainers to develop the loyalty, the responsiveness of this group. They're a creation I'm very proud of. The trouble is, breaking up a fem-hold by giving one fem away is a risk in itself, since you never know beforehand how the others will react to the loss of any one of their number." He sighed, and smiled almost apologetically. "But you haven't introduced me to your companion, Servan."

Servan said urbanely, "Senior Kendizen, it's a pleasure

to introduce one of my friends to another, always. This is Eykar Bek."

For an instant the Senior's smile stiffened. Almost at once, however, his expression warmed back into what looked like genuine hospitality, and he responded courteously, "You both look tired and in need of refreshment. Come inside, and let some of these pretty fems of mine prove to you that they're useful as well as decorative."

In the bathing room Kendizen bravely kept up his end of the gossipy conversation that Servan lazily indulged in. He seemed a decent sort of man for a Senior, the more so because of his undisguised embarrassment at Servan's outrageous comments, all liberally laced with innuendo and sarcasm at the expense of others whose names were for the most part unknown to Bek or else only vaguely familiar. Servan jibed at the growing tensions across the age-line, incidents of friction and violence that contributed to it, the tendency of Senior men to see rebellion and witchery everywhere, certain scandalous Senior-Junior liaisons in Lammintown, and so on.

Kendizen made one effort to change the subject, following Servan's remark about the monopolization of good-looking fems by men too old to sire cubs on them. The Senior pointed at Alldera, who was washing her hair discreetly in a corner of the bathing room as she had been ordered to do.

"Would you consider a trade for that sturdy little runner you have with you? I know several people who would be interested. Looks are so much easier to come by these days than real skills among fems."

This remark set Servan off on a detailed exposition of certain common abuses of fem-trainer status, which brought color to Kendizen's cheeks; it was not so long since the Quarterbacks had worked at Bayo. This teasing was intended to highlight, for Bek's benefit, the familiarity of Servan's relationship with the Senior. Bek turned his attention to the trays of food Kendizen's fems brought around.

When they all had reached a small sun-court outside

the bathing room, Bek finally broke in. "Senior Kendizen, have you any idea of our purpose here?"

The Senior turned toward him. "I can't imagine any purpose," he said, in a tone of reproof, "that would take the Endtendant from Endpath."

"I am looking for my father."

"So are a number of people," Kendizen replied. "His name is rumored to have come up recently at a Board meeting, not once but several times. You can hardly expect me to be of any help to you in your own inquiries. Senior Maggomas is a man of my years or more, and you yourself are both a young man and reputedly his son. You can't mean him any good, and I can't assist you in doing harm to any peer of mine or Senior of yours."

These older men who mixed a certain moral firmness with their vices Bek found hardest to deal with. He did not dislike Kendizen nearly as much as he should have, so he spoke as brutally as he could, in memory of Seniors he had known who were anything but decent.

"Servan, this man is a client of yours. Can that be proven to the Board through some informant, if necessary?"

The Senior opened his mouth as if to shout for assistance; instead, he ordered the fems, who were still hovering about with pitchers and plates, to leave. Then he turned to Servan, saying in a whisper, "Servan, you know it wouldn't be the first time; if I were exposed again—"

Putting his arm through the Senior's in a friendly manner, Servan drew him into a slow, unwilling stroll around the fountain.

"No one expects you to simply divulge Maggomas' whereabouts, even if you knew, which you plainly don't, or you would have volunteered the information to the Board long ago, as a responsible citizen. What we hope is that you'll put us in touch with someone who does know where to find Raff Maggomas, leaving it up to that person to decide whether or not to tell us anything. As it happens, we know of a likely informant, a man named Karz Kambl. We've heard that he's living in the City somewhere, and all we ask is that you use your considerable influence to arrange a meeting with him for us."

Senior Kendizen began to sweat. "You're asking me to risk more than you know," he muttered. "Servan, there must be others you can go to. I've broken too many rules for you and your friends already. I've let you use my fems, spoken for offenders, helped certain young men to escape being sent to Endpath—" He shot a look at Bek, coughed nervously and added, "I've been a friend to younger men; you know how I feel about certain injustices between the generations . . ."

His voice died; Servan was nodding, smiling, making it very clear without saying a single word how delighted he was that the Senior understood the precariousness of his position because of these same actions—one might say, crimes—that he was listing. It was not only for DarkDreaming that this Senior could be hauled before the Board.

This was not the first time that Bek had profited by Servan's skill at blackmail. He did not enjoy it any more now than he had in the Boyhouse. On the other hand, neither did he object or shrink away, let alone refuse as he had sometimes done in the past. He did not like this hardness in himself. But he could not afford to be balked in his search by tenderness of feeling.

XII

In the end, Kendizen agreed to contact a certain high man who could put them in touch with Karz Kambl, though he could not promise that anything would come of it other than immediate arrest for them all.

"Don't give this intermediary time to think about it," Bek said. "Bring him to meet us at the Boyhouse Library during the dreaming." The Boyhouse would be an ideal place, deserted for the afternoon. The boys would all be assembled on the roof with their Teachers.

Kendizen protested, "He'd never consent to miss a dreaming!"

"Servan will help you think up a tale to bring him."

At this, the Senior made a sound that was half-groan and half-sigh, glanced at Servan and said, "Yes, Servan can probably think of a way... Well," he added, with an attempt at a smile that came out very wry, "whatever happens, at least I know the Board won't send me off to Endpath, don't I."

"I'll leave you, then," Bek said. "I want to go and rest while I can."

One of the tattooed fems showed him to a sleeping alcove off the main court, while Servan and Kendizen continued to circle the fountain in the sun-court, talking.

The fem settled herself in a corner in case Bek should want anything of her. He tried to send her away. She didn't comprehend his wish to be alone and came back twice to apologize for having forgotten what it was he had sent her to fetch. The third time, he sent her for Alldera. Having furnished him with another fem to attend him, Kendizen's fem retired without further confusion.

After Kendizen's phantasmagoric femhold, the sturdy simplicity of Alldera was a relief. She had cleaned up and been given a fresh smock to wear. Now that she stood straight without the pack-basket bowing her back, he found her rather pleasant to the eye.

She knelt to take off his shoes for him.

"Look up," he said, remembering the curding-room fem's approach to Servan.

She turned up toward him a face like a round shield of warm metal. Instead of the sweet perfection of Kendizen's pets, this fem's face expressed a willful stupidity that was perfect in its own way. The muscles around the wide mouth were strongly molded and the lips cleanly edged, but instead of mobility the effect was one of obstinate dullness. Her eyes, not large enough for the breadth of cheekbone underneath, gazed blankly past his shoulder; she blinked only after a long interval, and sleepily. The total impression given was one of fathomless unintelligence.

Close up and undistracted, he studied her; and he did not believe her. He wondered how long it would take to penetrate this burnished smoothness that offered no hold for the lance of keen sight, and what sort of being would be found hiding. Her hands still rested on his ankle and instep. He felt their warmth and stillness. He began to get a sense of her solid body close to his own that Kendizen's decorated servitors hadn't touched in him. He drew back his foot.

"Go sit outside the alcove," he commanded, "and see that Kendizen's fems don't come disturb me."

"Please-you-master," she said in that vacant uninflected tone that he didn't believe either, and she rose and left him.

Bek could not hear the men's voices, only the faint splash of falling water. Servan would round out their plan and see that Kendizen didn't talk to the wrong people before the dreaming. Of what else he might do with the Senior, it was better not to think. Servan had always been promiscuous by nature.

He hadn't realized how tired he was, and he only began to feel it fully when he lay down in the hammock. But the body-brute was feeling too skittish and self-important to let go and sleep.

There was a theory that a man's soul was a fragment of eternal energy that had been split off from the soul of his father and fixed inside his dam's body by the act of intercourse. Being alien to everything that the soul represented, the fem's body surrounded the foreign element with a physical frame, by means of which the soul could be expelled. Seen from that perspective, a man's life could be regarded as the struggle of the flesh-caged soul not to be seduced and extinguished by the meaningless concerns of the brute-body.

Bek had been fighting that battle all his life. His body was his oldest and most constant enemy, often subdued but never defeated. It was powerfully armed against him. Starving, it would approach food with a mouth tasting like dust and then nag him with hunger-pains later. His body would ache for rest and greet the opportunity with subtle muscular discomforts that made anything but a shallow doze impossible. It warmed impartially toward men of any age and even toward fems according to caprice alone, as witness just now. With its inconsistencies, it sought to wear down and break his spirit.

He had nearly killed himself before discovering that it was a mistake to try to discipline the rebellious body with pain or any but the subtlest punishments. When crossed, his body could marshal a whole range of aches, cramps and rashes against him, and weaken him with fevers, sweats and racking chills. The only possible attitude to bring to the struggle was determination to endure and to prevail.

All this was a conceit he indulged, a sort of game. He knew well enough that what he fought so hard was merely the inertia and imperfection of any material lump, not a consciously malicious enemy. It had, however, become a habit of thought to consider himself split into opposites, particularly after he had realized that it was through the body-brute that the will of others could be inflicted on him. When his body was moved to Endpath, Bek himself, imprisoned in it, went too. The trick was to compel the brute-flesh to act as his own instrument, rather than the instrument of others or of its own appetites.

He lay on his back and soothed his eyes with the design of a fine mat-weaving that hung on the wall. To ease into sleep, he concentrated on how comfortable his body had been made here in Kendizen's house: the nails of his fingers were clean and shaped; his skin felt fresh and was clothed in first-grade hemp-cloth; his cheeks were smoothly shaven; his teeth were clean; his hair was glossy with washing and brushing (though he had avoided the fem with the scent-bottle); his travel-stiffened muscles were massaged into relaxation; his stomach was full . . . Only a slight sexual tension remained to be assuaged.

On cue—he was always on cue—Servan stepped into the alcove, drew the curtain behind him and came over to the hammock, all in silence; he knew that words had no place in the pleasures of the body-brute.

When Servan touched him, Bek did not turn toward him. He would turn soon enough.

Alldera woke them, calling, "Masters. Masters.

Masters," in that maddening, empty voice. It was time to go to the square in the bright noon for the dreaming.

Servan would not leave his fem in Kendizen's house, being unsure of when they might be able to return for her. So she came with them, walking with two of Kendizen's fems who paced along at the rear in tattooed splendor, their hair laquered into wide, glossy fans spreading down past their shoulders. Bek and Servan, exercising the guest-privilege of wearing blanks, walked behind Senior Kendizen, who wore a mantle trimmed with blond fur. As Kendizen's escort, the two of them augmented his standing.

Other men moved in the same direction though the quiet that always preceded a dreaming: the bells of the City were still. It was said that the silence could madden any man foolish or crooked enough to withhold himself from dreaming—which was only just, since what legitimate purpose could any man have to be awake and active while all his fellows slept?

First to converge on the square were these mantled Seniors attended by fems, young friends and peers. Heads were inclined this way and that in precisely measured degrees of respect and condescension. The ideal was to present oneself in a splendor of dress and company.

Young men in the Seniors' entourages eyed each other, from group to group, with haughty disdain. They were Juniors who had found favor in the eyes of elders important enough to flout the age-rules, though never so openly as at these ceremonies. A Senior's patronage brought sure meals, gifts of clothing and even sometimes of small items like jewelry that might be traded for rations later on, when the patron's favor had been withdrawn. In recent years, competition for Senior protection had grown fierce among young men handsome or clever enough to have good prospects. They watched each other for signs of slippage, sharp-eyed to press for their own advantage with a generous Senior or one likely to go to Endpath soon and leave property to his favorites. It was always this way in lean times; there had been lean times in the Holdfast for over a decade now.

Later the less fortunate Juniors would come, grouped by company in sullen ranks, far from splendid in the work clothes which was all most of them had. They were more in need of the comforts of dreaming than those who had gone before them. A man in a dream felt no hunger.

Bek remembered the appropriate stately pace, and in the same moment remembered who had taught it to him: Senior Bajerman of the Hemaways. He began looking for faces he knew and forgetting his salutes, which brought him cold stares from older men trying to identify him so that they could mark him for one of their young friends to challenge in the Streets of Honor at a later date. The suit of dress-blanks that Kendizen had furnished Bek included only a domino-type mask, but Bek wasn't nervous about being recognized. He'd been through that on the ferry. He felt, rather, exhilarated by the pageantry around him.

The square opened ahead of them. Every eye turned to the tables set up before the Boardmen's Hall and the figures standing beside them. Kendizen and his fems moved on with the crowd. Bek and Servan, with Alldera at their heels, cut swiftly to one side and into an alley, making for the Boyhouse on the south side of the square by the back way.

Nothing about the Boyhouse had changed; not the ease of slipping in unseen, not the sweaty redolence of the hallways, or the glimmering floors of the classrooms. The open cubbies lining the corridors contained the same sparse crop of personal belongings: a bright bit of cloth, a clay top or comb, a string of clay bells. In the corners of the classrooms, lecterns loomed under their burdens: books of the Ancients, chained securely down. Portions of these books were read aloud over and over, until each boy could repeat what he had heard word perfect. Some said that most of the Teachers couldn't read either, but it didn't matter. The books were only the palpable authority behind the lessons.

Bek had been a fanatical and gifted memorist, taking

possession of the heritage of men like a starveling at a feast, chewing everything over and over. He'd been a great one for the forms of things in those days, uneasily putting aside the discrepancies of content that he had occasionally perceived.

For instance, once he had made the connection: all boys learn how to get in and out of the Boyhouse unnoticed when they want to; all men have been boys; all men know how to get in and out of the Boyhouse unnoticed if they want to.

How terrified he had been over that, fearing that his father would come soon to kill him. He had conceived a gripping horror of dreaming, because instead of the stylized patterns he studied, he kept slipping off into fantasies of flight from invisible pursuers and of struggles with huge intruders bent on devouring him. It wasn't even possible to tell the Teachers about it, because they would have suspected a penchant for DarkDreaming—for which they had no cure, as Servan's case so clearly illustrated later on. Bek cured himself, with patience and self-control.

When this hysteria (and the sweaty bout of illness that its banishment cost him) had faded, what remained was the suspicion that much if not all of men's civilization was built on secret foundations that no one ever hinted at, let alone discussed—unarticulated agreements that might even run directly counter to the rules that were spelled out in the Boyhouse.

Not that it mattered in the long run. Bedrock truth, he had come to understand later, was found only at Endpath. He no longer believed that the purpose of the Boyhouse was to teach the truths that made men out of boys. It was to impose discipline.

How unpleasant it had been! These corridors were normally either empty as now (but reverberating to the chanting voices of classrooms full of boys on either side), or filled with lines of boys shuffling in lockstep from class to class with downcast eyes. Sometimes they were turned out into the halls to walk up and down after a whole morning of sitting and chanting, before returning to an afternoon of more of the same. They always had to wear those wretched grass sandals that could barely be kept on, so that moving quietly was impossible. Even upstairs on the dorm floor, where boys lived naked to be reminded of how like beasts and Dirties they were, the first thing to do on being wakened in the morning was to slip into those sandals; and woe to the boy whose enemy had kicked his pair away down the floor during the night. Always there would be a Teacher nearby, and even the ones who were most bored and impatient with Boyhouse work were alert to the sound of whispering among the ranks, or of bare feet on the worn and polished tiles, or of blows and gasps when a couple of boys surreptitiously tried to settle a feud.

And then there was the ceaseless gnawing of hunger in the gut. Only later did a boy learn that the deprivation he had been taught to regard as valuable discipline was a constant factor in the lives of most Holdfast Juniors.

"In discipline is belonging," the Teachers said. "In discipline is solidarity among men against the sly evil of the void with which your dams have infected you." And again, "Discipline is the firm ground on which rugged individualism stands." And again, "We are here to help melt the fem-fat from your spirits and toughen you into men."

There are lots of punishments, and whatever a boy was caught doing reasons were found to punish him for it. Most often, the culprit was docked a meal. Those who finally turned their backs on punishment forever by giving up and turning their backs on life were deliberately forgotten. Their names were erased from the Boyhouse ledgers.

By and large, a boy settled for hating his Teachers (and shining up to those who had food to spare for favored boys); stewing in guilt over steamy affairs with older or younger boys; betraying other boys to Teachers and to each other; and generally passing on all of the grimness of Boyhouse life that he could to boys who were junior to him. The Teachers knew all this. They said it was better than in Ancient times, when boys had been left to their filthy dams to raise. (Was it any wonder they had turned Freak, and attacked their own fathers!)

Ah, the stories, the threats, the casual insults and deadly hatreds! Incredible, Bek thought, that one lived through it.

At the doorway to the Deportment room, he paused. There were lines painted in white on the floor; they shimmered in the sunlight striking in through the clerestories. The lines marked out patterns of precedence in the meetings and dealings-together of the various age-ranks of men. Under the tutelage of Bajerman or his like, boys learned to keep the proper distances, and to present the proper expressions, stances and salutes for this or that encounter. Bek remembered practicing the correct manner of approaching the Endtendant at Endpath. History gave the reasons; Deportment instilled the behavior. He could still recite the chant called "Roberts Rules," which described some long-lost game in archaic language.

There was no proper manner, however, of being an ex-Endtendant.

Bek saw his own reflection glimmering at him from the wall-wide mirror, spare, straight-backed, even elegant in the understated trimness of dress-blanks. He seemed a model of the Cityman, a successful graduate of the Boyhouse (he who had never graduated), the body-brute triumphant. No wonder he hadn't been recognized in the street, even only half masked. He scarcely recognized himself.

Servan's reflection came and stood beside his.

"Do you remember," Servan said, with mock-nostalgia, "when I came along in time to whip off that bunch who had you pinned on the steps, right after Anzik killed himself? Poor Anzik, he was no realist! Even if you'd returned his feelings, there were so many higher-ranking suitors ahead of him that he'd have hung himself anyway in the end, out of jealousy." He grinned and put his arm across Bek's shoulders. "Poor Eykar, you did spend a lot of time limping through these hallways, what with one thing and another."

Trust Servan to bring everything down to its lowest level. Their double reflection looked out of the shadowed glass, like the manly lovers Bek had seen in a fine glaze-painting once; the peer-couple, handsome and well matched, linked faithfully together from boyhood on in spite of all obstacles and partings, like two heroes of a love-chant. They were in reality a parody of that ideal.

Bek's education in love had begun in the Boyhouse, as was common. Though frail of build, he had often been called to the Library to help with the heavier drawers and bins. As he was setting an armload of books back onto the shelves, he would hear the sound of squeaking wheels as a book-cart was drawn across the end of the aisle, guaranteeing privacy. In theory, inter-age sex was banned by Boyhouse rules. Adults were supposed to confine their love affairs to their own peers, and so were younger men. In this way, those who were more mature avoided the possibly corrupting influence of younger, less masculine lovers. In practice, many Teachers seemed to seek out such corruption, and not always against the will of the boys they preyed upon.

There were men who later claimed that their first contact with true, manly love (as opposed to the counterfeit kind represented by a fem's bewitchments) had occurred under the influence of beloved Teachers exercising what were known as "Library privileges." For Bek, the Library had been the scene of his first contact with aggressive lust, and his experience had not stopped there.

Among the boys themselves there were similar conventions, copied from their elders. Those who had been most intrigued, and perhaps most frightened, by Bek's singular parentage used the crudest possible methods of proving themselves unshaken by his presence among them.

Through such forced encounters, Bek had first learned to differentiate between his treacherous, lascivious and vulnerable body and the outraged spirit trapped inside it; and he had learned to hate. At Endpath, he had had to school himself to give the cup without a tremor to men whom he recognized from those times; they came to him in pilgrim gray. The only one he had truly dreaded to see on the Rock had been Servan, because Servan was the only one to whom both body and soul had responded—still responded.

Even then, Servan had had the awful integrity of a DarkDream; his actions rose cleanly from the pit of his being through the medium of muscle and bone without the slightest distortion by scruple. In other words, he did what he wanted without any concern for why he wanted it or the effects of his actions on others. He seemed subject only to the objective limits of possibility, within which he gracefully made his way. In the Boyhouse he had bent the rules where he chose, creating spaces of comfort around himself and those whom he protected. He'd been a hero to some, for that. Many had felt the beauty of his ruthless, uncomplicated egotism.

To Bek, he'd been (and remained still) a shameful but irresistable indulgence. Bek had thought of him oftener at Endpath than he had admitted that night on the causeways. Now he could have laughed, remembering how he had tormented himself with images of Servan in the hands of vengeful Teachers; Servan mutilated, starved, destroyed. Look at him, with his sleepy, knowing grin, his easy self-assurance! At the deepest levels of his soul, there were no conflicts to wrench him apart. His effortless coherence kept him alive and flourishing while everything around him fell to pieces. Contact with him was like the promise of immortality. Perhaps it was that completeness, at base, that the body-brute loved.

The buoyant, confident Cityman who stared back at Bek from the glass was simply his physical self infused with Servan's assurance and vigor. This was the price: each time Servan lay with him, beguiling him with comfort and delight, the carnal being became more real; the farseeing and austere soul gave ground.

Deliberately, Bek moved out from under Servan's arm. With a grin and a shrug, Servan followed him on down the hall, picking things out of the wall-niches and replacing them in the wrong openings. He knew this morning-after remorse for what it was worth.

At the end of the corridor, light shone under the tall double doors to the Library. Those lights were never all blown out, day or night. Images and records of the unmen were kept here. Darkness was the element of their kind, and though all of the unmen were dead except the fem's descendants, no one wanted to take chances. The aisles between the stacks were like cool doorways down the sides of the great room. At the far end was a large window, curtained with sun-blazoned drapes.

But there was no order here. The floor and the study-tables were littered with books and loose sheets of paper, as if vengeful ghosts had torn through the shelves. Everywhere, obscene images faced them from the scattered pages; crouching creatures covered in fur or scales, or sprouting incredible appendages; swarms of monsters, in motion or laid out in dead rows; gesticulating figures that looked like men, but were actually Dirties dressed in skins or rags; grubby Freaks with hair to their shoulders; fems actually brandishing their fists and waving placards with writing on them.

Servan waved the fem back. "Looks like there's been a fight." Steel flickered down into his hand, as a thick-shouldered, gray-haired figure emerged from one of the aisles. Bek's heart clenched.

But it was Kelmz, not some filthy-handed Senior Teacher.

"Nothing to get excited about," the captain said. The words were for Servan and the knife in Servan's hand, but Kelmz' eyes were on Bek—an eloquently sympathetic glance. Kelmz had passed this way too, in his own youth.

Having discarded the false mantle somewhere, he stood simply-clad as any Junior despite his lined face and gray hair. Because of this—or because in traveling together they had used the age-rank structure as a tool

and a disguise instead of as a system of truth, or because
of the havoc wrought in this hated room by Kelmz'
researches—the years that stretched between him and Bek
suddenly seemed not to be a barrier but a spectrum which
included them both.

Looking down at the papers spread in his thick hands,
Kelmz said, "You two are late, the dreaming's already
started." He jerked his head in the direction of the
window. "If you're careful, you can look out from behind
the curtain without being seen."

The square was packed with a crowd asway with
solemn, silent movement, above which floated the voices
of the chanting boys and the smoke of the witch-burning
which traditionally opened the dreaming ceremonies. The
bodies of three fems, the conventional number, were
angled sharply out from posts set into the central trench.
They were already contorted and black in the grip of
flames that could scarcely be seen in the bright daylight.

Bek flinched from the sight of them. He had always had
that reaction, an involuntary sympathy rooted deep in the
body-brute. He forced himself to look again.

On both sides of the smoking trench, long lines of men
moved at a slow gait toward the Boardmen's Hall at the
end of the square. Heavy earthenware tables had been
placed on the steps of the portico. Behind each table stood
a Senior of the Board, his head and shoulders massively
framed by a highstarched mantle of office. Each of them
had a company bellringer in attendance, whose present
job was to dip up mannabeer from the well in the table top
and pour it into the cupped hands of each dreamer in turn.
The man would drink, have his hands dried by the same
young bell-ringer, and then kiss the palm of the Senior of
the Board by whose grace he dreamed. He then would
pass by to enter the Hall and find his assigned cubicle,
where he would lie on fine matting to dream his heroic,
soul-strengthening dreams.

Fems and Rovers were carefully locked away for the
occasion, while the entire population of men in good
standing dreamed. Although men did not lawfully dream

together, all had their dreams at the same time. When everyone had been served, the Seniors of Board would have the ringers drink, drink the last themselves, and then go in, closing the tall doors behind them and leaving the streets of the City empty.

The voices of the boys were muffled by the thick, bubble-specked glass of the window, but by the rhythms Bek knew what chant they were doing. His memory supplied the words: the names and characters of the unmen, who were only properly spoken of under the bright noon sun at a dreaming. Having just done the beasts, they were telling the names of the Dirties, those gibbering, nearly mindless hordes whose skins had been tinted all the colors of earth so that they were easily distinguishable from true men: "Reds, Blacks, Browns, Kinks; Gooks, Dagos, Greasers, Chinks; Ragheads, Niggas, Kites, Dinks..."

They chanted the Freaks, commonly represented as torn and bloodied by explosions their own bombs had caused: "Lonhairs, Raggles, Bleedingarts; Faggas, Hibbies, Families, Kids; Junkies, Skinheads, Collegeists; Ef-eet Iron-mentalists," the last a reference to the soft-minded values of the Freaks, iron being notoriously less strong than steel.

Finally, the chant came to the fems, huge-breasted, doused in sweet-stinking waters to mask uglier odors, loud and forever falsely smiling. Their names closed the circle, for being beast-like ("red in tooth and claw," as some old books said) they had been known by beasts' names: "Bird, Cat, Chick, Sow; Filly, Tigress, Bitch, Cow..."

A counter-chant was being raised now by the Teachers, enumerating the dreadful weapons of the unmen: "Cancer, raybees, deedeetee; Zinc, lead and mer-cu-ree..."

The floor underfoot seemed to vibrate as the passionate voices reinforced each other with righteous power.

Servan said, "Remind you of old times?"

XIII

Bek remembered standing with the others on the Boyhouse roof, staring at the billowing smoke, and chanting. The smoke stank (it was by that same cooked-flesh stench that he had recognized the purpose of the Bayo Rendery); but the boys breathed it joyfully. It was the smell of evil being punished as no boy could ever be punished, for only witches were burned, and only fems were witches—always excepting, of course, the special case of DarkDreamers, but what boy ever imagined he would be one of those?

The chants naming the wickedness of the Ancient fems were always shouted with extraordinary venom by the younger boys, who were closest to the separation from their own dams. The older boys were privileged to bellow out the list of the virtues of men, virtues which fitted men to master fems and boys in the name of order. Most boys of any age never came close enough to fems to observe their dreadfulness personally or knew many truly decent adult men among the Boyhouse Teachers; but they were convinced, and they chanted their throats raw.

Bek thought of gray-robed pilgrims along the narrow trail that led out over the black peninsula of stone to Endpath. The intervening step—that of walking to a dreaming at the Hall as one of the adult brotherhood of the Holdfast—was missing from his own experience. Watching now, he felt less substantial than the coiling smoke.

"Well," Kelmz said, glancing out once, uninterestedly, "what's been arranged?"

"Do you know Senior Kendizen of the Quarterbacks?" Servan asked.

"That famishing fem-lover? Sure."

Servan gave him a narrow stare; Bek was startled too. Mature men did not ordinarily run down their peers before Juniors. "Kendizen is bringing someone here who can tell us where to find Karz Kambl."

"And you think Kambl will tell you where to find Maggomas," Kelmz said. "Well, maybe he will." He rubbed at his eyes, which were red-rimmed from hard use. "I'll keep watch at the doors. You don't want that fem sidling in here; and your contacts may be less dependable than you think. Like everything else."

Frowning after his broad back, Servan said, "I told you it was time to get rid of him. I've seen men torn loose from their certainties before. They generally end up as wreckage on Skidro, and starve in an alley, if they last that long."

"Not Kelmz," Bek said, curtly.

"I grant you," Servan said, settling himself on the deep sill of the window, "he's full of surprises for an old man. Take that dream of his; people do sometimes dream of beasts—the other unmen were still men of a sort, after all, but the beasts were entirely different. The lure of the alien is strong." With his foot, he stirred one of the pages on the floor. The picture showed a stick-legged, brownish creature in mid-leap, its placid face in strange contrast to the urgency of its movement.

"Most men don't go so far as to dream that they

literally are beasts themselves. That takes a degree of imagination that I wouldn't have thought Kelmz had."

He sighed. "You'd be surprised at the level of most DarkDreaming; I was. I used to think everybody used it the way I wanted to, to give imagination free rein and really dig down into the spirit. Well, men don't; or else imagination and the core of the soul are mostly so petty that its hardly worth the bother.

"I'm good at my work, mind you. I could give my clients beasts more marvelous than any that ever really lived. I could give them gilded courts of power and splendor, steel cities roaring with wealth and crowds. But the quality of the dream depends on the visualizing capacity of the dreaming mind that I have to work with. Most of them are pretty puerile—as you must have noticed, back there on the ferry."

Bek paced past him, back and forth. The Library disturbed him; the dreaming disturbed him, and Kelmz disturbed him. What disturbed him most of all was the possibility of meeting Raff Maggomas soon. Irritably, he said, "I'm surprised you didn't stay with the Scrappers on some congenial basis—such as taking over their leadership yourself."

"There are too many famishing Scrappers already," Servan said, fiddling with the fringe of the window-curtain. "And when they've dug up everything worth salvaging that the company men have missed, they'll have nothing left but the bondboy business—not my style."

"You nearly died of dreaming in the Boyhouse. Why do you stay with it? You may have built up a tolerance by now for a DarkDreamer's low dosage, but someday you'll take something stronger than you expect, and it will kill you."

"Oh, I like my work," Servan said, cheerfully. "In spite of everything. What could be more amusing than bringing to the surface the nasty little men who live inside our grandest, most noble-natured and mature brothers?"

"Almost anything, surely," Bek grimaced.

"My clients come back for another dose, which is more than can be said for yours!"

Bek paced, thinking of the ambivalence of men's attitudes toward Endpath and the man who brewed deathdrink inside its black stone walls. A peaceful death in the mists of dreaming, under the assurance of eternal remembrance in the Chants Commemorative, was said to be a good thing, worth striving for. Yet men came shaking to the Rock, babbling their sorrows in spite of the rules. And after they drank, they were no less dead than those who died outside, unremembered.

The Endtendant was custodian of perhaps the most important ceremony of Holdfast life, and he was served as such. Though the companies' ranks grew thin in the wake of faltering harvests, supplies of food for him and the Endpath Rovers came regularly. Yet each Endtendant was sent to the Rock as a kind of punishment; his Rovers were his jailers, and in the end each Endtendant in turn took the death-drink himself—as if to pay for his offense in having given good deaths to his superiors.

It hadn't taken Bek long to see that it was for his own death that he had been sent there. He had decided not to let himself be so easily discarded.

Not that there was anything wrong in the soul of a man choosing to shed the bodily husk after a lifetime of battle with the void-stuff of which the world was made. Endpath itself was a recognition of the rightness of such a choice. Only by years of self-discipline and right action did a man know himself to be ready to die. However, Bek's problem was precisely that he did not feel that he had yet engaged in a significant struggle. It seemed to him that he had only endlessly made ready, and that it was wrong to step out of the world before arriving at the meeting place he'd been preparing for all his life. So when he had found himself lifting the warm, lethal cup to his own lips, he had seen the necessity of leaving Endpath, and taking the shaping of his life into his own hands.

Yet he missed the Rock. He missed it so hard that it

made his eyes ache with trying to see something different from what was going on out there in the square: not magnificently glazed walls and deep arcades and a solemn procession of dreambound men past a smoldering trench, but bare and sweeping lines of rock, sea and shore. The wind always blew at Endpath out of the wide sky. The sea rolled vast and barren and clicked and chattered unceasingly among the pebbles at the foot of the Rock. All was simple, clean and final.

For a moment he seemed to feel the touch of the black mask on his face and the weight of half-filled cups in his hands. The words of the Endpath offering sounded in his mind: "Here is the sleep of the body, the freedom of the spirit and the everlasting naming of the name."

"—paradox," Servan was saying, in his lazy, negligent manner. "What you do is supposed to be a good thing, but everybody knows in his heart that it's rotten. What I do is supposed to be a crime, but everybody suspects that it's a good thing, a service, even. It's so stupid to say that a man will be remembered if his name is stuck into a chant for the famishing Juniors to gabble through every day as fast as they can so they can get to breakfast."

"How will you be remembered?" Bek challenged. "In the songs of fems, that only corrupt men will ever listen to?"

"That's the only kind of man whose recognition I'd have any use for," Servan airily replied.

Bek laughed, the dark mood broken. "If the Board had caught you during these past years, they probably would have sent you to me at Endpath to punish us both at a stroke, knowing that you don't believe in the efficacy of the chants."

"What would you have done," Servan said, "if I'd come to you there?"

"I'm surprised you didn't visit me to find out."

"You'd have handed me my poison without a blink," Servan grinned, "after letting me coax you to bed first, of course, for old times' sake. Eykar, relax, will you? Your pacing is driving me rogue. If you won't sit somewhere, at least lean a bit."

Bek snapped, "Must I drape myself gracefully over the furniture in order to talk with you?"

"All right, I admit it: in you, ease would be an affectation. But you ought to learn to be more appreciative of comfort, Eykar. Why are you so enamored of hard edges and sharp corners? If I didn't know you better I'd say you were in constant danger of falling asleep without a bit of pain here and there.

"Why are you so impatient? Don't let the tensions of ordinary Holdfast life get to you. Things must have been very peaceful in your kingdom on the Rock, complete with four devoted retainers and swarms of suppliant subjects. Was it hard for you to leave Endpath?"

Servan was watching him with that connoisseur's look, appreciating the effects of his words. Bek tightened his lips and said nothing.

Shrugging, Servan shook the knife down out of his sleeve again and entertained himself by carving spirals into the plaster of the Library wall. The spiral was the sign of the void, of fems, of everything inimical to the straight line of manly, rational thought and will. It would infuriate the Teachers to find that symbol here tomorrow, not least because within an hour the boys would be terrifying each other with whispers that unmen-spirits had visited the Library during the dreaming and had left their mark.

Bek looked around at the pictures scattered everywhere. As a frequent visitor to the Library in his Boyhouse days, albeit under duress, he had seen some of them before. Then how was it, he mused, that he hadn't noticed that the fems in the pictures were not particularly huge breasted, nor magically alluring as the chants said? Some did seem to have a red stain on their lips that might have been blood, but actually it looked more like the paint that Kendizen's pets wore for decoration. To tell the truth, many of the fems in the pictures didn't look much more dangerous than Alldera—less dangerous, in fact, since they seemed much softer in body than she was.

And here was a picture of a long-striding lion (the label was torn off, but he remembered the beast-name) taking what appeared to be a companionable stroll, not with some witchy fem or even a young Freak, but a white-bearded man of mature years.

Baffled, Bek frowned at the pictures. Could he have been so blind with his terrors of this place as a boy that he had looked without seeing any of this? Then what of the Teachers? How would they have explained these extraordinary images? No wonder Kelmz seemed shaken, even aged by his hours alone here today. What esoteric mysteries were hidden here, passed over and tucked away by men who had no use for anything but the simplest, crudest evidence supporting what they taught as truth?

"Here they are," Servan said, sliding off the sill.

Kelmz had eased open one of the heavy doors, and Senior Kendizen slipped inside. Behind him came another Senior, who wore a high, fine-spun wig which forced him to bend in order to enter without knocking it off.

In a hasty whisper, Senior Kendizen made introductions. When he came around to Kelmz, he said, "Is it Captain Kelmz of the Hemaways? A pleasure to meet you, Captain, outside of ceremonial occasions, so to speak." And he smiled his rueful smile.

His companion he presented as Dagg Riggert, an old Angelist whose name Bek knew to be an important one. Senior Riggert studied Bek in critical silence. Looking into the man's deep-seamed, haughty face, Bek recognized the beginning lines and colors of illness. He thought, pain will bring you to Endpath soon. The thought made him feel older than the Angelist.

"I can take you to Karz Kambl," Senior Riggert said. "Do you know just who he is?"

"Raff Maggomas' friend," Bek said, still somewhat disoriented, so that he neglected the proper honorifics due in addressing an older man.

"Before he was ever a friend of Raff Maggomas," Riggert said, icily, "he was a friend of mine; he was a man of great promise. Thanks to Maggomas, that promise will never be fullfilled. But Maggomas is gone, and Karz Kambl is my friend again.

"I will do whatever I can to prevent Raff Maggomas from doing my friend any further injury, to the point of absenting myself from this dreaming and conspiring with Juniors against a man who is only a few years younger than I am."

"Since the Senior speaks of friendship," Bek said, giving up any thought of trying to mend matters of courtesy between them, "he will recognize that there is no conspiracy in a man being helped in a crucial matter by his friends."

"I had heard," Senior Riggert replied, "that you were clever in argument. You certainly seem to have won over as steady a man as Captain Kelmz here, who was, I believe, assigned to bring you before the Board for judgment?"

Kelmz said, "I was assigned to accompany d Layo. There he is. Here I am."

Before Senior Riggert had time to fully consider this remarkable, not to say insulting, reply, Servan said smoothly, "I am sure that Senior Riggert has his own goals, which are served by this expense of his time and knowledge with us."

"Justice!" snapped Riggert. "Retribution!"

Kendizen spoke up, unhappily, as if he would rather not have, but couldn't keep silent. "Certainly the Holdfast could use more of the first, but as for the second, surely the manly ideal of generosity—"

"You're soft, sir," Riggert said, harshly. "I've always said so, and I say it again, in front of these young men."

"And I say that there are those who are so eager to be tough that they become cruel," Kendizen retorted, turning pink like an angry boy.

Ignoring him, Riggert continued, "Vengeance is owed to my friend Karz, though he wouldn't say so himself. He has an open and forgiving nature—perhaps a trifle too much so, like Senior Kendizen, here—and would no doubt have Maggomas' friendship back if it were offered, a possibility that I mean to prevent—or rather to help you to prevent. In return, I will require some token, some proof that Raff Maggomas has been destroyed."

Was that what moved this fierce old man, jealous rage at having been robbed of a lover? Anger with himself for accepting Maggomas' leavings again afterward? Bek saw himself as a weapon in another man's hand, a sharp edge to cut an enemy. He didn't like that.

"Your token must be my word, Senior, that I mean to find Raff Maggomas and deal with him as I see fit."

Outside, the boy-voices mounted in praise of the manly virtues: pride, courage, strength, patience, reason, loyalty... Senior Riggert chose patience.

"We will discuss this later," he said. "Just now, we have only the interval of the dreaming in which to deal freely with Karz. If he thinks it's to protect Raff Maggomas, he'll tell you where to find him. Can you think up a story that will put that appearance on your questions?"

"Nothing simpler, Senior," Servan said. "Let's go."

"One thing," Kelmz said. "Seniors, when you came in, were the streets clear? Is everyone but the boys inside the Hall now?"

"All but a handful of young rowdies who were turned away for arriving half-drunk," Riggert said, disdainfully. "They'll have staggered off to keep each other company somewhere until the silence is over."

Kendizen frowned. "There is a rumor that some young Tekkans went up to the Rock, and that one of them swam up a vent-pipe and let the others into Endpath. So it's known that the Endtendant, far from having barricaded himself in, has left Endpath and is at large. Possibly the young men we saw were only feigning drunkenness and are actually on the watch for suspicious movement in the City during the dreaming—in hopes of capturing the renegade, and with him some extra points."

Eager and apprehensive now at the prospect of actually closing in on Raff Maggomas, Bek said shortly, "I accept the risks. Let's waste no more time."

"Good." Captain Kelmz looked over the confusion of

paper that he had created. "I'm sick of this place. There's nothing here but pictures of dead things and a stink of lies."

Servan laughed and said it was really wonderful, how you couldn't so much as set foot inside the Boyhouse without learning something, no matter what your age.

XIV

Their passage from the Boyhouse through the silent City was swift and uneventful. The two Seniors put up their mantles to hide the sight of the empty, sunny streets. They hurried ahead, unmindful of the dust swept up by the hems of their dress-mantles. The stillness oppressed them.

Bek had developed a taste for stillness at Endpath, and he would have liked to walk alone and slowly. But Kelmz worried him. He dropped back to walk with the captain. "Did it go all right with the Rovers?"

"Fine." Kelmz kept his eyes moving, watchful of alley-mouths and shadowed doorways. "Tell me something. If you were the descendant of beasts that somehow survived the Wasting, would you stay anywhere near the descendants of men?"

"There were decendants of the beasts," Bek said, slowly, "the monsters. But the refugees' descendants exterminated them."

"From the Holdfast," the captain said. "The world was a big place in the days of the Ancients. It still is."

"A hostile place, Captain. Sometimes men who go out on the wood crews go rogue, have you forgotten?"

"I'm just giving you notice: after this you're going to be on your own with your friend d Layo. I've got a trip of my own to make."

"But what can you hope to achieve—"

Kelmz snorted. Servan heard and glanced around at them. "You've got balls to ask that! Look at your own expedition, your own purposes!"

"I want to talk with you before you go."

Kelmz smiled. "Your turn to advise me? All right."

It was none of Bek's business, he had no reason to be concerned. But he was. And Kelmz seemed to accept his concern.

They stepped into shadow, and thick doors closed them into a spacious, cool quiet. The Seniors had brought them to the company compounds. This was the common-room of the Angelists' Hall, high-ceilinged, gloomy and islanded with groupings of high-glazed furniture that were strewn with rugs and cushions for the comfort of Seniors at table-games or conversation. No one talked or played now, no old men gossiped by the hearth today in their accustomed places. Like everyone else, the Angelist Seniors were off dreaming in the Boardmen's Hall. So who were the men chanting down at the hearth-end of the room, masked by fire-glowing screens of woven grass?

Senior Riggert turned toward the screens with nervous eagerness. He seemed to have forgotten all his anger.

"Wait here," he said, and strode off down the length of the room.

To the others, Kendizen said tensely, "You understand, a lot of cults like this one have sprung up in the last three five-years, as in other troubled times. The cultists come here for the blessings of the sun; they say the rite can help some men more than dreaming can. And the cult's existence enables a man like Karz Kambl to support himself as its leader, in spite of his condition—or because of it, I should say."

A sun cult, Bek thought, with contempt. Appealing to a sun god for power against a moon witch was an old man's game, like the taste for magic, another weakness of age. A man would do better to come to Endpath.

Kendizen read his expression. "Sometimes you young men are as intolerant as the most tyrannical Senior," he said. "Try not to show too much shock when you see Kambl. He was burned once, and he has healed badly."

Rejoining them, Riggert said, "When we join the circle, I'll tell Karz that he has visitors. He'll dismiss the others, and they'll be glad to go. They can't afford to stay together and risk discovery by prowling youngsters. The Board is not lenient with sun-worshippers. Are you prepared?"

Servan said, "Tell him who I am by name. I'll do the rest."

"What about her?" Kelmz pointed at the fem, who was skulking in the darkness of the great doorway.

"The cultists will be furious if they see a fem here," Riggert said.

Servan went and spoke to her. She hesitantly took a place on one of the long, cushioned couches—a small figure obscured among the blocky shapes of seats and tables around her.

"She'll keep watch on the door for us," Servan said, "just in case. I've pointed out to her the reason for everyone's interest in not being surprised here—we wouldn't all pay together or in the same way, but by Christ-God-Son, we'd all pay!"

On the other side of the screens, a group of blank-suited men, masked, walked in a long oval, chanting. They paced gravely, not looking at one another or at the newcomers, for whom room was made in the line without apparent concern for age-standing. The chant consisted of a set of lines extolling the world as a fitting place for men, watched over by a benevolent Being: "To the Sun, Earth is a small stone; the sea is a drop that films it; the sky is a glass ball enclosing, that the Sun holds in his hands to darken; and in daytime he looks within, one bright eye."

Bek, taking up the words describing a deity who

peeped in at the world of men like a boy at a keyhole, could scarcely keep from smiling. The rest of the ceremony was not at all amusing.

Now and then a man would leave the line and go to kneel before a figure seated on a block between two small braziers in the ashes of the high-arched hearth. The figure was a horror: the body was hidden in a robe of dull red and yellow patches, but Bek could see that one arm was drawn up in a twisted crook against the chest, while above it cheek and shoulder were squeezed together on a seal of scar-tissue. The face was an unreadable snarl, wound tightly around the off-center vortex of the one milky eye.

He had seen such deformities at Endpath and could scarcely credit that a man would choose rather to live on in this state. Involuntarily, he thought of the fems he had seen burned today in the square; they were surely better off than this ruin of a man!

Senior Riggert stepped forward as others had done and knelt before the burned man. He reached out and took the figure's one sound hand between his palms: a lover's gesture, simple and direct. Kneeling so, he spoke in loving treachery. Bek, watching, felt his own flesh creep. When Riggert rose, the burned man spoke aloud. Bek didn't understand a single word, but the cultists did.

The chant died. Swiftly and in silence, the line of men filed past the burned man, who briefly clasped the hand of each of them. Then all dispersed; the Hall doors closed with a soft booming after them. The visitors were alone with the burned man.

He spoke to them. Bek watched his fire-scarred mouth, and this time, despite the distortion, he made out the meaning: "I'm told that a young man, a friend of Raff Maggomas' son, is here."

Servan stepped forward, bowing his head in an appealing manner that suggested pride and independence struggling with awe. "What was once friendship between Raff Maggomas' son and myself," he declared, with becoming boldness, "was betrayed by him and has become a bond of debt. He turned me over, in my moment

of weakness and boyhood foolishness, to my enemies. I've
lived an outcast since then. I owe him for that."

It was, Bek thought, an interesting interpretation of
events. He made a small sound of appreciation,
something between a snarl and a laugh. Kambl, moving
his upper body all in one piece as if fire had fused his
joints, turned toward him; how much did he see out of
that one clouded eye?

"Who is that?" the burned man asked.

"A true friend of mine," Servan said, and he managed
to imply with his modest tone the effort of a man to
suppress unseemly pride as he showed off the one he
loved. His delivery was masterful. A whole relationship
was conjured up, a golden transmutation of the reality
between himself and Bek. It was so convincing that even
Riggert, with murder on his mind, looked up with a flash
of quick sympathy and pleasure.

Kambl said, "Good. It will help you to do well what
you have to do, if your friend is looking on. His presence
will remind you of what is best in yourself. A man's
revenge should never be polluted with spite or cruelty."
He did not sound pompous, like a Boyhouse Teacher
launching an exhortation on the Streets of Honor, but
rather as if he really believed what he said, never having
doubted or examined the truths of Holdfast life. Bek
would have preferred some good, healthy bombast. He
could not despise this wreck who spoke so simply of
virtue. "You understand, I owe Eykar Bek, too; but my
grudge is not personal, like yours. It's only that by the
Law of Generations he is the first and most dangerous
enemy to my first and most precious friend."

Then he said, "Dagg?" And when Riggert, who stood
just behind him, touched his shoulder he added, "I'm
sorry, but truth is truth."

Saying nothing, Riggert leaned down and pressed a
handkerchief into Kambl's hand. Saliva sheened the
lower part of the burned man's face. He seemed to have
hardly any control of his lips at all and probably did not
even feel the moisture, the scar-tissue being insensitive.

With an audible sigh, Kambl used the cloth to blot the shining film from his face.

Servan, to Bek's sardonic amusement, looked rather dismayed. He was accustomed to grotesqueries more figurative than literal through DarkDreams or to quick, straightforward and bloody reality. A prolonged nightmare like this shook him up.

But he caught up the thread of his performance again. Briskly, he said, "I'm afraid the danger to Raff Maggomas from his son is more than theoretical now. Are you under the impression that I'm on my way to find Eykar Bek at Endpath to settle our differences there?"

The handkerchief hovered beside the ruins of the burned man's mouth. "I take it, then, that you're not?"

"No, sir; coming back from there. Eykar Bek has bolted like a fem, the whole City knew that this morning. I think he's gone looking for his father."

"'Rebellious sons rise,'" intoned Riggert, "'to strike down first their fathers' ways, then their fathers' lives.'"

Kambl sat very still, like one who hears a sound for which he has long listened. In a strong voice, he said, "What do you need from me?"

"If you can tell me," Servan said, "where to find Raff Maggomas, I'll intercept Bek on the way to him. When I've paid Bek what I owe him, he won't be fit to trouble Maggomas, or anyone, ever again."

Standing very tall behind Kambl's chair (like the shadow of the man Kambl might have been, had he been able to stand erect), Riggert said, "Tell them everything." The glow of the braziers reddened his dry, grooved cheeks and the mass of hair hovering above him like a sunset storm. "Young men should know that the quarrels which heat their blood began long before them and have more history than a Junior's tally of injuries. They should know for whom they act, and why."

Kambl said, "It's nothing of any great importance, except to myself and those kind enough to concern themselves with me. I was at Bayo with the Quarterbacks when Raff came down from Lammintown. He was bitter about his troubles there. He'd been trying to reorganize some phase of the way the Tekkans were handling the weaving shops, and he'd been making some headway—and then the scandal about his claimed son broke, and his influence was wiped out, though the rumor was never proven. I don't think he ever got the chance to answer the accusation formally.

"He came to Bayo in a hurry, afraid that he wouldn't have time to start over again and achieve something as great as he meant to before he died. He distrusted his health. He had no use for Endpath immortality, though. He used to say that a man should be remembered by the works of his hands and mind, not by generations of ignoramuses babbling his name by rote.

"Our Seniors," Kambl went on, "had heard the rumors, and considered Raff a trouble-maker. But he was a Senior himself, so they had to take him in. From the beginning he was full of notions that set him apart. He insisted once that fems' milk-curd could be turned into a hard substance useful for making into buttons and buckles. The Quarterback Seniors were laughing behind his back for weeks afterward.

"So he used to talk with us younger men. He said the Seniors were too soft anyway, not men enough to be really intent on Reconquest, which was his goal. He wanted to explore the waterways south through the marsh, looking for solid land to be the site of a new town, a base for expansion beyond the present borders of the Holdfast. He spoke of winning back our pride by winning back the world. It was very exciting. We liked to think of ourselves as new heroes, turning our backs on everything we hated: our Seniors, the Rovers, the marshes, the smell and sound of fems around us all the time...

"What we hated we also feared. Some of us came to love Raff for his enthusiasms, his brilliance and for his—misplaced—faith in us. But we never did do what he planned for us to do.

"Toward the end of that five-year the lavers failed again. Raff was enraged to see the fems being decimated for witchery in retaliation. He said they weren't to blame and that killing them was a stupid waste. That got him into more trouble. Some of the Seniors began saying that he had brought the blight with him, that he was in league with the fems. But he was tough and clever, and he got back to the City with us at the end of that unhappy five-year and began working to amass new power—which he did.

"Then, a few years later came this other upheaval: news that his son was mixed up in a DarkDreaming. He went to a Board meeting about it and came back very keyed-up, but he wouldn't say anything. He began to get ready immediately to go to 'Troi in a boat that he'd been fitting out for that journey for some time. Nobody knew he was doing it, except me. I don't know even now where he found all the metal he needed to make the machine that drove it. At the time, I didn't dare ask—he had no scruples at all about things he thought were necessary.

"He needed a helper for the journey and asked me to come. It was amazing, to travel so swiftly and steadily against the current of the river! A fire burned in the machine. I remember wondering if that signified some holy tie with the sun."

It was impossible to tell whether the burned man was smiling or not as he said this.

"The trouble was, I had no aptitude for mechanical things. Also, those were full-moon nights that we traveled. Maybe the Moonwitch was watching, remembering the machines of the Ancients that had violated her in the old days...

"Anyway, I stayed behind when we stopped near Oldtown, and Raff went to get some more fuel. The machine exploded. I went floating down the river in a mass of wreckage, until a hemp-barge picked me up and brought me back to the City—and into the hands of my good friends.

"Now, this is the part that we argue about, Dagg and I. I've heard nothing from Raff since then, and I haven't tried to get in touch with him. But he's alive and doing well in 'Troi, it's perfectly obvious. Rumors have been coming down the river ever since, of invention, excitement—the kind of stir he's always made wherever he's gone. And then there are the Boardmen, responding as they always do to signs of unusual power and organization. They've been asking nervous questions everywhere and sending spies upriver. Raff is already beset, without his son being after him besides."

More traveling, then, Bek thought, dismally; Maggomas isn't in the City at all. When we get to 'Troi, where will they tell me he's gone to? To the mines, to the moon—anywhere but where I am.

XV

"What's the matter?" Kelmz said, speaking close and quiet at Bek's shoulder. "You look washed out."

"Does it amuse you, Captain," Bek rasped, "to gull a cripple and his friends? I hate to have to go further—I don't like what this trip is making of me."

"Nothing worse than those you're dealing with," the captain said. "These are all grown men, you're not responsible for what they do or say. Riggert, there, is trying to use you to wipe out a rival he's too thin-blooded to murder himself. As for Kambl, he looks to me as if his brains got a good cooking in that fire."

"They seem to care about each other."

"Oh, you can call that caring if you like. I've taken orders from men like them all my life, run my Rovers to death for their little quarrels and jealousies. You find this kind of petty stuff at the bottom of every inter-company skirmish, if you dig deep enough."

Kendizen joined them. "Well," he said accusingly, "you have what you need now, don't you. And here I am, helping Riggert achieve something he's had in mind for a long time—to his discredit, and my own now that I'm involved, thanks to you."

"I'm not the cause of Senior Riggert's bloodthirsty passions," Bek retorted.

"But you'll get your use of them all the same." Kendizen looked back to where Servan and Riggert stood still attentive to Kambl's twisted form. "I don't like Riggert and never have," he muttered, "and that goes far beyond this specific mania of his about Maggomas. But I hate worse to see him helped to realizing the worst in him, because there's so much else. Look at this relationship of his with Karz, of such long standing and in spite of everything . . ." He gnawed at his lip.

"Aren't they done yet?" Kelmz said.

"Karz wants a promise that no one will tell Maggomas that he's still alive here like this. Your friend Servan is making a pretty show of reluctance." Kendizen gathered the folds of his mantle over one arm and turned on Bek with a bitter look. "Well, you won't forget to send back some kind of token for Dagg, will you, so that he can convince Karz that Maggomas is dead?"

In his mind's eye Bek saw Riggert's tall wig dipping forward in a stately manner as the Senior bent to deposit a white-haired, severed head on the lap of the burned man.

He said, harshly, "Let him come make a corpse of Maggomas himself—then he can choose his own mementos!"

Too late, he heard his voice crack sharply out in the sudden quiet—the others had ceased speaking.

Karz Kambl heaved himself upright, lunging past Servan and knocking Riggert staggering with his outflung arm. Roaring incomprehensibly, the burned man came hurtling down on Bek, brandishing aloft in his sound hand the brazier that had stood by his chair, a solid metal box that glowed with the fire it held.

Kelmz rammed Bek aside and met the burned man's charge in his place. The brazier smashed down on the captain's neck and back, and he fell against Kambl's knees. Kambl stumbled backward, the brazier tore out of his hand, and Bek sprang and grappled with him. Somehow, the burned man kept his feet. The two of them wove in a tottering circle, gasping, straining against each other. The arm that was clamped across Kambl's torso pressed against Bek, blocking any clean body-blow. With his good hand the burned man clawed for Bek's hair, seeking to drag his head back and dig at his eyes.

Bek braced his forehead against the ropey scar-slick of Kambl's neck and lunged with all his power. They toppled.

He forgot about his eyes, his head snapped back, he screamed. His thigh was jammed against the brazier's scorching lip—he could smell the burning. Frantic, he heaved himself free of Kambl's struggling weight and rolled clear of the searing pressure on his leg.

His cheek and mouth were pressed against the cool tiles, he could see his breath misting the shining surface. Why hadn't he passed out? Why didn't Kambl return to the attack? He felt only a numb ache in his leg. He closed his eyes, trying to remember just where he'd felt the burning—

"—Up!" That was Servan, speaking urgently into his ear and pulling at him. He pushed Servan's hands away, rolled onto his back and sat up, supporting himself with rigid arms.

Servan bent, blocking his view of the wound, and began cutting off Bek's pants-leg with his knife.

Right next to them, Karz Kambl lay crumpled on the floor, his terrible face turned down into the blood that had pooled from his body. He looked like a hunchback because he lay on the arm that was clamped across his belly. Bek remembered being pressed against that unnatural bar of bone. He looked away, feeling sick.

The brazier stood tipped against the far wall on two of its legs, smoking a dark spout of soot up the glazed bricks. In the hearth, Kendizen was trying to help Riggert to his feet. The Angelist, whose wig had fallen off, kept patting around for it, raising a fine dust of ash. Kendizen looked

up at Bek, his features shock-whitened, his brindled hair
standing up in spikes.

"Where's Kelmz?" Bek croaked.

"Behind you," Servan said, "but leave it. There's
nothing to do, or if there is someone else will have to do
it."

Bek twisted to look.

"Hold still," Servan protested, "I haven't finished
binding up your wound."

"He's breathing." But Bek knew how bad the captain's
breathing sounded, and how bad his color was.

"His skull's smashed, and his neck may be broken.
Move him a foot and you'll kill him for certain. We've got
to leave him and get to where we can lie up quietly for a
while."

Looking at Kelmz' slack face, Bek thought of the
words of the Endpath offering. He didn't speak them; it
wasn't as Endtendant that he had traveled with Kelmz. He
wanted to say or do something, but there was no time to
find the right words for his feelings.

What he did say, finally, was, "I can't stay." Stupid; it
was just as well if Kelmz couldn't hear him. Was this the
way men met the sudden and violent destruction of
friends, gaping like fools and stammering inanities? How
could it be that Endpath had not prepared Bek to do any
better? It was a relief to be hauled upright by Servan and
half-carried away.

"No, no, look," Servan said, tugging at him, "put your
arm across my shoulders, do you think you're going to
stroll off to 'Troi on that leg tonight? He put his brand on
you, that Kambl. No, don't try to put any weight on it at
all, lean on me; lean, Christ-God-Son! Who would have
imagined a ruin like that could move so fast or be so
strong? I had to stick him twice. He must have been really
something before he got burned. Bitch it!" He elbowed
the obstructing screens out of the way. "Everything was
going so well! In another minute I'd have had us a boat
upriver even—and you had to blow up like that!"

Before they had gone very far in the sunblind streets,

downhill toward Skidro, Bek began to flash faintness and
fall against Servan. Someone came up on his other side
and helped to support him. Not Kelmz; Kelmz was back
there dying. It was over the slim shoulders of the fem that
Bek's arm was drawn.

He came to with a wrench. He was lying, stripped, on a
blanket. People worked by lamplight over his leg. Who
were they, standing around to watch, commenting to one
another? Was someone kneeling on his leg, to make it hurt
like that?

"Get off!" he shouted.

Servan bent close over him, pinning him back by the
shoulders. "Stop that!" he said. "Listen to me: every hair
and every bit of charred thread has got to come out of that
wound. Otherwise, you'll end up with an infection and
lose your leg, maybe your life. If it hurts, so much the
better. That means there's still some skin there with live
nerves in it, something to heal from."

Bek clamped his jaw shut. He watched the drops of
sweat form among the hairs on Servan's temple, heard his
own breath sobbing, was embarrassed, wished he could
stop his muscles from jerking and thrumming. The warm
pressure of Servan's hands gave him something to steady
himself against.

"—cold water," a voice said, "until the pain lets up, if
he's to get any rest. That will help prevent scarring, too,
and muscle-shrinkage. That's not cold; you call that
cold?"

"You wanted it boiled," responded another voice, "so it
was boiled. We have no ice to cool it again, so that's as
cold as you're going to get it."

It was cold enough. Bek nearly howled at the first
contact. Then the pain went deep, spreading away from
the coldness and seeping into his bones. He could hardly
feel anything at the injury itself, except for the pressure of
the wet cloth. Cold water ran down his skin; the blanket
was soaking.

Above him, Servan sat back on his heels, blotting at his

own forehead with his sleeve. When someone remarked
that the burn looked like it was well down into muscle on
one side, Servan said furiously, "Shut up, you!"

Bek tried to look at the wound. He saw the fem bending
over his swollen leg, a dripping pad of cloth in her hand.
He let his head fall back again, panting, "Get her away
from me!"

"All right," Servan said, moving down to take the fem's
place. "I'll do that. Somebody show her where to find
something she can cook up into soup."

The room was full of shifting footsteps as people
moved away.

"Dinker, don't go," Servan said. "You and I have some
things to talk over."

A shaggy-headed man of indeterminate age stayed,
glum-faced. There were bright-glazed armlets on his lean
biceps. He kept turning these glittering ornaments with
his grimy fingers.

"Last time I helped you out," he said, resentfully, "as
soon as you'd gone two pair of Rovers and a squad of
patrolmen busted in on me at the old place and killed
three of my lads. I don't have to tell you what kind of good
stuff I lost in that raid—six weeks' worth of scrapping
right at the edge of the Wild."

"Dinker," coaxed Servan, "look at the favor I'll be
doing for you. Who else is going to carry freight for you in
times like these?"

"Carry for me?" cried the shaggy man. "Steal me blind,
you mean! Double my trouble for half the gain!"

"Think a minute, Dinker: the patrols have been rough
lately, and they're going to get rougher; bands of lads go
roaming the streets during a dreaming; the Seniors are so
nervous they'll strike out every time a rock rolls. Now,
your face is known and your lads are all known, at least
the ones you know well enough yourself to trust them.
Who would carry contraband scrap to 'Troi for you but
me?"

Silence, while the Scrapper mulled that over.

"As for myself," Servan added, "I have no choice. I

have to go to 'Troi, so why shouldn't you take advantage of that fact? You let me use your set-up to get there, and I'll carry your stuff for you."

Plaintively the Scrapper inquired, "When are we going to be paid up, you and me?"

Bek lost track of the conversation after that. Several times they propped him up and slapped him till he was awake enough to swallow instead of choking, and they spooned soup into him. He couldn't taste any flavor to it, but it was hot, and afterwards they let him sleep.

Eventually he woke clear-headed and jerked his face aside from the slaps that were meant to bring him around.

Servan squatted beside him, with a steaming bowl of soup. The flame of the floor-lamp nearby was washed out in daylight that shone in through a frosted window. The room, a bare cell with cracks in the walls, was part of some abandoned complex of buildings in Skidro.

"I don't want any more soup," Bek said.

"You're sure?" Servan drank it up himself. He wiped his mouth on the edge of Bek's blanket. "How does your leg feel?"

"It hurts." The leg was one great, nauseating ache. Bek looked at the opaque windowpane. "Is it morning?"

"Afternoon, and so far everything's quiet. Dinker went with a couple of his lads to clean up the mess we left behind us. Things could be worse. The sun-cultists won't be eager to come forward with information. Eventually, though, Riggert will have to answer some questions, high as he is. So will Kendizen. They'll put aside their pride and throw the blame for everything on a notorious Dark-Dreamer and a renegade Endtendant whom they somehow got mixed up with—in their sleep or something.

"But it will take some time before the Board even figures out what questions to ask. Dinker's men will cut up Kambl and Kelmz and sling them into the alleys on the other side of town. They'll lie on a rubbish heap for days before—"

"What about transport for us?" Bek said.

"Transport where? You're supposed to rest and heal

up, and this is as good a place as any. When the time comes, I'll take care of getting us on to 'Troi. It's all set up already."

"How long do you expect me to lie here wondering what kind of deal you can work out to sell me? I know you, Servan. This burn will take time to heal, and you'll get bored. A friend doesn't put his friend into the way of temptation."

Sighing, Servan held the soup bowl up to the light, studying its translucence. "This is the finest piece I've ever seen in Dinker's hands. I'll have to find out where he dug it up and who told him it was worth hanging onto. Normally he has miserable taste. But even Dinker shows better sense than you do, by Christ! Are you feverish, or what? You're hurt, my friend; what do you want to do, crawl up to Maggomas and bite him on the foot? Be sensible, man! You need to take time out to mend, whatever the risks."

"No. We must go now, while Maggomas may still be in 'Troi. That information cost too much to waste."

"The burn must be very painful," Servan remarked. "You didn't used to set much value on your injuries."

"I meant Kelmz. That blow was meant for me." Bek could see, in memory, the fiery brazier sliding down a curve of air, spewing bright spots, rebounding from Kelmz' shuddering back with a momentum that tore it free from Kambl's grip.

"Ah," said Servan blandly. "Of course, Kelmz stepped in to save you. Noble Captain Kelmz."

"You didn't see—"

"I saw. You don't think it's possible that he was merely responding to an attack according to a lifetime of training?"

"It's possible."

"'It's possible,'" Servan mimicked. "But you know Kelmz better than that, right? I couldn't put out a hand to help you last night without your calling me by his name and pestering me with nonsense meant for him."

"What nonsense?" Bek said, not believing. But his

mind floundered back, trying to remember its own delirium. What had he said? What had he dreamed? "I was asleep, how could I—"

"And you should have seen your face just now when I told you what the Scrappers will do with his body. I wonder if you'd look like that and change the subject if it were me, rotting in the garbage behind some screw-joint in Skidro. There, there it is again—I wish I had a mirror."

"I will not discuss this now with you," Bek said, shutting his eyes. The leg was throbbing insistently, the brute-beast of a body was using its hurt against him. He couldn't fight that and Servan at the same time.

"Well, never mind," Servan said, equably. "It just makes me wonder whether to turn you over to Bajerman after all, since our relationship—yours and mine—seems to be something less than it once was. But I can see you're not fit to chat about such personal matters. I won't hold your unfriendly attitude against you. You might think about this business of you and the captain, though. I didn't make it up. Not that I'm going to run around blatting to everybody that Eykar Bek has leaned across the age-line. It's hardly flattering to me; though you're certainly not the first to succumb to the glamor of Kelmz' reputation, his strong and silent manner, and all those romantic scars. I just never thought I'd see you crumble so easily."

He stood up. "Since you're anxious to get moving, I'll go put the finishing touches on our travel arrangements. Alldera's there in the corner, if you need anything."

And he walked out, whistling.

The question for Bek had never been whether he would get where he was going. His driving will (or whatever he sometimes thought he glimpsed standing behind his will—Fate?) would not be turned aside, no matter what the costs. The question was how to bear his losses.

ALLDERA

_____

XVI

Sometimes she wished herself back in the Rendery. This open sky, with its sweet and sweeping winds, was hers to enjoy only by the whim of the masters. The stink of the Rendery had emphatically belonged to fems and only to fems. There was something to be said for honest ownership, even of a charnel.

On the whole, however, the journey was going well. The Rover officer had worried her at first. A good Rover-runner with experience around fem-gangs could develop an instinct for wrong notes in femmish behavior. Fortunately, his attention had been divided between his own concerns and his concern for the Endtendant. Still she felt better with him gone. The remaining two were absorbed in each other. Meanwhile they all moved toward 'Troi, as Alldera's own plans required.

The river would have carried them faster, but with a wounded man and a load of scrapper-loot to transport, the men had judged the easy conviviality of the river-barges too risky. The Scrappers had provided a two-man camper and a fem-gang to carry it.

They had the southside road to themselves. With summer's "forests" of tall green hemp cut down, the dusty line of the horizon was exposed beyond the bare and broken fields. The friendly hemp camps, noisy and active all summer, were shut down now. After harvest men traveled on the river, protected by the high levees on either hand from the disquieting sight of the stripped fields, which brought the Wasting to mind.

From the road, you could look right past the borders of the Holdfast to the scraggly trees that hemmed in the territory of men. Similar trees had been cleared from the Holdfast long ago, and the men had proud chants telling how they would cut and burn the trees from the face of the world one day and would claim all the bared land for themselves. What they would use in place of wood, the chants did not say. Nor did they mention that among the companies' expeditions to the Wild for necessary supplies of wood, there were always some men who went rogue and did not return.

It was the silence, they said; it was the endless series of empty tablelands stretching away north and south, and the mountains rising in the west. They said the Wild was worse than the sea, which at least had a patterned motion. On a windless day in the Wild, all a man could think of was the stillness of the void.

When there was wind, so much the worse. It sounded like the sighing of the countless men lost in the Wasting. Or, men sometimes said in lower tones, like the whispers of the ghosts of the vanished unmen, stirred up by the intrusion of living men who chanted as they came, to drive away either sound or silence. Men were romantics, of course—they could afford to be—and they loved to magnify the significance and danger of anything that happened to them. With considerable effort, fems had gleaned from them over the years some useful information about the Wild.

The land beyond the Holdfast appeared to support no life whatever, other than spiky trees and a mixture of hard-stemmed grasses that were of no use to men. The wood raiders carried provisions with them, but there was water which men could drink. Sometimes they went rogue afterward, and it was claimed that spirits fouled the springs and streams in spite of the care men took to recite the Chants Cleansing before drinking.

As for ghosts and demons, few but the most humble and credulous fems believed these to be anything but mental creations of the men themselves. As a rule, men hated most those they had most wronged; it followed that they hated—and therefore feared—their ancestors' victims, and imagined vengeful unmen where there was nothing but vacant desolation.

None of this was reassuring. Fems thoughtful enough to consider the Wild at all dismissed it as of no use to them, since it seemed to offer no sustenance for fems who might try to escape into it.

And yet the brightest fems could not help but think about the Wild sometimes, wondering what it might hold that men were blind to. Those who bolted and actually reached the edges of the Holdfast vanished among the twisted prickly trees forever. Thoughtful fems wondered, but held their ground.

Alldera looked southward often as they traveled, squinting at the distant blue of the tree-line. She had no intention whatever of bolting, however.

She paced along at the rear, the drover's position, giving the carry-fems a step-song to keep them together under the weight of the camper. It was a riddle-song, half nonsense now that many of the word-meanings were gone: "Why is a raven like a writing-desk," it began. And what was a raven? The newer parts lent themselves to as whimsical and subtle a consideration of the concept of likeness as the singer could devise. She sang in femmish softspeech to obscure the words from the men's hearing. She was not interested in entertaining them, and besides the song was not "clean"—free of insults to masters in general. The pity of it was, the song was undoubtedly incomprehensible to the carry-fems as well, being too complex for them.

They were a mixed bunch of tough worn discards and runaways whom the City Scrappers had stolen or caught wandering and kept for their own purposes. Though not matched for size like a proper crew, these fems carried the fully laden camper smoothly. Their ragged smocks showed dirty, scarred skin at the rents; their feet were pads of callous. Only Alldera's intelligence had saved her from being beaten into just such a shape herself.

At noon she sat with them and shared their food. She dipped her hands last in the washbowl, dedicated the meal to Moonwoman, and spilled the water out (water being sacred to the mistress of the tides). Alldera didn't believe in Moonwoman herself, but the prayer was a bond among fems.

The carry-fems grunted and reached to touch her hands, thanking her for speaking on their behalf. Two of them opened their mouths to show that if their tongues had not been cut out, they too might have been speakers. Muteness in fems was a fashion in demand among masters. These two fems did not look bright enough to have been speakers in any case, but after a fem had done time in the labor pools there was no telling how well endowed she once had been.

Alldera would not have spoken of her plans to them in any case. Fems had been known to betray their own kind for this or that paltry advantage or out of spite or simple stupidity. Intelligence had been bred out of the majority of them along with size.

Even in Kendizen's house she had said nothing beyond routine inquiries for the news-songs that carried information back to Bayo. She had had even less in common with those tattooed pets, though several of them had been speakers. The trouble with pet-fems was that they came to take pride in their disfigurement—a technique of survival practiced by most fems to some extent. But in its more blatant forms, when it extended to identification with the interests of masters rather than with the interests of fems, it sickened her.

Besides, Alldera had a strong contempt for and distrust

of the merely decorative. Her own tough body, small in breasts and hips and well muscled, predisposed her toward valuing utility. She had learned to be glad of her broad pan of a face, which served both to mask her intelligence and to repel the interests of men perverse enough to pursue fems for the gratification of sexual appetites. There were times when she wished herself beautiful, of course; her own kind took their standards of beauty from those of the masters, and Alldera had spent lonely times because of that. Generally, though, she was well pleased with the virtues of her looks, and she continued to prefer the company of hard-used labor-fems like these, battered and stupid though they were.

On the second day there was rain, and the footing on the road was too slick for travel at any decent speed. At d Layo's orders, Alldera ran the carry-fems in training eights in a field to keep them from stiffening up. D Layo sat in the entry to the camper and watched them splash through the muck. He hectored and shouted criticism until he grew bored with them and went inside. Alldera used the opportunity to practice some speed-running while the others were slapping along in eights. She circled them at a hard pace, welcoming the exertion.

D Layo had her in, soaked and stinking, to cook for them that evening. He occupied himself by sitting beside the Endtendant's cot and telling ferryman stories.

First was "How Ennik Rode the Deeps"; then, a short story that Alldera had never heard called "Degaddo's Trick"; and finally part of an endless cycle of myths about a hero of just-after-the-Wasting called "Wa'king of the Wilds." This character's body was made up mostly of replacement parts carved for him by his incomparably devoted ferrymen friend, Djevvid, to remedy mutilations suffered in battles with the monsters. Following this, d Layo began a long, brooding tale of a forbidden affair across the age-line, in which the younger man inevitably misjudged and betrayed the elder and then perished on the Lost Ferry. D Layo trailed off before the ending and looked at his friend from under lowered lids.

The Endtendant said, "Servan—" He seemed to hover on the verge of a long protest and explanation, but finally said simply, "No."

D Layo put his hand on Bek's forehead as if feeling for fever. He stroked downward into the open collar of Bek's sleepshirt.

Coldly, the Endtendant said, "Are you really reduced to forcing yourself on an injured man?"

Withdrawing his hand, d Layo remarked sarcastically that it would certainly be embarrassing if the Endtendant should pass out under his tender attentions. Over the lean meal that Alldera served them, he began recalling the events of their stay in the City, mocking the parts played by the older men—particularly Captain Kelmz—with wicked style and verve.

Bek ate meagerly and made no comment, as if the effort of eating exhausted him. Alldera thought he was doing fairly well, considering the seriousness of the burn on his leg. That was good; when men died, fems burned, and she couldn't afford to be charged with witching this man into a decline.

Later in the evening, after she had completed the washing-up and lain down with the carry-fems, d Layo came out and called her from among them. He hustled her a little distance into the fields and shoved her down in one of the gang-paths.

She knew her part as well as any fem in the Holdfast, having been through the usual training at Bayo; but she had not had to play it often outside of the monthly stay in the breeding-rooms, thanks to her looks. In this case she was lucky; the DarkDreamer was young and vigorous and probably free of the incapacity for which men blamed and punished fems. On the other hand, if he were annoyed by his friend's rebuff, he might be cruel. Nothing could protect her if he decided to beat her or even strangle her on the spot. If need be, she would have to bolt and take her chances as a runaway fem, to be hunted by Rovers.

He knelt and ran his hands over her. "My friend has a

streak of cunt-hunger, I think; he'll get to you sooner or later. So let's see what he'll be getting."

He took endless time with strokings and touchings that were plainly modeled on the gentle practices of fems among themselves. To her horror, she realized that there was not going to be the ordinary swift assault, designed to carry a man triumphantly past the dangers of a fem's body by sheer force and speed. He seemed totally unconcerned with the possibility of being robbed of his soul by the femmish void (through the medium of her body), a risk that men spoke of running if they fucked a fem outside of the breeding-rooms. To some young men this was a danger to be dared for the thrill of it.

This DarkDreamer was working on another level entirely. He obviously derived some special gratification from his effort to stimulate her to pleasure. What kind of a pervert was he?

She was too stunned and disgusted to feel very much in spite of his knowledgeable manipulations; how could he have learned just where and how to touch her, if not by forcing fems to lie together in front of him? That seemed to her to be a violation far uglier than any common assault.

Anxious to put an end to his insistent handling of her, she performed a set of moanings and writhings that she hoped would persuade him that he had forced her to a climax. He was taken in, for he mounted her briefly afterward for his own satisfaction and then withdrew to lie relaxed beside her. He began humming a femmish love-song, of all things; flat, but recognizable.

She stared up at the cloud-dimmed stars and tried to consider calmly how this peculiarity of his might be useful. It was not entirely unknown for the news-songs to carry word of some pet fem who had gained a hold on her master by exploiting a vein of perversity in his character. But that was something that came only to those of legendary beauty and cunning, and those fems generally ended up being burned as witches anyway. How much better could she expect to do, out of her depth as she was to begin with?

Suddenly he jerked her head up by the hair and twisted, so that she had to turn on her belly or have her neck broken. She turned. He pushed her face against the wet, hard-packed earth.

"Eat," he said.

She bit at the mud. She coughed. Grit got between her teeth.

"What's the lesson?" he said.

What he wanted was recognition of his god-like unpredictability. The trick was to furnish it without drawing attention to the fact that total arbitrariness was also an attribute of chaos and the void. It was not for a fem to point out paradoxes that men chose to ignore. The best Alldera could do at the moment was to mumble, through bruised and filthy lips, a stock response: "The master is always the master, and he does as he pleases according to his will."

Saying nothing, he let her go and got up. She followed him back to the camper, wiping mud off her mouth with the cleanest part of her hem.

The carry-fems greeted her with murmurs of concern and light pattings over her body and limbs to assure themselves that she had not been injured. Then they sank back into sleep around her. She was grateful for their warmth. The back of her smock was wet through; the night was cool, and a fem who fell sick was likely to be abandoned. But she felt alone among them. Even if she had explained, not one of them would even have begun to comprehend the special unpleasantness of her encounter with the DarkDreamer.

She would simply have to put up with him, and with anything else that came her way during this journey, without help. That was nothing new. Her skills had always set her apart from all but a few of her kind anyway. At least she had a mission to serve by her endurance these days. If she failed, fems who survived the coming holocaust would be broken by their masters to become like these sleeping brutishly around her. There would be no more fems capable of organizing even the most timid and well hidden resistance.

That new pogroms were coming no thinking fem could doubt (though there were many who preferred to deny it). The lammin-failure and a consequently hungry winter made that inevitable. Moreover, the fems of Bayo knew something that the men had not yet realized: the lavers, too, would be coming in thinner than ever this year. The men would cry witchery and turn on the fems, as they always did when things went badly.

This time, certain young fems had sworn to fight back. Cells of young rebels had sprung up everywhere during the past five-year, possibly triggered by an especially strict weeding-out process in Bayo which had alienated the young fems from their elders.

The older fems, the Matris, made a secret culling of each class of young fems due to leave the Bayo kit-pits for training by the men—and by the Matris, whose teaching ran secretly alongside the men's training. The Matris saw to it that these kits submitted first to the underground authority of their own elders to assure full acceptance of the breaking-techniques of the men. In the past one or two youngsters had responded to the standard, initiatory beating by attacking male trainers. Each time, the reaction of the men had been immediate decimation of the femmish population in Bayo. So for the safety of all, young fems who showed signs of rebelliousness had to be cured of it before they fell into the hands of the Bayo trainers. Those judged incurable were simply killed by the Matris themselves; giving rise to the legend among men of kit fems so wild-natured as to bite open their own veins and bleed to death, rather than be brought up out of the pits for breaking.

Faced with new crop-failures on top of the old, the Matris had grown stricter than ever. They had been savage, hoping to avert the worst of the men's unavoidable rage by permitting only the most docile young fems to live. One result had been the opposite of their intention: warning had somehow gotten round the pits, and many kits had successfully dissembled their true attitudes. Once dispersed among the labor pools and private femholds beyond the direct reach of the ruling Matris in Bayo, these youngsters were swearing among themselves that this time there would be no slaughter without a fight. They sang songs of their own, saying that death was better than survival to no other purpose than the production of new generations of fems for a worse oppression than before.

Hearing of this, the Matris had sent out warnings by way of the news-songs, saying that men would be so enraged by even token resistance that they might well kill all fems without realizing the meaning of what they did. And the recalcitrant youngsters—who were now calling themselves The Pledged—had replied: let them.

Alldera herself doubted that the defiance of The Pledged would prove as bold or as farreaching as either side claimed. With many youngsters, taking the pledge was sheer bravado and would not hold up. Yet she found them very appealing. If she hadn't been a few years older than most of them, and experienced enough to know that she was neither a joiner nor physically brave enough to be a leader, she might have pledged herself. Instead, she kept track of them with anxious hope, seeing in them a potential organization of active but subtle resistance and dreading that they would sink in a welter of their own blood when the killing began.

So she had agreed to the Matris' plan.

There was an old tale that in the mountains west of 'Troi, deep in the heart of the Wild, lived the so-called "free fems," runaways who had learned to stay alive beyond the borders of the Holdfast. A token message brought from them might persuade the pledged fems to give up their plan of suicidal resistance in favor of simple endurance until armed support could arrive from the free fems. By the time it became apparent that no help was coming (for neither Fossa nor any of the other Matris actually believed in the existence of the free fems), the

men's rampage would hopefully be spent. The disillu-
sioned young rebels would then have to come to terms
with reality and settle down to make the best of their
situation in the tradition of their kind.

Alldera didn't believe in the free fems either. Yet it
seemed to her that if any young fems could grow bold
enough to dare a concerted and determined break into the
Wild under the mistaken impression that they would find
allies there, then they themselves might of necessity turn
into free fems. That was her hope, though not for herself.
Her skills—speed and fluency—were fitted for spying
against the masters, rather than for being part of a group
that would depend on cooperation and planning to
survive in the Wild.

So she had settled for the job of journeying toward the
mountains and back again. The news-songs were already
carrying hints of her mission to prepare acceptance of the
message she would bring back. That it was a false
message, made up by the Matris and memorized by
Alldera before ever leaving Bayo, was a pity, but
necessary. She could hardly count on finding real free
fems in the Wild, let alone foresee their reaction to a plea
for help. Fems knew if anyone did that having been
victimized was no guarantee of courage, generosity or
virtue of any kind.

So she carried with her the hope-inspiring message that
she was ostensibly traveling to beg of the legendary free
fems. She accepted this dishonesty as she accepted the
dangers of accompanying these men merely because a fem
could not travel sizeable distances alone without arousing
suspicion. There was a difference between lying and
bending her neck for the privilege of continuing to lie and
bend her neck, and going through the same motions so
that some other fems might not have to do either any
more.

XVII

The next day, d Layo took charge of the carry-fems and ordered Alldera to ride in the camper with the Endtendant. For himself, he said, he wanted some exercise. If the fem failed to please Eykar, a complaint from him would bring swift discipline.

She climbed inside and squatted down at the foot of the bed, her eyes properly lowered. Outside, the fems heaved the camper up onto their shoulders and began to run with it. Trapped together in the musty interior, the two passengers were silent for a time.

Finally the Endtendant said, "Make yourself useful. Tell me about that night at the Scrappers'."

Alldera gaped at him and poked her tongue into the corner of her mouth as though trying her best to concentrate—without great success. If a fem showed herself to be in possession of what a man regarded as his secrets, she invited death in the witch-fires.

"As the master says," she ventured.

"Servan says I talked in my sleep. Is it true?"

"As the master says." She blinked at him.

"Tell me what I said."

"As the master says," she quavered, puckering her face as if about to weep in fear and confusion.

"I see," he said, comtemptuously. "I misjudged you. I thought I detected a glimmer of intelligence. You must be no more than a brute with a memory for others' words after all."

Now that she had convinced him, she was tempted to blow it all up. She wanted to tell him what he asked and a lot more, yielding to the prime fantasy of all speaking fems—that of becoming the one who, by sheer eloquence, drove through the barrier of the men's guilt and fear.

Others' words? Her own words would blast his cursed bones—or at least it was gratifying to think so. The Matris said that the men already knew that fems were wrongly blamed for the Wasting, but that for men there was no truth but that which served their upraised fists.

Alldera ducked her head. "As the master says."

He stared coldly at her. His dislike was hard as stone.

"I've seen you doing exercises," he said. "They seem to be for stretching the muscles of the legs."

"As the master says."

"Spare me that sniveling cant!" he exploded. "Just show me what you know that would work the muscles here." He laid his hand gingerly along the side of his injured leg.

"These are femmish exercises, please you," she said, cringing to disguise the fact that she was offering a correction to a master, "which this fem hopes she can perform to the master's satisfaction—"

"I want you to teach them to me," he snapped. "I'm not interested in a performance."

Alldera had, and knew she had, considerable muscular grace, a side effect of speed-training. The exercises he required could show off her body without leaving her open to a charge of attempted seduction—while helping to accomplish the fact. Judging by d Layo's remarks the night before, he had put her in here to seduce the

Endtendant. To please d Layo seemed the sensible course.

Yet she would have to go carefully. Men like Bek—high strung, tightly controlled, inexperienced in the reality of fems as opposed to Boyhouse nonsense about them—were potentially dangerous to the first fem to break through their defenses. They sometimes went rogue and killed the offending fem or even themselves. Either way the blame was laid at the fem's door.

How sick she was of this process of figuring out the subtlest, safest course to take with them! It used up so much time and energy, and to no avail. No matter how carefully you weighed up men's motives and probable reactions, you ended with the same helpless gamble you'd started with. A man's whim was law, and knowing this made men capricious.

She channeled the energy of her anger into the exercises, showing him with beauty and smoothness how to stretch, to turn, to bend the legs from the sitting position. Runners had to know how to keep fit even when penned in tight quarters for long periods as punishment or in the line of duty. She made a masterpiece of the routine. That was her defiance.

Slowly and clumsily, he imitated her, keeping himself decently covered with the blanket and the long skirts of the bedshirt that he wore. His prudery was comical at first, but as he sweated and fought to follow, he seemed to forget her, almost, in his absorption with another enemy: his own body. He strove against the stiffness of his muscles with grim concentration, so that she could not help feeling a grudging respect for him. Respect was not something she gave willingly to men. It annoyed her.

As they were about to go through the routine for the third time, there came an outbreak of terrified wailing from the carry-fems outside. The camper lurched forward, its canvas walls flying.

Alldera glimpsed a stranger in Hemaway colors standing over the forward-offside fem who had sunk down, clawing at his knees. He was sawing at her neck with a knife. His hissing breath was audible between her screams.

Then Alldera and the Endtendant were spilled together under a shroud of tangled canvas, rope and poles. They fought to be free of each other; they scrabbled for light and air.

The wreckage was wrenched aside.

"Look! Raff Maggomas' son entwined in the arms of a fem!" exclaimed their discoverer, a high-mantled, round-faced man whose eyes were squeezed nearly shut with mirth at the sight of them. He was speaking to a group of hefty Hemaway Seniors, not one of them more than a couple of years across the age-line. Two Hemaways held the DarkDreamer by the arms, which they had twisted up behind his back. They had taken his knife from him. One of them kept turning to spit blood from his bruised mouth.

Five carry-fems stood huddled around the dead one. They glanced furtively over at Alldera. She lay quite still, hoping by example to keep them steady. They would be pulled down and butchered if they ran. These were strong men, not dodderers, and had already been primed for blood by one femmish death.

At their leader's orders, three Hemaways hustled the Endtendant and Alldera to their feet and out of the collapsed camper. Because of his bad leg, Bek had either to lean on Alldera, or to sit on the ground and look up at his captor and at the sun.

He clamped his hand on her shoulder, glanced once at the Hemaways as they set about rebuilding the camper, and turned a bitter look on the senior Senior.

"Senior Bajerman," he said, "I had hoped to meet you again sooner."

"Oh?" inquired the other, brows arching in mock perplexity. "Were you planning to catch up with me by running away from the City where I live?"

"I meant that I had hoped when I was still at Endpath to meet and serve you there, Senior; though in fact it is by leaving the City that I have found you, isn't it?"

The Senior sighed and looked him up and down. "I remember you more kindly than you remember me, I think. You were less lean and sharp-faced in your

Boyhouse days, Eykar, but, I must add, no less arrogant. To grow older without maturing is a dreadful waste."

D Layo laughed. "You should know, Bajerman."

The bloody-mouthed Hemaway gave d Layo's arm a wrench. D Layo grinned at him, part pain, part promise.

"You two young men," Senior Bajerman sadly remarked, "are a great reproach to me. You never did learn basic consideration for your elders. You've been slow—we've been waiting for you since dawn." He nodded in the direction of the levee, which was pierced at this point by the thick-woven cables of a bridge linking the north and south river-roads. "Our boat is down under the bridge. It's too small, unfortunately, to carry us all but I see you have thoughtfully furnished transport yourselves. We knew you would come by on your way to 'Troi, so we were patient, and here is our reward.

"You must have guessed, Eykar, that your father's whereabouts have been known to certain members of the Board for some time. We were hoping that you yourself might be useful in curbing Maggomas' ambitions. He's been gathering considerable power about himself in 'Troi, more than seemed to us healthy for the general life of the Holdfast. Your flight from Endpath indicated to us that you were ripe to be used against him, if we could lay our hands on you and point you in the right direction."

"And now that you have—laid your hands on me," Bek said, with a curl of his lips, "what direction do you have in mind?"

"Oh, we'll go on to 'Troi," the Senior said. "There is noplace else to go. An army of young madmen is at our heels now. The Juniors of the City, having discovered that there are no great hidden stocks of food and supplies there, have turned toward 'Troi instead, where other hoards are rumored to be hidden away.

"Their rebellion apparently began with some quarrel in Lammintown between 'Wares and Chesters over a question of unauthorized passengers and lammin-theft. The 'Wares took the matter to the City for the Board to adjudicate. Some young Chesters followed, were turned

away drunk from the dreaming and returned to break into
the Boardmen's Hall and maltreat some of the 'Wares.
Two men died. Other companies leaped into the dispute,
and yesterday there were riots in the City. By noon, young
men were cutting down their elders in the streets."

"It's very gratifying," d Layo said, "to know that a
man's actions do count for something in this world."

Senior Bajerman nodded: "I thought that tale of the
raid on the lammin-stocks and a daring escape by sea
might have involved you; it had your touch. But I
wouldn't take credit for setting off a generation-war if I
were you; it's been brewing for a long time. Anything
could have ignited these City punks. The lessons of the
Wasting have been too lightly remembered lately, and
hardly taught to the young. If Juniors don't understand
the meaning of work or discipline or honor any more,
why, I suppose we Seniors must bear some of the blame
for that.

"Now there will be a battle of 'Troi, I think, an historic
event—which we will attend, hopefully, from a vantage
point inside 'Troi walls. We will arrive bringing word of
the approach of the degenerate City rabble, and I'm sure
that Raff Maggomas can find proper places for myself
and my friends in exchange for that; and for the person of
his own natural enemy, Eykar: yourself."

"But," d Layo said, with exaggerated astonishment,
"where were the Seniors' famous Rovers during this
upheaval, where were the Rovers' even more famous
officers?"

"The Rovers proved a great disappointment," the
Senior admitted. "Some of the young men had made
distance-weapons—strictly forbidden, of course, but
these things are so hard to control. These boyos stationed
themselves on the rooftops and picked off the officers
with stones whirled from slings.

"After that, it was not too difficult for them to lure the
uncommanded Rovers into the alleys where barricades
were thrown up to pen them in, and they were harrassed
and bombarded from the rooftops until they went rogue

and turned on one another. Of course, the caliber of the younger officers wasn't all it should have been; it's been declining lately with the caliber of all young men. I've come to regret having sent Captain Kelmz with you, Servan.

"And I must say I am shocked at the way you treated him—to throw him aside like a worn-out shoe! A shocking end for a prominent man, to be struck down in the course of some obscure, illicit brawl when all decent men of the City were dreaming!" Kindly, he added, "Yet I can see that Eykar feels his loss, and misses, no doubt, Kelmz' courage, his experience, perhaps even his close friendship in spite of the disparity in ages? I'll do what I can to take his place."

"You?" Bek said, and he uttered a raw bark of laughter.

"Do you scorn my good will, Eykar?" murmured the Senior. "I could leave you to the mob, remember. You served the Board at Endpath for six years. I doubt those degenerate City cubs will look kindly on that career, so many of them having lost friends and lovers to the Rock."

"Don't be stupid," Bek said, flatly. "You'll take me to 'Troi because that's where I'm going, with or without your aid. Do you think it matters whether I arrive there walking, crawling, or dragged by an enemy?"

Senior Bajerman gazed earnestly at the bright sky, assuming an expression of pink-cheeked magnanimity.

"I was once fond of you, Eykar. I thought you had great promise. For the sake of our past closeness, I'll put these ravings down to the effects of your wound. As for this DarkDreamer, I think I have a place for him quite close to me, for which he should be grateful. He needs lessons in behavior as badly as you do, since what was taught to you both in the Boyhouse evidently didn't take. You should count yourselves fortunate in finding a qualified Teacher to help you correct your errors. We'll hold class in the camper for you two as we travel.

"As for this fem of yours, Eykar—"

"She's not mine."

"Whichever of you two she belonged to," the Senior

said, "it's a good thing that someone thought to bring her along. She can take the place of the carry-fem that my friend Arik killed. These over-trained personal fems are going to have to get used to honest work in the future. The City lads included fems in their rampage, apparently incensed by reports of fems actually attacking men. Only idiot boys would credit such tales, of course, but you know how rumors like that get about whenever there is any unrest. When the dust of this chaos clears, fems will be in short supply. So I must thank you young men, I suppose, for your forethought in providing me not only with your charming and invaluable selves, but with a useful bit of property besides."

XVIII

The morning was already spent when Alldera joined the carrycrew. By midafternoon a dark and gritty wind began to bite at them from the west. As they ran, the carry-fems showed her the rhythm that was least tiring, how to balance the load over her spine and let her hips do the work, how to fold her carry-cloth on the run so that it provided the best padding under the yoke.

The trouble was that she did not have the strength to support her share of frame, canvas, and the weight of three male passengers. The carry-fems were built square, for lugging heavy loads. Alldera was long-muscled for fluid motion.

Eventually, she fell. The others managed to keep the camper from dropping and crushing her. They prodded her with their feet when Senior Bajerman descended from the camper, but she couldn't even draw her legs under herself to rise. It made no difference; her mission had ended when fems began dying in the City, for the Pledged would be the first to be killed. She only hoped that these men would cut her throat cleanly, rather than break her legs and leave her there, as some drovers did. It was a mercy that her eyes were so puffy from squinting into the driving dust that she would hardly be able to see the knife.

Standing over her, Senior Bajerman did not draw a knife. He said that it was crowded in the camper. He had been told that this fem was speed-trained, and he was not going to let such potentially valuable property go to waste; that would be unmanly. She would ride in the camper where she could attend Eykar while she got back her strength. Perhaps a man running with this crew of hulks could make them put some decent speed on. Bajerman would go on foot outside with his men, he said, and observe the performance of Alldera's replacement: d Layo.

The DarkDreamer was pushed into position, and the Hemaways slung Alldera into the camper. The dim interior smelled of Bajerman's perfume, for the ceiling-vent had been shut to keep out the blowing grit. Alldera crawled into a corner and huddled there, too cramped to move or speak, drawing painful breaths of the stale, sweet air.

The camper was lifted and carried into the teeth of the wind. A man's voice, hoarse and panting, struck up a step-song concerning the foolishness of old men who insisted on showing off their dwindling physical powers to younger companions. D Layo was singing.

Later, in the blowing dusk, the carry-crew staked down the camper into tent form for the night. The Hemaways fashioned a rough shelter for themselves of their mantles and staffs a short distance away. The fems were left within the bare area between the two structures, where Hemaway sentries could keep an eye on them.

Alldera was thrust among the carry-crew for the night. She squatted stiffly and used her carry-cloth as they used theirs, as shelter from the wind. She had not slept; the Endtendant had not said one word to her all afternoon in the camper, but she hadn't dared to doze off for fear of being punished for inattentiveness. Now the carry-fems took turns kneading the ache out of her shoulders, back and legs. A bald one, scalped too closely at some time by fur-weavers, offered her the moist center of a portion of curdcake, keeping the tougher skin for herself.

In a tight circle, using their hip-packs of provisions as cushions, they settled for a night of shared warmth. The carry-fems began to hum, weaving tone and amorphous rhythm into a plaintive, wordless request for a song for the dead one.

Every song needed one fem in the group who knew the words, and could sing them under the camouflage of gutterals and trills set up by the others to mask the sense of the song from men—most of whom could follow softspeech if they tried. Alldera was not a singer. Her work had been largely solitary and not conducive to music. But her trained memory had retained every song she had ever heard.

She sang a mourning song for the slain carry-fem. It was an uncommon one; she had never heard all the words, for some of them had been lost. She loved the tune, however, which was unmistakably grieving: "Goodbye, all pain, something-something Shy Ann."

When that song was finished, the carry-fems kept up their vocal pattern, building on the mournful melody. Alldera wondered if some inkling of the meaning of Bajerman's remarks had gotten through to them—that the massacre of fems had already begun. All the carry-fems and Alldera herself had come very close to dying by the bridge. They owed their lives—for however much longer they would be permitted to keep them—to Senior Bajerman's judgment of their usefulness.

It was unfair for her to be left with a bunch of carry-fems who could scarcely comprehend the dimensions of the disaster and of her own failure. They were not the type with whom she would have chosen to spend the last of her life. They smelled and were dim-witted, and they looked to her—foolishly, in her opinion—for leadership.

And so? A dead bitch is a dead bitch, what difference

whether she had brains or not? What use had Alldera's brains ever been? She might as well be one of these carry-fems as not. They remembered their dead, at least, in spite of the brutality of their lives, and showed kindness when they could afford to. If these poor scarred hulks wanted songs, she would sing for them.

She began with the traditional singing-invocation, relating how men continually brought their own houses down on their heads and then looked around for some one else to blame. With the beasts and the Dirties all gone and the idea of gods discredited as a femmish hoax, there was no one to blame these days but the fems and their young. The words asked for strength to bear the blame. Alldera sang them ironically, using the shortest form, and then swung into the jeering rhythm of songs mocking the Ancient men for the brainless greed that had perverted their inventiveness and strength.

These songs told of rotten water, ravaged hills, air made unbreathable by noxious gasses, cities uninhabit- able because of the noise of machines—all of it, the product of the men's own wonderful knowledge and their obsession with breeding more sons on their fems. Dying of the men's assault, the Ancient world had rotted, and its decay had released poisons. The first to die had not been the men whose avarice for the riches of the world caused it all; they had had wealth with which to buy protection, while there was still protection to be had. It was the beasts who died, all unknowing; and it was the Dirties. Those of the unmen who realized what was happening and rose up to fight, the Ancient men slaughtered, using flying fires and earth-smashers that only compounded the damage suffered by the world.

At last, seeing their own kind falling to the increasingly widespread and indiscriminate destruction of wars and poisons, the leaders of men had bravely made the choice of sustaining themselves in the Refuge so that mankind would not utterly disappear.

The carry-fems slapped their knees to make the beat for the mock-heroic songs that told of the Holdfast-

making: how the descendants of the world's mur-
derers had stepped out into the open again to build a new
life on the bones of the dead and the backs of their fems.
In the time-honored manner, the descendants had
become heroes in their turn by pursuing and exterminat-
ing the pitiful creatures that had survived the Wasting
outside, the so-called "monsters." So the river-plain had
been claimed for men again, from the hills behind 'Troi to
the sea.

The decendants' courage had been rewarded. They had
found life-sustaining gifts of the sun on which to nurture
their society. There were the edible seaweeds, the metal
mines, the pits of coal for fuel, and the hemps for food and
fiber. Not to mention the last gift, the docile compliance
of fems in their own suppression.

"Heroes!" the songs mocked. "The unmen are not
gone; you are more predictable than the thoughtless
beasts, though not as beautiful. You are poorer than the
Dirties, though less wise. You dream the drug visions of
the Freaks, without freedom. You are more vain and
jealous than the fems, and weaker." The formal closing of
this sort of history-cycle was an admonition to all fems
who heard: choose your hatreds with care, seeing how the
men have become all that they hate! And then came
urgings to patience, promises that the men would find
their sanity and humanity again in time. Meanwhile, fems
must keep themselves sane and fit to meet them again as
people when the time came. The way to fight your enemy
is not to become like him, they said.

Alldera could no longer even finish the words. She
broke into another song instead, one that asked how was
it that the fems the leaders saved from the Wasting
accepted degradation instead of swallowing their tongues
and suffocating in defiance?

Every one of the carry-fems huddled against the wind
knew the answer to that, for it was the first and last lesson
dinned into all fems by the Matris: for the survival of the
race.

"And to save their own lives," Aldera added, hoarse with hatred. She too had learned to snivel and whine and creep softly about in order to stay alive. She ended with a proscribed song called the Cursing Song:

"Moonwitch's daughters, enticers of men, bloody-mouthed cub-makers—if only we had the power! Ogres, man-eaters, ravening monsters, drinkers of blood and strength—if only we had the power! Bringers of evil gifts, fountains of chaos, stinking, merciless, wild-hearted haters—if only we had the power! Unchangeably ancient, corpse-crones, child-eaters, justice-blind and mad as blackness—if only we had the power!"

The carry-fems weren't happy with that; it made them uneasy. They let their accompaniment lapse when it was over and curled up to sleep. The wind had died. From the camper came intermittent sounds of conversation, even laughter.

Alldera lay awake a while, wondering if the femmish songs had been sung for the last time tonight.

In the morning, there was a shadow on the plain behind them. It was Oldtown, the remains of an Ancient City. They had missed the hemp-stink and the rumble of machinery because of the previous day's wind. Over decades, fem-gangs had been brought in to strip the site of usable materials. Scrappers had scrounged furtively after them. Nothing remained but heaps of rubble among which a complex of water-mills had been built to catch the strength of the river and to use it to help process the hemp harvested from the plains.

Morning also revealed the distant, hurrying figure of one of the Hemaways, who was making for the town. He must have had enough of traveling that empty road toward an uncertain reception in 'Troi. The others looked after him scornfully and spat on the ground, but there were envious and speculative glances too, when Senior Bajerman wasn't watching.

He sat unconcernedly in the sun. D Layo knelt behind him and rubbed his back with scented oil. Occasionally, the DarkDreamer leaned forward to murmur in the Senior's ear. Then there were smiles and laughter between them.

So that was why the Endtendant sat apart from them both and hardly touched his food. Alldera thought his behavior absurd. What did he expect from his friend? D Layo was merely demonstrating that he knew how to make the best of a bad situation—a femmish quality, but there were plenty of men who would make fine fems, given the opportunity.

Bek turned, extending his hand for the water-cup, and saw the contempt on her face. His eyes narrowed; but there was no shout, no blow. She blinked and looked away. He took the cup from her hand, not touching her fingers. She knew she would not get away free. She hardly cared.

With the flaps buckled down around them for privacy and the journey resumed, Bek settled himself among the cushions at the head end of the bedding. He picked at the blanket, tracing the shape of the bandage on his leg underneath. He said, "I'm still thirsty. Pour me some more water."

Oh, these conscientious types, she thought. He needed an excuse to exercise his rage because he was ashamed of it. Instead of coming right to the point and beating her because her expression had angered him, he would give her orders and watch for the least sign of insubordination—which he would find, one way or another. Then why play the game of submission? In a convulsive gesture, she turned the pitcher upside down, and its cold contents splashed out over the bed.

He jerked his legs back with a gasp of pain, rose onto his knees and wrenched the pitcher out of her hand. He raised the pitcher over his head, his face twisted with fury.

Alldera fell back. She spread her legs and clawed up her smock with both hands in the last, mindless defense: when threatened, present.

For an instant, he hung over her; then he flung himself down on her. It took all her concentration and skill to help him carry through his assault. He was clumsy and in pain, and when he entered her, she heard his groan of mortal terror. Their coupling was painfully dry for her, but brief. Almost at once a strained cry burst from his throat. He pulled away and rolled onto his stomach in the sodden bedding, his ribs pumping in and out like a blown runner's.

Mechanically Alldera took stock: one sleeve was half-torn from her smock; a bruise was swelling warmly under the skin of her left temple; there were other aches and abrasions, none serious. She finger-combed her hair and blotted her sweaty face on the skirt of her garment. A fem must never offend a master by appearing messy if she could help it.

She thought what a good thing it was that she had never joined the Pledged. Let this man, not much taller or heavier than herself and wounded besides, only raise his hand to her and all her courage disappeared into the habits of survival like a rock into a swamp. A clever fem sometimes needed a reminder of her true positon, and there was nothing like a good swift fuck to set firmly in her mind her relation to the masters again: the simplest relation of all, that of an object to the force of those stronger than she.

Fem, she thought, you only think you think. The pitcher the man drinks from does not think. The camper that carries his weight does not think.

She felt hollow in body, which was fitting in one who was merely a receptacle for the use of men; and she felt hollow in mind, for there was nothing she might imagine, feel or will that a man could not wipe out of existence by picking her up for his own purposes. Any fem drifted helplessly, awaiting their actions and desires until one of them inadvertently authenticated her by seizing her to himself—if only to run an errand or repeat a phrase—for an instant. That she could have a mission, a direction of her own—or that others like herself to whom she was in some way bound could—was an absurdity. A man's usage conferred existence.

But this man didn't know his part. He should have ignored her or briskly ordered her to change the bedding, signifying that the incident had no importance for him. Instead, he surged back onto his knees, though the pain drove the blood from his face, and he took the front of her smock in his hands and shook her so that her teeth snapped together.

"You haven't made a cub off me, have you?"

The question was unheard of. If a man intended to breed, it was assumed that he did so unless interfered with by femmish magic. Breeding was a matter entirely out of the control of fems, who came into estrus as time demanded.

Panicked by his agitation, she stammered automatically, "Not if the master wills not."

"Nor stolen my soul," he said, giving her a shake. "Is that all there is to it, then?"

He had gone rogue; he was going to kill her. Her head was full of flarings of blackness from the violence of his handling. She couldn't speak.

"Then it's nothing!" he cried, and flung her backward against the end-wall of the camper. One of the carriers outside staggered at the sudden shift in weight.

Alldera lay where she had fallen. She'd bitten her tongue and tasted blood.

Very low, the Endtendant said to her, "Listen, fem. I couldn't stay in the camper last night, so I slept outside. I heard your songs. I heard how you sang them. I came closer to listen. In the Boyhouse, they taught me that fems' songs are nonsense. They also taught that coupling with a fem outside of the breeding-rooms is a dreadful peril, but here I am, no different than before; so maybe the songs are not nonsense.

"Now you talk straight to me, bitch, or I'll break your neck, for I'm fed to the teeth with tricks and lies!"

XIX

Exhilarated, she almost laughed. She dreaded a crippling injury too much to oppose him physically, yet here the man bade her take up words, her only weapon.

"The master has heard all the songs I know," she said, and stopped, struck by her own daring, saying silently to herself, "I. I." She could hardly believe she had spoken the magical pronoun aloud to him, the equalizing name for the self.

He didn't even notice. "No more songs," he said. "One version of the past seems as likely as another. Tell me about now. Tell me about your own experience."

That meant, tell about your life. Alldera's life was the only thing she owned, not to be had for the asking. But she saw that she could use parts of it, and parts of other femmish lives (he wouldn't know the difference), to beat him down. He was not armored against her in the callousness that most men acquired by customary contact with her kind.

Was he disturbed by the suspicion that he had been

taught lies in the Boyhouse? Excellent. She decided to begin with what young fems were taught in the kit-pits and training-pens of Bayo and let him draw his own conclusions. She began to speak evenly and matter-of-factly, as if she were delivering a long message.

She told about life in the pits, where young fems lived till the breaking age of nine. They scrabbled naked in filthy straw for food that the trainers threw down, and only strong and cunning fems survived. She made for him the sounds of the pits: the grunting signals that the young kits learned from those a little older, for no one spoke human language around the pits. The theory was that fems' capacity for language was generally so limited that they must not be confused by exposure to any more words than the basic command and response phrases.

Learning to speak more than the minimum was a risky maneuver. Alldera described the care she had taken to disguise her natural aptitude, so that it would seem to the men of Bayo that her verbal achievements were entirely to the credit of her trainer. Otherwise they might suspect witchery, by means of which she would be supposed to have raised herself so far and so fast above the norm for her kind. She had made her trainer work to discover her mimetic abilities and her grasp of the structure of complex speech.

A pity, they had said, that she wasn't pretty enough to be trained as a pet, some of whom were taught to tell stories and jokes in an entertaining manner. The Bayo men had altered her diet to improve the quality of her hair and skin, and they had succeeded to some extent; but she would never be pretty, only presentable.

So they had taught her how to memorize messages, how to find her way from place to place, how to identify other men than her master by clothing, mien and surroundings, and how to present a message properly. Then came the wonder of her first trip from Bayo to the City on a barge with a dozen others ripe for the bidding of the companies; the glory of the highstanding City, paved streets after mud-walled Bayo, and the majestic and terrifying peal of the company bells, which she had taken at first for the voices of monsters clanging out over the City.

She spoke of her pride in being selected to serve an important Senior (to a fem fresh from Bayo, all Seniors were important to an equal, exalted degree): Senior Robrez of the well respected Squire Company.

How impressed she had been with the size of his femhold: a private squad of seven fems under the domination of Fossa, who at that time had been only a year away from discard. At first, Alldera had not perceived the sly politicking among the other fems of the hold, the jockeying for favorable positions from which a lower fem could hope to vault into Fossa's place once it was vacated. Gradually, young Alldera had recognized the aping of men's hierarchical concerns among the fems, even though rank for them could only be a pretense; no real power—beyond the reach of a master's whim— accrued to any femmish position.

Then there was Senior Robrez himself. With time, his pomposity, his pettiness and his spite had all revealed themselves, and the godlike virtue of masters (real masters, not trainers brutalized by life in Bayo) had been toppled forever in her mind.

She told how Senior Robrez had had her painted up one night as a pet, so that he could humiliate an unfavored guest by assigning a hideous fem to attend him. Delightedly, the other fems had decorated Alldera for the occasion, not permitting her to see herself or to guess the true purpose of her assignment to personal service that night. Only later, in the privacy of the guest-alcove, she had glimpsed her own face in the surface of the water she brought the man for washing.

They had lacquered her hair into a spiky crown; her skin had been covered in blue and green spirals; her eyes were pallid gleams set deep in pits of livid color and her lips had been made up into a great bruise-colored weal. No wonder the guest had regarded her with such disgust, once they were both hidden from the amused eyes of others.

After that, Alldera had redoubled her efforts to acquire

the speed skills that Senior Robrez had hired a man to teach her. Her trainer had been a Skidro derelict who had once trained young men of the Squires Company to race in intercompany games. She remembered the good pain of pushing herself to the limit, the wind of her own speed (though her steps only brought her around again to her trainer in the end).

She stopped speaking. She hadn't meant to tell about that last part; it was a private thing, and therefore treasured. She remembered the glory of racing through the streets of the City early in the morning or late at night alone. That the messages she carried were most often trivial (plaints of love and jealousy, protests at infringements of standing, claims on others' time or property or loyalty, simple gossip) didn't seem to matter then. Neither did she care that the chief use of her hard-won speed skill was to race after some departing guest, arrive at his door before him, and greet him there with messages from Senior Robrez, whom he had just left.

When she had realized that messages of any urgency could be sent more quickly from rooftop to rooftop by means of coded flags, she had fallen into her first despair. The skills of which she was so proud had no real purpose. Rather than live as a luxurious symbol of her master's wealth and status, she had decided to run herself to death. Her chosen method of suicide had proven a poor one; she had only exhausted herself and come down with a cold . . .

None of this was for this man to hear. Her purpose was to disturb him, not to cause herself pain. She had an uneasy feeling that his stillness and concentration, while permitting her to omit the phrases of submission, were drawing more from her than she had intended to give.

, "And?" he prompted. "How was it that you were returned to Bayo?"

"To Oldtown first," she said, "for work-discipline."

He frowned. "What is there for a fem with your talents to do in Oldtown?"

"Nothing. That's why it's discipline."

Oldtown was the processing center for the hemp

harvested from the plains. The hemp yielded not only all fibers from fine thread to cable-rope, but a variety of foods made from the seeds, roots and leaves. Manna for dreaming was a product of the taller, more widely scattered highland hemps grown west of Oldtown and handled entirely by male crews. Fems were forbidden to have anything to do with the plants which made the dreaming drug. Nevertheless, the winds blew westerly, and during hemp harvests the plain breathed a sweet redolence that could give even Oldtown fems strange visions.

Alldera's job had been at the take-in sheds where the leaves were pulled from the stalks and fed to the curding-mills, and the hempseeds were beaten out, pressed, and ground into flour. The sheds, having no walls, let in the stench of the rotting ponds, where the stripped stalks decayed under water until the fibers came loose.

She hadn't minded. She found herself describing her time there with nostalgia.

Of her fantasies—and she had had her share—she said nothing. To recall the dream in which no one—man or fem—could understand a word of her speech was still terrible, a rending betrayal of the first great astonishment at discovering that communication need not be confined to the grunts and snarlings of the kit-pits. She had wakened sweating and gasping from that nightmare. The longing to run until her heart burst had recurred, no less impracticably than the first time.

Finally the Matris had sent a message to her in Oldtown, saying by way of the news-songs that they had a job for her to do. She had feigned loss of her speech skills (due to lack of practice in the take-in sheds), so that when her work-discipline at Oldtown had been completed, she had been sent back to Bayo for retraining.

There she had discovered the existence of the Pledged rebels, and she had grown restless. All winter arguments had raged among the Matris about her suitability for the mission of going inland and all the risks of sending such a messenger at all. If she had been steadier they would not have taken the time to maneuver her into the Rendery as a chastisement and a testing. They would have sent her west sooner, with a shipment of newly trained fems to the City. She might not have been caught like this, her job half-done and the murder of fems already begun, if she had been more dutiful toward the Matris and less proud. Knowing that she was the only speed-trained messenger they could get hold of just then, she had hesitated and argued, instead of bowing at once to the Matris' plan and getting on with it...

She had fallen silent, thinking of these things. The Endtendant was watching her.

"Did you think of running away?" he prodded.

"From Oldtown? To where? What should a fem eat in the Wild, stones? As for bolting to hide inside the Holdfast, that just gives men a fem to hunt for sport. I have never actually seen a formal fem-hunt; the last time they caught a runaway and set her loose in the City for the Rovers to catch I was in Oldtown, so I missed it. There are plenty of stories of such hunts and songs about them—locked doors and crowds of men on the rooftops to cheer the Rovers on and to see to it that their own fems watch the futile flight of the quarry.

"But I saw a fem bolt in Oldtown. It was early in the morning. She just put down her beating-stick, took off her apron, and ran. The men sent Rovers to pull her down and kill her. Work was held up for a while so the men could watch and gamble on the result. The rest of us paid for her moon-madness—the moon was up that morning—by having to work double time until her replacement arrived."

"Why did she run?"

"Fems are creatures of impulse."

"Nonsense," he snapped. "That's obviously the last thing you can afford to be. Did Rovers guard you there on the Oldtown work floors?"

"No, they patroled the perimeters of Oldtown, more on the watch for Scrappers than for escaped fems. Where we

worked, the noise and activity of numbers of us would
have put Rovers too much on edge."

"Yet Captain Kelmz held those two Penneltons in the
depths of Bayo without evident strain."

"He was a first-class officer. We had few of those at
Oldtown. The companies like to keep them home in case a
skirmish is called."

"You fems can tell a good officer right away, can't
you."

"It's important to us. At Oldtown, we could even spot
Rovers trained by Kelmz. He turned out clean killers,
quick, accurate, no hesitation or flailing about. It's worth
the effort for fems to know roughly what kind of behavior
to expect from a given brace of Rovers."

"Like the Juniors," he remarked, sardonically,
"though most young men would not be pleased to see the
similarity. You can't have enjoyed traveling with Captain
Kelmz."

"No."

"Yet you came with us, in spite of his being one of our
group."

"Old Fossa told you; I had to get out of Bayo."

He looked at her, and said nothing.

The camper was being carried up the steep portage
road which ran from the plain to the upper plateau
through the defile cut by the descending river. The slow,
lurching progress, already more than an hour old, was
bothering the Endtendant's wound. Dark patches of
sweat stained and spread from the armpits of his shirt. He
kept shifting his bandaged leg from one position to
another.

He had not asked her again to repeat what he himself
had said of Kelmz at the Scrappers' that night; he did not
ask now. Instead, as if he were still pondering his
connection with the dead man, he asked about love and
friendship among fems.

In carefully chosen generalities she sketched the
explosive style of relations among people whose lack of
security intensified their loves and hates to extraordinary

levels. There was no time among fems for the ripening of delicate affinities. Fems went where their masters went, often without warning or time to send messages of farewell to lovers in other femholds. Did this man feel sorry for himself because his friend d Layo was inconstant in adversity? Alldera told of betrayals, disfigurements, even murders among femmish lovers.

"And fems who love—masters?" he probed.

"Fems who bewitch their masters? They are burned for it."

"Do fems ever love masters as some men fall into loving fems? Tell me what your songs say."

"They make fun of such perversions."

"Ah," he said, with a sour twitch of his mouth. "Books of the Ancients on the subject say much the same. But sometimes they suggest that such perversion could be a great glory."

"How could it be?" she said, thinking of d Layo in the hemp-field.

He moved his shoulders in a shrug or a shiver, she couldn't tell which. "Love between fems or between men certainly seems less grotesque; the relation of like to like." Again the crooked smile: "Or so we are taught."

"Your teachings are not things for a fem to know."

"Nevertheless," he said, "It must amuse you, all this carrying on among us—Kelmz, Servan, myself, and now this filthy brute Bajerman."

"That's men's affairs," she said, stubbornly.

"Oh? I'd have said it was just the sort of thing you've been describing as typical of fems, but less intense; the loves and hates of dilettantes, as opposed to those of devotees. You have no need to look so sullen; I like the comparison less than you do."

Exchanges like these provided them both with distraction. Alldera saw the danger in it and would have stopped, but she couldn't. Even among her own lovers and friends she had never had any one to talk to like this. There had never been any security, any time, even when she found another fem with true verbal facility. This was her first experience of speech as self-expression with any degree of complexity, eliciting responses of similar quality. It gave her an extraordinary feeling of power, of reality.

That was the danger.

XX

They camped on the upper plateau for the night. D Layo brought over his fellow-prisoner's ration of food and stayed while Bek ate. Then he announced Senior Bajerman's invitation: that the Endtendant come and sleep in the camper tonight.

Bek, sitting wrapped in his blanket against the highland chill, shook his head. "The entertainment isn't to my taste."

D Layo sighed. "I'm not exactly enchanted with it myself, but it's better than having my throat cut. So my little fem, here, is proving more fascinating to you than our esteemed Senior? A function of familiarity, I suppose. He won't be delighted to hear it, though."

"Did he do this?" The Endtendant touched very lightly a line of raw sores on d Layo's shoulder.

"No. That's from lugging you half the length of the Holdfast. I can't get the trick of padding the yoke exactly. Bajerman does like to beat on me a bit, but I don't mind that as much as I mind not being able to wash up at all. He seems to get a thrill from dust and sweat; I don't remember him having been like that back in the Boyhouse, do you? And then that reeky stuff he wears gets all mixed in, I can hardly stand the smell of myself any more. You should be grateful that I haven't made a run for it, Eykar."

"Why haven't you?"

"What, and leave you to Bajerman? He'd be on you in a flash."

"I have also noticed," the Endtendant said drily, "that there's no place to hide out here, when the hemps have been cut."

The DarkDreamer gazed off at the darkening horizon, hugging himself for warmth, and sighed. "I worry about you, Ekyar. You're turning into some kind of wretched realist. It's distressing." He looked toward the camper. "I'd better go back; he'd love an excuse to come out after me and give me a whipping in front of you. It's cold up here! The old cur won't let me wear a shirt, either. Someday I'll wear his famishing skin."

Alldera slept among the carry-fems, as usual. When she served the Endtendant in the morning, she found him so stiff-limbed from lying curled up in his blanket that he could hardly straighten up. Irritably he accepted the Hemaways' rough help in getting into the camper for the day's ride, and he sat slumped in a corner and brooded on the squares of sunlight falling on the blanket through the roof grill. When the camper was lifted and moved on, he looked up at Alldera. His eyes were red-rimmed and gritty-lashed, as if he hadn't slept.

"Where do they go, these talks between us?" he said.

She was silent. Deliberately she waited until he invited her to speak, giving a sort of sanction in advance to what she had to say. That might even be truly effective in the case of a man as scrupulous as this one tried to be, if she did eventually go too far even for him. Besides, his bending to her unspoken rule filled her with a feeling of righteous power.

He looked exhausted and downcast this morning, and

that was her doing; hers and d Layo's. Bek would no more tell her to shut up and leave him his peace than he would avert his eyes from the flirting between d Layo and Bajerman. He just took it and took it, like a fem taking her punishment. She despised him for it.

"Ah, that look again," he said. "If I beat you for looking at me like that, you'd show some respect, wouldn't you? Servan, in my place, would whip you till you bled. Would that impress you? You don't accept us at our own evaluation, do you? No, surely you're too clever, entirely too clever not to see through us."

She made no answer. He prodded the thickness of cloth wrapped around his upper leg. "Change this; it's wet again."

The wound, though less swollen, was still draining, and the bandage was stuck at the center and had to be worked off carefully. She looked up once and saw him watching her hands with the same steady, straight gaze she had seen him turn on Kelmz, Bajerman, even on d Layo. He just looked: not for what was gratifying, not for what was useful, not merely to fill time or distract himself from less pleasant matters, but to see what was there.

For a moment, she let her imagination fly, thinking, what could seeing eyes see in her? Anger. Beyond that—anger, grief for her helpless dead—she couldn't see herself. It was no wonder. She, after all, had no experience with that sort of looking. She could not afford to attend to anything other than what was helpful to her own survival.

Her hands drew away the pad of cloth, revealing the glistening wound.

"Isn't this ever going to heal?" he said.

"It is healing," she said.

"But the process could be slowed down—or speeded up—by a spell, couldn't it."

"I'm no witch," she protested, alarmed by the direction his remarks had taken.

"Tell me," he said, leaning back and resting the back of his hand across his eyes, "how you're not a witch."

Briefly, while she tended his wound, she told him.

The Seekers had been a club of young fems in Senior Robrez' femhold. She had joined them, drawn by their intense conviction that the fems of Ancient times had indeed caused the Wasting by witchery, just as the men said. If the powers of the martyred Ancestresses could be rediscovered, men would have good reason to fear witchery again—from the Seekers. These youngsters had met at great risk to exchange rumors and recite spells that came to them in dreams. During hours stolen from rest periods, and often in the company of fems who had slipped away from other houses to join them, they would huddle passionately together over pathetic scraps of "news": that a fem in Lammintown had brought up a mandrowning storm at sea with a song; that another had breathed life into a lump of Bayo mud.

Soon Alldera had reluctantly seen that the powers the Seekers longed for surely would have won the Wasting for any who had possessed them. Her friends were not searching out true weapons, but spending their courage and energy in the pursuit of nonsense concocted by fearful men. That did not mean that masters only pretended to believe fems might (or at one time had been able to) change shapes, steal souls, control weather, move objects and thoughts through the air, send sickness and death from a distance, speak to past and future generations, and so on; it meant only that men were dupes of their own ideology.

She had tried to dissuade the Seekers from their path. They had not wished to be influenced, least of all by logical argument. They had labeled her a traitor and banned her from their meetings.

Of the rest, she said nothing. One of the younger members of the group, whom Alldera had loved, shortly afterward had leaped to her death from a rooftop, attempting to fly down a shaft of moonlight. Alldera's reaction—withdrawal into lethargic sullenness—had gotten her packed off to Oldtown for discipline. Senior Robrez, an experienced femholder, had been lenient with her, not least because of the size of his investment in her training. To turn her over to the hunt would be to lose it all. The other fems had been glad to see her go; her reckless mood had endangered them all.

Bek said, "But if I accused you—"

She shrugged. "I would burn."

"With no evidence, just because I said I suspected you?"

"It doesn't have to be you who makes the complaint. The fem who bore you was burned for witching your father into breaking the Law of Generations, but it wasn't your father who made the charge. The Boardmen accused her themselves."

Once his interest was engaged he couldn't be stopped; show him horrors, and he asked to see more. "Have you had cubs?"

"Twice lucky," she said, briskly. "That both were little kit-cubs and didn't have to be chopped out of my belly by your Hospital men; and that I had little milk and didn't have to languish forever in that boring hole, the milkery. That's all the luck, and all the cubs, I want."

"Do you know which ones they are in the kit-pits?"

She sat back on her heels and looked at him. "Why should a fem want to know that it's her grown kit-cub crackling in the witch fires? Or, for that matter, her boy-cub matured to manhood and fucking her in the breeding-rooms?"

"Then how could anyone know which was my dam?" he said sharply. "The mark on her neck must have been gone long before the rumors of the broken law began, and she wouldn't have known herself."

"One of the Hospital-men noticed a dye-mark on her neck when she came in and dropped her cub, and he spoke to her master about it. Her master questioned her, couldn't get a sensible answer, had her beaten and forgot about it. She was valuable property, a speaker and fine looking. Later, when the Boardmen started asking questions about this story of Raff Maggomas and his claimed son, her master remembered that identifying mark. She was older by then. He turned her over to the Board, and they burned her."

"What else do you know about her?"

"What I've heard in a few songs."

"What was she like?"

"She wasn't like anything; she was what she was trained to be—as all fems are."

"As you were trained to be insolent and bitter?" he rapped out.

"I'm nothing that I haven't learned from my trainers and masters," she muttered. Let him hit her, at least she knew where she was with a blow.

"The same could be said of others," he said. "Men."

"Men have some choice when they are old enough to see what's happening," she said. She turned to put the used bandage into a bowl of water for washing.

He rolled onto one elbow and reached to secure a buckle on the camper-flap. In mid-action he seemed to freeze, his hand still extended. Without looking at her, he said, "Suppose I told you to take off your clothes?"

She'd been expecting this. Often when she tended to his bad leg he became aroused. Both of them had ignored this till now.

She began to pull off her smock.

He caught her wrist: "Don't!" Thrusting her arm back down, he held her beside the bed, kneeling, with the bowl of water next to her and the bandage trailing out of it.

"When Bajerman put his hand on Servan," he whispered, "that first night in this same camper, for the instant before he began being flippant about it Servan looked the way you do now. I think I know that expression from wearing it on my own face in the aisles of the Boyhouse Library, when Bajerman or some other like him said, 'Kneel down, boy,' or 'Come and kiss me, boy—'" He stammered with rage and disgust. "Or, 'turn, turn around, boy, and stand right there.'

"Now you look the same, and you have every right—I was going to turn and pass it on to you—Bajerman's style of routine, callous rape!"

"Men do not 'rape' fems," she said. "They use them. The act then has a certain cleanness, reminding a fem that her duty is to receive whatever a master chooses to bestow on her."

"Don't you speak that way to me, not about him! To use another person as a convenience is nothing but filth."

"You're not speaking to a person," she spat, "only to a fem—whom you have already used in just that way, surely without staining your fine, manly honor!"

"That was before!" he cried. "Look around: where do you see 'men,' where do you see 'fems' in here? There's nobody but us, you and me. I know you now from everything you've shown me and a little that you've tried not to show; I know you almost as well as you know me. But it's worth nothing while I have the power of death over you." He unwrapped his fingers from her wrist, leaving white pressure-marks on her reddened skin.

Bitterly, to himself, he added, "Nothing that passes between us can be anything but rape.

"I'm not Bajerman!" he burst out, "I won't be like Bajerman! There has to be something clean left in me when I come to face my father!" He lay back amid the pillows, staring up at the roof grill, and muttered, "Everything must be jettisoned, then, even valuables I didn't know I had." He turned toward her again, and said in a tired, reasonable tone, "Only in dreams can a man be an all-purpose hero. I don't have an extra lifetime to spend helping to heal up the horror between men and fems—or even just between us two. I'm on my way to meet Raff Maggomas. Everything must go toward that meeting."

He closed his eyes and hissed his breath in. Then he said, in his old, harsh voice, "There must be no horror, no rape, nothing outside of the ordinary, superficial relations between men and fems. Therefore I can't permit you to be a person. What you haven't told me, keep. The rest I'll do my best to forget—unsuccessfully, if it's any comfort to you. Do you understand me?"

She understood him perfectly. She had beaten him into a retreat. She bent her head: "As the master says."

DESTINATION

XXI

It was said that two suns lit the high country skies: one that rose in the east, another flaming low against the dark western hills and shining through the nights. The second sun was 'Troi itself, whose concrete buildings were sheathed in the flattened, polished bodies of Ancient machines extracted whole from the mines—the single boast of wealth that the 'Troimen allowed themselves. After dark 'Troi shone with its own lights; the skills of 'Troi took light from the river, men said. Looking at the brilliance of the lamps burning all along the roads that ran north to the coal pits and south to the mines, Servan believed it. Those were no coal-fueled flames. One could say it was witchery, except that it was the work of men.

The supply roads were empty now, though the purpose of the lights was reputed to be to enable a constant flow of fems to bring coal and metal to the furnaces of 'Troi, night as well as day. A dull, heavy pulse beat out from the glittering town: the mutter of machines, 'Troi's music against the silence at the edge of the Holdfast.

High above the steep westward summit of 'Troi hills the sun rode low and dusky in the sky. Smoke obscured the mountains, which were only discernable as long, looming shapes. The late light struck points of brilliance from their tops, as if the 'Troimen had sheathed those heights with metal too. The town itself was built with its back to the Wild, as if in disdain of a conquered enemy.

The river, which fell steeply from the hills behind the town, ran through the center of it and on away east to Oldtown and the City. The lower slopes on either side of 'Troi valley were terraced with stone walls and footed with heaps of black slag from 'Troi furnaces. Across the lower valley, a palisade of metal plates had been newly erected, shielding the town from the rest of the Holdfast. Heavy metal grills set into this barrier blocked the river to traffic. The north and south river-roads were shut by similar gates set into the palisade just outside the eastern margin of the town.

The carry-fems set the camper down in a riverside loading-yard in front of one of these steel grills. A concrete tower had been reared behind the palisade. From the upper tier of the tower men could be seen looking down.

Standing well back from the palisade, the Hemaways offhandedly pointed out this and that about the new fortification to each other, as if they were all Rover officers and veterans of every skirmish ever fought. Senior Bajerman held himself aloof from the discussion. He regarded the sunset rather than the town, while Servan helped him adjust his wilted and travel-worn mantle to maximum effect. Even without starch, the folds could be arranged to frame the Senior's face and head, giving an impression of extra height and bulk.

The taller you stand, Servan thought, the more pleasure to bring you down. He hummed to himself.

Eykar got out of the camper (he wouldn't be caught like that again, all tangled up with the fem) and braced himself firmly upright, one hand on the roof-frame and the other on Alldera's shoulder. And how he stared when a gray-haired 'Troiman let himself out through a narrow doorway in the tower's base and strode to meet them: unmantled, tough-looking, the man wore the wheel insignia of the 'Troi Trukkers.

Not Maggomas, Servan decided; there was no resemblance, no spark of recognition. Eykar relaxed visibly almost at once. What interested Servan was something the Trukker carried in one hand: a dull metal tool, pointed like a finger toward the ground. A weapon, Servan thought, if he had ever seen one.

A dozen paces from the camper the 'Troiman stopped and looked them over. "Which of you—" he began; but Senior Bajerman stepped forward and effortlessly over-rode his question with a sonorous announcement:

"Tell Raff Maggomas that his son has been brought to him by Gor Bajerman and certain other, lesser, Senior Hemaways. We offer him Eykar Bek in exchange for power and privilege here in 'Troi."

Haughtily high-mantled, Bajerman stood with one hand spread on his chest, the picture of a man awaiting a salute from another of inferior standing. A breeze stirred his wispy white hair.

The Trukker did not salute. He shook his head. "My orders are to let in Eykar Bek, his friend d Layo and any fems they have with them. That's all. We don't need any Citymen here. Plenty of them will be knocking at our gates soon enough."

He raised the metal thing he carried and pointed it at the Hemaway nearest to him. There came a crash, stunningly loud and close; and there lay the Hemaway on his broad back, arms and legs outflung, blood running from under him.

Two other Hemaways bolted for the palisade. The watchtower issued thunder, and they fell. It was too much for the carry-fems; they raced for the high grass growing at the edge of the loading yard. The rest of the Hemaways scattered. The air was full of boomings, crackings and strange wild whinings. Other 'Troimen along the palisade whooped and pounded one another's backs in their excitement as the darting figures were felled by invisible thunders.

The noise stopped; the voice of the Trukker could suddenly be heard, roaring abuse at the men in the tower. Ribbons of smoke dissolved in the air overhead. None of the Hemaways had even reached the palisade. One carry-fem still tried to drag herself into the sheltering grass, leaving a smear of blood on the flagstones behind her.

Bajerman stood stupefied; beyond him Servan could see Alldera crouching under Eykar's white-knuckled hand.

"... have your asses for this!" the Trukker was bawling at the men in the tower. Red-faced, he turned back to the newcomers who were still standing: "Stupid sonofbitches, they think a weapon is a toy! Give them a moving target and they can't resist. Even then they don't finish the job!"

He jerked up his own thunderer and clicked it at Senior Bajerman. Swearing, the Trukker peered down the tube of the weapon.

Servan thought, am I a fem or a cub to stand shaking in front of this old wolf because he wields powers he can't even control? He said, "Not that I mean to be critical; but since when do 'Troi Seniors kill their own peers for being from out of town?"

"It's necessary," the 'Troiman said, truculently. "We've abolished those divisions anyhow. This matter has nothing to do with age. We'll be under siege by the Citymen sometime tomorrow. We're pared down to the bone now, so nobody comes in that we can't use; and we can't use him."

"Then," Servan said, with a joyful laugh, "I'll attend to the Senior for you. Have you got a knife?"

The Trukker handed him a blade from his belt, muttering, "Sometimes I think we would be better off with knives than with these fancy distance weapons." And he shook the recalcitrant pointing-killer in his hand.

"We're of an age, you and I!" Bajerman cried.

The Trukker considered him again. "Do you know any technics?"

Senior Bajerman composed himself and said, "I am an expert in Deportment, a Master of the Field of Hierarchies—"

"That's no good to us," the Trukker said.

Servan stepped between them, turned on Bajerman and did swiftly with the knife things he had been dreaming of doing. The Senior shrieked and staggered backward. Belly slit, red hands knotted into his groin, he fell twitching on the flagstones. Servan knelt to wipe the thin film of pinkish blood from the Trukker's blade, using Bajerman's mantle. The knife was a good one, with a full new blade and a handle of some hard substance ribbed to give a grip. He pivoted, still crouching, and offered it back with some reluctance to the Trukker.

"Aren't you going to finish him off?" the Trukker said.

"He is finished."

Eykar held out his hand. "Give me the knife."

"Oh, no, Eykar," Servan flipped the knife for the 'Troiman to catch. "You're forgetting which of us has had to put up with Bajerman all this time."

Seizing hold the the Senior's mantle, Servan heaved him to where the edge of the paving sloped down to the river. Bajerman twisted to blink up at him. Servan shoved him down the incline. Sloshing noisily up onto the flagging, the water took the Senior and tugged him away. The weight of his stained, soaked mantle dragged him down. Servan dipped his bloody hands into the water.

Two 'Troimen from the tower were searching the dead Hemaways for weapons and private caches of food. Servan considered demanding that his own knife—or some other, in its place—be returned to him. It would look better, though, to enter Maggomas' stronghold empty-handed. Besides, maybe he could get one of those crashing killers instead. Anything was possible now.

In the broad streets of 'Troi not many people were about at twilight, and none of them were either very young men or mantled Seniors. There were no Rovers and no fems, only men of middle years clad in sober clothing. Some wore wide belts from which hung metal tools, and one man passed by with something resembling a polished skull in the crook of his arm—a helmet of some kind.

The streets were surfaced from wall to wall with a smooth, dark substance; down the centers ran parallel flanges of metal, shiny as ice. No refuse littered any of the alleys or doorways, but a layer of grime outlined the mosaics of metal that covered the facades of the buildings. Overhead, thin black cables of some kind loosely laced the sky between rooftops and upper-story ledges. The central buildings towered all along the river's course, straddling the water. Lamps projected on metal arms from the walls, blindingly bright now that darkness was descending. Everywhere, streets and structures seemed to vibrate with the ceaseless growling of the engines of 'Troi.

No wonder men used the streets briefly and with purpose. It would be difficult to loiter and chat in these stark passages, that were plainly for the transport of materials first and only secondarily for the movement of men.

Servan was impressed. He took in everything—the massive architecture, the combination of efficiency and grime. An ugly place, he thought, but effective; pity it was wasted on Eykar, who looked for only one thing here. Watching him limping ahead, leaning on the fem, Servan felt a wave of warmth for his friend.

At a massive complex of buildings, the Trukker turned aside. 'Troimen standing sentry in a broad doorway slid back the metal leaves of the door into the walls. Two of the sentries fell in behind the strangers. The silver bars on the collars of this escort marked them as men of the Armicor Company, ruthless by reputation. Each of them carried one of the thunder weapons in a special pocket slung from his belt.

Glass globes set into the ceiling shed a harsh, cold light. The Armicors' metail-tipped boot heels snapped against the floor.

Stairs led up onto a railed gallery that ran high along the wall of a huge, roaring room. The room was lit by the familiar warmth of firelight—but what fires! The entire wall opposite the walkway was a tangle of metal tubing, struts and plates in which a row of revolving kettles was mounted. The giant kettles glowed red with heat and thundered as they turned. Men in helmets and heavy clothing moved around the machines, carrying long, fire-blackened rods with hooked ends. Others bent or climbed to examine glass-faced dials, making notations on tablets fixed to their sleeves. They spoke with their heads close together amid the tremendous noise.

In front of a lighted doorway at the far end of the gallery, a man leaned out over the railing, pointing and shouting at someone down on the work-floor. There was imperious vitality in his stabbing gestures, though he was the first really old man they had seen in 'Troi. His close, curling hair was like a design tightly engraved on silver. From beneath his long apron of shiny material there emerged limbs as lean as ropes. His voice, keen and reedy, was audible even over the rumbling of the machines.

A whistle shrilled. On the work floor men tipped one of the kettles with the bent ends of the long poles they carried. Liquid fire spewed out, with darting sparks and a sharp crackling sound. A man poked black scum from where it gathered in the spout and obstructed the outpouring. The hot, glowing stream turned dull red as it congealed in channels in the floor beneath. In the air a fresh pungency tingled.

The Trukker strode out ahead and spoke to the old man, who turned, glancing first at Servan. With an abrupt gesture, the old man waved them forward.

For a moment, Eykar hesitated, his expression a study. Whatever he had been expecting, Servan thought, it had not been this skinny, axe-faced old fellow! And he would not have missed the sobering of the old man's eager look when the Trukker pointed out that it was Eykar, not Servan, who was the Endtendant. Father and son would have to revise some preconceptions.

"I see," shouted the old man over the noise of the

turning kettles, "you're injured—not so badly as to keep you off your feet, at least."

"It's healing," Eykar shouted back.

Maggomas rounded on the Trukker, barking, "Go turn over your gun and your squad to Anjon, and let's hope he shows better control over the tower post than you have." The Trukker flushed red and stalked away.

Turning as if he'd forgotten the man already, Maggomas led the others through the door behind him into another corridor. The Armicors, when he waved them irritably back, fell in at a discreet distance, still an escort.

Eykar said, "You knew I was coming."

"I sent men to find you as soon as I heard you'd left Endpath. I see you didn't need my help. That's good. Self-reliance and capability are respected here in 'Troi."

"What do you expect from me?"

"Ah," the old man said, approvingly, "but it's not such a simple matter. These are complex times. What did Bajerman tell you, that we're in a generation war? He would; he was always a cheesebrain.

"It's not a political squabble between old men and young that we're faced with this time. This is going to be a great famine, a literal famine. Tell me, how do you think the seaweeds we live on survived the Wasting? I know that's not the kind of question you're encouraged to think about in the Boyhouse; don't be embarrassed by your ignorance. The answer is, the seaweeds were tough, fairly simple organisms that already were living on the rubbish of the Ancients' civilization to some degree. They were able to adapt to using the large quantities of poisons released during the Wasting as a side-effect of the men's efforts to defend their civilization.

"Our problem is, the lammins and lavers have now metabolized and dissipated most of the contaminants left over from the Wasting, and these seaweeds are finding much less of the kind of nourishment they've come to depend on. So each succeeding crop is scantier, and the situation is going to get worse, not better. Oh, some seaweeds will survive on the sewage from the City, and others may adapt again to clean conditions; but not in the profusion we're used to for a very long time, if ever. And we don't know which of the other plants moving into their place we can use. That change will also take a long time. Meanwhile, as men have become so heavily dependant in turn on lammins and lavers, they must also starve."

"Unless," Servan observed, "they've prepared. Bajerman said you have all kinds of food stockpiled here in 'Troi."

"That's one way to prepare," Maggomas said. "There is another—as I tried to tell the Board, but they wouldn't so much as give me a decent hearing—and that's to diversify the food supply so that we don't need the lammins and laver so much. That's what we've done here; we've stripped down, lived lean and stored up food to carry us over the transition period until new staples we've been developing are available in quantity.

"Mind you, we have no margin; we can't take any more mouths to feed. I haven't had a lot of time to get things ready. We have had setbacks; some of the information I needed was locked up in the Boyhouse where I couldn't get to it. Still, we're set to go just as we are, which is more than can be said for the rest of the Holdfast. We mean to ride out the crisis.

"Then, when the time is right, 'Troi will take over what's left and will start building a new, better and truly rational society. All of which will require leadership from dedicated, intelligent men: heroes."

He opened a door on the outside, where a bridge of metal linked the furnace-building with another, taller structure a street away. A sooty wind plucked at their clothing and stung their eyes. Down below illuminated glass globes stippled the empty street.

"Heroes," Eykar echoed, limping out onto the thrumming metal walkway. He raised his voice against the wind. "And what am I to be, then?"

"Look down there," Maggomas said. "Look over my town. It will still be here, strong and vital, when the rest of the Holdfast is rags and bones. That's my doing.

"Why do you think I've bothered? So that I can stand here for a while, until you come to kill me—unless I kill you first—because that's what you've been taught you must do? You're too valuable to use yourself up in dramatics. If I didn't know it for a fact, I could read it in you now. Your injury pains you, your surroundings are strange and threatening, you have only your wits for weapons; but you haven't asked for rest, or for time, or for help. Inner discipline is the beginning of a man's power."

"You haven't answered my question," Eykar said.

Servan swore silently. What was the matter with Eykar? Couldn't he see that they were home-free? Nothing could stop them. It was all going to be worth every famishing step of the journey and more. Legends? They would be gods. Even Eykar's beautiful, absurd pride would have to bend before the superb artistry of events.

Maggomas thrust open the door on the far side of the bridge and led them into a suite of littered rooms. There were papers and books everywhere. Lop-eared drawings and charts hung from the walls. There were stilt-necked lamps clamped to the desks and tables, one even to the back of a chair, so that beams of light crossed each other at every angle through the dimness of the rooms.

"Consider, my son," the old man said, "what rational motive do you have for opposing me? You can't be any more ambitious yourself than I am for you." He swept out both arms, indicating the chaos through which they made their way. "This place of disorder will become the center of the new Refuge and someday of a new Holdfast. From here I control 'Troi now; the entire river and much more besides will fall to me in time. I am the master of this and creator of its future.

"My place here will be yours. You're to be my successor. Did you think you were bred for anything less?"

XXII

One glance showed Alldera that no fems kept this place in order for its master. Could all of 'Troi's fems have been sent to the mines or locked up somewhere else in preparation for a battle with the City men?

"Not that there won't be problems about the succession," the old man continued. "I've already run into resistance trying to persuade the 'Troimen that my son need not be my born enemy. We'll work out some demonstrations of unity. For a start, you'll drop your name and take mine. Your DarkDreamer friend can design a ceremony to mark the new legitimization of lineage."

Bek said, "Suppose I am your born enemy?"

Maggomas made an impatient gesture of dimissal. "If you think of yourself that way, it's not by nature but out of ignorance. What would I do, rationally, if were your antagonist? I would stand in your way. But I've made your way for you!"

"This is grotesque!" Bek grated.

"Not at all. It's a very sensible custom. In the old days a man used to have a son to take over his property, further his plans and generally see to the honor and prosperity of his bloodline, after—when the time came." Maggomas stood glancing restlessly about him, took up a stack of papers from a table and began looking through the pages as he continued.

"Mind you, sons turned against their fathers even before the Wasting. But I'm convinced that that was a result of the warping influence of their dams. Ancient men very carelessly left the education of their young boys primarily to fems.

"Still, the Ancients knew the basic principle: a man smart enough to amass wealth and power has a good chance of passing on his talents to his son. That's important, if a great lifework isn't to fall into the hands of quarreling louts or idiots. And idiots there are in plenty, no matter how carefully you try to weed them out. Take the lads I've been training here; they still turn in trash like these reports.

"You two get cleaned up. You'll find clean clothes in the alcove; something in there should fit you. I have no one to send in with you—we're used to doing for ourselves here in 'Troi—but your fem can attend you. I'll join you shortly."

In the small bathing-room d Layo scrubbed quickly, miming his delight in scouring off the grime of the journey and bowing in mock-obsequity to his companion the Crown Prince. Bek ignored him. They chose not to shout over the rushing of the water for any one in the corridor to hear.

The DarkDreamer had already shaved and dressed in simply cut shirt and pants of a soft gray when Bek and Alldera entered the dressing alcove. D Layo's jaunty, graceful carriage lent a touch of elegance to these severe clothes. He was too eager to wait for Bek, so he went off to find their host.

Bek sat down before the mirror and began to shave with grim-mouthed care. "Go get yourself washed," he told Alldera.

The hot water, which sprang from holes in the wall at the touch of a knob, nearly put her to sleep. She hadn't realized how exhausted she was. She went through a series of warm-up exercises, delicate slidings and tightenings of muscle, and the water washed away the sweat of exertion and left her feeling fresh. Decorously wrapped in one of the men's damp, discarded towels, she returned to the alcove.

Bek, looking lean and taut in dark shirt and trousers, stood bleakly studying himself in the long mirror. "I thought I'd look older," he said.

There were no femmish smocks in the alcove. Alldera chose a shirt that was long enough to serve, one that had correspondingly enormous sleeves. But Bek was in no mood for the ludicrous. He had her take it off and wear shirt and pants like his. The significance of his own somber clothing and his austere and deliberate preparations was clear: he was armoring himself in his ritual status: it was as Endtendant of Endpath that he meant to face his father.

The sound of voices drew them to the great front room of the suite, which was in darkness. Its furthest wall was a transparent sheet incised with a glowing design which seemed to shine with light from lamps outside in the night.

Alldera's messenger training had included recognition of maps. This one she understood at once: there was Bayo, there Endpath, there the City. Deeper inland gleamed a gridwork representing Oldtown, a larger one for 'Troi—and further up the river, further than shown by any map she had ever seen, stood steeply pitched figures that seemed to be actual descriptions, not mere symbols, of mountains.

D Layo stood tracing the mountain-marks with his fingertips. He said, "Then the Reconquest has actually begun?"

Maggomas, crouched over a table laden with papers, glanced up and laughed angrily. "What Reconquest? I've sent out a few exploring parties of my own, that's how I know this much. There is no Reconquest, it's a myth.

"Everything the Board does—or fails to do—is

calculated to insure that nothing happens to shake its control. That means no new ideas and no new territories and not too many young men! I'm surprised that neither of you has figured it out. What's hierarchy for, or the endless maze of games and standings, if not to dissipate young men's energy? Which is kept low anyhow with an insufficient diet, since the old men take more than their share of the pittance of food that the Holdfast furnishes. You know, in the Refuge men had to play games to keep from going rogue. Sport is an acquired taste which the Seniors have encouraged in the Holdfast for the same reasons: to use up energy.

"You, my son; what do you think Endpath is for? When the Board decides that there are too many restless youngsters around for the maintenance of stability, it's not difficult for them to manipulate the standings or break up certain love affairs, so that pride and misery send a number of Juniors off to die at Endpath. Dueling in the Streets of Honor takes care of others.

"Then look at our economy: a model of institutionalized inefficiency! The old men pool the surplus of a five-year's production and take off the top themselves for their own comforts. Not that the Holdfast offers much more than subsistence—rotating the companies from work-turf to work-turf every five-year means a lot of unskilled clods do everything badly in an effort to do each thing better than the last lot of unskilled clods did it.

"The point, young men, is to prevent the Junior population from growing large enough, rich enough or educated enough to burst the boundaries of the Holdfast, begin a real Reconquest—and perhaps turn around afterward and take the Holdfast for themselves, with their newfound strength and confidence. Now, I maintain—"

Interrupted by a string of faint popping sounds from outside, he held up his hand and listened. "That's got to be first contact with the City men! Come on outside."

They followed him out onto a paved terrace overlooking the plain. A table had been set up, its surface a mosaic of magnificent green and golden tile glittering in the light of two squat globe lamps that were housed in the parapet. The light of the lamps gleamed steadily on the gear of four Armicors deployed by Maggomas along the length of the terrace. He himself went to confer with a stocky young man of the same company, who reported without lowering the spyglass through which he was studying the plain below.

"No problem," the old man said, joining the others around the table. "There's been a little skirmish some distance down the river. We saw the flashes of our people's guns. Our patrols are too small to stop that mob, but the guns will stagger them! You're going to have a fine view of an interesting night.

"How do you like this?" he added, running his palm over the gleaming tiles of the tabletop. "'Troimen are realists, but you'd be mistaken to think they have no taste. This is a product of your own kilns."

"You've built kilns here?" d Layo said, with interest. "You know, we had just the thing to give you as a guest-gift: some plates and platters from Oldtown ruins, Scrappers' loot. They were stowed in the body of the camper we came in, which was left outside the palisade."

"Then they will have to stay there a while. The gates of 'Troi won't open again for a long time. Tell me, though: what would you have asked for in exchange for your guest-gift?"

"They were fine pieces," the DarkDreamer said, considering. "Very old, I think. A fair exchange would have been one of those weapons." He pointed to the shiny weapon belted to the hip of the nearest Armicor.

"Well chosen," Maggomas said, plainly pleased. "Not that I'm entirely happy with the guns yet; but even imperfect as they are they'll shake up that City mob. Sit down, I've got a meal laid on for us. Have that fem sit, too. I hate having people hang over the table while I eat." He raised his voice: "A bowl of wash-water and something to drink while we're waiting!"

No fem appeared at the service-hatch. Instead, one of the sentries descended and returned bearing a tray with glasses, a metal bowl and a large carafe of water. The bowl, poured half-full, was for Maggomas' use. He fumbled for a moment at the ties of his apron, swore and sat down to wash as he was, the apron-bib standing out stiffly under his chin. He dried his hands on a stained rag from his pocket. Several small, colorless objects fell from the rag's folds, clicking and bouncing on the table top.

Maggomas off-handedly explained that they were cubes of something called "plastic," which the Ancients had made out of coal and other substances. He had recently produced these samples from the leavings of the Oldtown hemp-mills.

He shot a sly look at his son as he spoke of this, but Bek spared the intriguing little objects scarcely a glance. He kept his eyes on his father. D Layo was the one to pick up the cubes and juggle them on his palm. He rubbed the "plastic" surfaces and remarked wistfully and with awe on the powers of the Ancients—and again his eyes turned toward the guns the Armicors wore.

Maggomas sniffed at the soup that had been set in front of him. "About time," he said, and ladled some for the men and a bowlful for himself. Alldera was relieved that none was served to her; the soup had dark, shiny shapes in it and a musty odor. The young men sat and looked uneasily at their portions.

"You just don't know what you're talking about," Maggomas said, "when you glibly rattle off a phrase like 'the powers of the Ancients.' They were men of might, not scrabblers in an ash heap. Listen, just as an example: the Ancients had so many fibers, natural and man-made, that not only could a man change his shirt every day; but they even had to put labels in their garments, to tell the owner which of the many methods of cleaning was appropriate to that particular fabric! Extend that kind of versatility into all fields, and you begin to get some idea of the wealth and power of the Ancients."

"Yet," Bek said, harshly, "they were overthrown."

"Oh, yes," jeered the old man, jabbing his spoon in Alldera's direction, "and next you'll tell me that it was by the magical powers of her kind!

"Let me tell you something: the Ancients weren't overthrown; they fell down—in their understanding of their own incredible powers. They should have forseen the Wasting soon enough to have prevented it. Ancient science was so far advanced that they had machines to do the work of the Dirties, artificial foods and materials to replace those they had from plants and beasts, even man-made reproductive systems that would eventually have cut out the fems from their one supposedly necessary function. But the men didn't see where it was all leading."

He drank down the remainder of his soup in one draught, and turned to serve up a stew of mixed lammins and lavers on fresh plates for the men. The stew smelled strong. A bowl was filled for the Armicor officer, who ate standing.

Alldera's mealtime would come when the men were finished, according to the traditions of formal dining. Her mouth welled sweet juices. She had never seen so much food assembled in one meal in her life. The coldness of the night breeze on her damp hair seemed to spread all through her body as a hungry ache. She could barely stand to watch Bek, across the table from her, poking uninterestedly at his portion with his fork and frowning as if he didn't even see it.

"The science of the Ancients," Maggomas went on, around a mouthful of food, "was so highly developed that they were about to cut through the tie of dependence on this mortal bitch of a world altogether and become gods—not your famishing mystery-god who passes understanding and coping-with, but real, rational, deathless gods wielding real, rational power. The Ancients invented artificial body parts and anti-aging drugs that would eventually have made sons themselves obsolete. Who needs posterity when men are immortal? And given eternity, they could have discovered everything else that there is to know or do."

Rapidly, after a swallow of beer, he went on: "You can see that the fems couldn't have that. They were committed—still are—to an endless, pointless round of birth and death. They knew that once they were no longer needed for reproduction they would be dispensed with altogether. So they attacked first.

"How do you like the stew?" he asked, with sudden solicitude. "I noticed before that neither of you finished your soup. The black bits were only fungi. We've learned to grow them in quantity in our cellars and how to weed out the poisonous ones that have given all fungi a bad name. You get to like the flavor in time, as with so many foods. The Ancients, when they sat down to an evening meal, prized highly a wild variety of these same fungi, though of course they had so much else to choose from.

"If neither of you young men minds, I'll have your fem fed now."

Alldera shivered. When he had been speaking of fems in the time of the Wasting, his tone had chilled her. She had begun to feel the absence of her own kind like an added coolness in the air.

A steaming dish was set down in front of her by the Armicor. It did not contain curdcake or even seaweed, but was filled instead with a brown, grainy mass much coarser than hemp-root taydo. A sweetish scent was rising from it. Alldera's hunger vanished.

"Eat," Maggomas said.

She ate. The food was chewy but yielding, thick on the tongue.

"What is that?" Bek asked.

"The basic sustenance of the new Holdfast, and of the world in times before even the Ancients. It's a low-energy, high-bulk food, but an old and honorable one. We make it not from leaves like our curd-cheeses, but from the seeds of mature grasses: 'grain,' it's called. We've already raised two successful grain crops in the high meadows west of us—without the Board's knowledge, of course. In time, the whole upper plateau will be given over to grain-growing. That's our first step, when we take over."

"Then where will you grow manna-hemp?" d Layo said. "Or is this 'grain' good for dreaming?"

"Dreaming!" the old man scoffed. "Mind melting, you mean! Men with a whole real world to explore won't have any use for dreaming. There will be no manna in the new Holdfast."

With a glance at the Armicors, d Layo said, "Do all 'Troimen share your opinion?"

"There hasn't been a real dreaming in 'Troi for two and a half years," Maggomas said, "only mummery to satisfy the Board. I told you, 'Troimen are realists. To them a food-crop is obviously more valuable than a drug."

D Layo sat back, radiating polite incredulity.

"Come on, young man," Maggomas chided, "haven't you any ambition to be more than a DarkDreamer, scrambling through the alleys from one cheesebrained client to another? That's no life for an able young fellow. I can offer better. You lived to come through the gates of 'Troi because you have a place here—but not as a DarkDreamer. My son will need practical advice."

D Layo smiled and began some modest disclaimer, but the Armicor officer strode over at that moment and pressed the spyglass into Maggomas' hand.

"Look at the docks," the Armicor said, pointing. "The main body of the City men have come upriver from Oldtown by boat."

Even without a glass the first of a fleet of barges could be seen butting out of the darkness among the wharves. Citymen leaped out and ran along the palisade, looking for a weak point. A volley of thunder from the 'Troimen sent them scurrying from the reach of the lights. 'Troimen standing on the palisade walkway waved their fists and weapons in the air. The sound of their cheering rose unevenly on the night breeze.

Maggomas took the Armicor officer by the elbow and walked the length of the terrace with him and back, talking excitedly. The other Armicors brought up a large box through the kitchen hatch and strapped it to the back of one of their number. Cables dangling from the box were attached to places in the parapet. Maggomas wound a crank-handle projecting from the side of the box and talked into a hand-piece (also on a cord) that hitched into a bracket on the other side.

A small, crackling voice replied from the box.

Men's magic, Alldera thought grimly. Who was it who turned out to be able to speak to others who were not present? Not femmish witches, but the Ancients themselves, from whom Maggomas must have harvested this wonder along with all the others.

When the old man rejoined them, Bek said, "You've done astonishing things here. How is it that the Seniors of 'Troi allowed the development of such advanced machines?"

Maggomas sat down again and leaned back, a picture of comfort and confidence.

"Good question. Once I accepted the fact that real innovations were doomed, it was easy. I simply presented an idea that seemed designed to reinforce the status-quo. I offered to arm the 'Troi Seniors so effectively that they'd never again have to depend on Rovers for protection or worry about the energy and aggressiveness of young men. You remember that bow-and-arrow scare a decade ago? You can't let a Rover loose with a distance-weapon, so nobody else can have one either.

"These 'Troi Seniors trusted me because I was a Senior myself. They gave me a free hand. I used my freedom to make sure that the men who actually made the new weapons also knew how to use them—and who to thank for them. So here I am."

"And where are they?" Bek asked him. "The Seniors of 'Troi?"

"You met one at the watchtower; he, and a few others who were useful, were asked to join us. The rest we killed along with the Rovers and their officers. It gave my men a chance to try the new weapons before any major clash, and we were relieved of a lot of dead weight in our ranks. None of this should bother you; more men have died at your hands in Endpath than at mine here in 'Troi."

"There is no comparison—" Bek began savagely, but checked himself. "I won't argue that point. I have only one question that matters. Didn't it ever occur to you, while you were making your—preparations, that I might decline to succeed you?"

.

The old man began to frown, and Alldera thought, he is going to make the wrong answer.

Now she knew why she had spoken so freely to Bek in the camper, more freely than she had ever intended. Bek knew how to pay attention, however imperfectly and intermittently. It was to this offer of ultimate respect that Alldera had responded. But the idea of looking straight at a thing—or a person—to see what it was, rather than what use it might be to him, was alien to Maggomas. Schooled by years of examining the past for whatever he could turn to his own purposes, he had no conception of disinterested regard. Utility, bald and degrading, was his reality. His answer must be disastrous.

Looking from the blind old man to the desperate son, she felt a shiver of sweet dread.

Impatiently, Maggomas said, "You don't understand. You've passed every test: the Boyhouse, Endpath, even the timing of your arrival here. Your presence is my vindication, not that I ever had serious doubts. I set up the course, and you've run it, and the rest is all arranged. I had everything worked out before I ever marked your dam's neck."

"Thank you," said Bek scathingly, "for putting my life into its proper perspective. But if you've done all this for me, then you've done it for nothing. I accept nothing from you: not your name, not your place, not your future!"

XXIII

Now, thought Bek, be calm for this battle.

Maggomas scowled. "I see we're further apart than I'd thought. Maybe I was wrong about the maturing influence of Endpath. You would have no future if I hadn't risked my soul to plant yours in the black pit of a fem's belly; if I hadn't used my influence to keep certain Seniors from having you killed at once in the Boyhouse; and if I hadn't saved you from the consequences of your own foolish behavior later on."

"By having me sent to Endpath."

"Yes," the old man barked, "and not without cost to myself. You owe me, boy."

"There are more unpaid debts than I think you know. Do you remember Karz Kambl at all?"

"Of course," Maggomas said sharply. "A good friend, but an incompetent engineer. I never meant to bring him upriver. In return for posting you to Endpath, the Board insisted that I leave the City immediately—and there was no one else I could call on for help at the time. That Karz ended up back in the City in spite of having blown himself up with my boat's engine simply justified my original judgment that he was the wrong man for the job."

"You knew he was alive afterward," Bek said. "Yes, I guessed it. Why didn't you get in touch with him? He died in your defense, as he imagined it, not two weeks ago."

"Ah. Poor Karz." Maggomas brooded over his plate. "I've thought of him often. He would have been miserable up here. He was too idealistic, impressionable, literal-minded in an innocent and vulnerable sort of way. I doubt he would have understood one single thing I've had to do here in 'Troi—any more than you do, I suspect. Now look here, boy; this is no game where we outpoint each other for standings. I am the first real and true genius in generations to be born into this ass-end scrapheap of a world and to grow up with his brains unscrambled. The most has got to be made of my talents. That's the reason for your existence, which is more reason than most men have for theirs. You're needed here, and I'm treating you accordingly. You come as my enemy, as you've been taught; but have I had you drugged or chained, for my own safety?"

He shoved aside his plate, planted his elbows on the table, and leaned closer, intently. "Your pride is smarting; you're drowning in a puddle of self-pity over nothing! I've been a misfit and an outsider from my birth, with capacities that no one understood. I've had a few followers, fewer friends, and none who could keep up with me. I've spent my time in every dirty corner of the Holdfast and beyond, sniffing out fragments of the past that other men couldn't see the use of but made me pay for anyway. After one Scrapper burnt a book in front of me because I wouldn't meet his price—a book he couldn't read, let alone comprehend—I paid what was asked and let them laugh."

Bek broke in fiercely: "How could you mark me for an outsider's life, knowing yourself what it was like?"

"What are you talking about?" Maggomas demanded. "There's no comparison between what we've been through! You were born to be shaped to your capacity; I was born to shape myself. You've lost nothing by the help I've given you. No one could help me. In another age, I'd have been a rich man among rich men, a leader among leaders; I'd have had an empire to bequeath to you instead of a hidey-hole and a plan for taking a big step backward without breaking a leg!"

"What I don't understand is what a man like Karz Kambl saw in you to love."

The old man snarled, "What do you care? All I want from you is respect, nothing else."

"You have that; how could I fail to respect your brilliant handling of my life, so that you've had only to wait for me to come here"—Bek's voice cracked out of control into an anguished cry—"and be a monster like you!"

Maggomas retorted, "You make me sound like some kind of criminal! Control yourself! You're distracting my men from their duty with this display—shaming yourself in front of your friend."

For a moment Bek longed to plead with the old man to think again, to put his hand in the fire of his son's rage and say, yes, it's a dreadful conflagration I've created in my ignorance . . . But the feeling was smothered under the invasion of vast and chilling grief for something irreversibly lost; a grief colder than the void. When Bek spoke he said calmly,

"How soon . . . are you expecting to die?"

The old man shrank away from him. "I've struggled along with bad health for years," he said defiantly. "I can last a while longer."

"You stuff yourself like a gluttonous boy and have a Junior's energy," Bek observed coldly. "There's at least another decade in you. You don't need me yet. But I would like to know what you have arranged to keep me occupied meanwhile. Something to toughen me up some more? Perhaps imprisonment in a cage hung from your terrace?"

Gruffly, Maggomas said, "I've loaded you with too

much at once. I apologize. It's just that I've wanted to talk
with you for so long—"

"Of course, you could hardly have dropped in for a
chat at Endpath; you might have been taken for a pilgrim
and not come out again. But don't worry, you've said it
all. I only hope you have someone to put in my place—or
rather, someone else to put in your place. What about
your Armicor officer there? He undoubtedly believes in
your plans and ideas more than I ever could anyway."

The officer, who was speaking into the talk-box, gave
no sign of having heard.

"I don't understand you!" Maggomas cried, slapping
the table so that the dishes rattled. "Would it be so terrible
to be the instrument that saved mankind?"

"Mankind," Bek replied, with chilly precision, "has
nothing to do with this. You want to save yourself from
extinction. You want me to be your dead hand, crushing
the future into your design for you. You're transparent,
old man. Don't you think the Endtendant of Endpath
recognizes the dread of death when he sees it?"

Watching the painful wincing blink of Maggomas'
wrinkled eyelids, Bek felt an ache of wintry pleasure.

"I have a point, perhaps," interjected another voice,
Servan's of course, "at which you two could possibly
come together over your differences."

How relaxed Servan looked. He exuded friendly
concern, sitting there with his beer mug in his hands and
smiling so winningly at them both. We're no more than
dreamers for him to manipulate, Bek thought wearily,
drunk on emotion instead of manna, that's the only
difference.

"It seems to me," Servan went on smoothly, "that
Eykar is perfectly well suited to the exercise of power that
you offer, sir, but he doesn't yet see any personal interest
of his own in it to attract him. I think Eykar might be
amenable to overseeing your new Holdfast for you if he
could have a free hand in, say, formulating the place of
fems in that design. During our travels he's appropriated
my own fem to himself, and he sometimes even shows

concern for her welfare. I imagine that he has a whole book of notions in his head about her correct treatment. Am I right, Eykar?"

Oh, helpful Servan, to offer bait for Maggomas' trap! Beautiful Servan, eager for power he wouldn't know what to do with; clever, treacherous, beloved, blind Servan.

Bek kept silent, refusing to be drawn.

"The whole matter of the fems," Maggomas said, "is one of the few things that hasn't gone too well in the preliminary stages." He rushed into a history of the problem, plainly relieved to bring the conversation back to some sort of technical level.

"When we began slaughtering fems in preparation for the long siege, a couple of them actually turned and attacked my men. It was an incredible affair, and my people reacted as you might expect. By the time I got control again there wasn't a fem left alive in the town. Even my lab population had been shot down in their cages, and all the mining-fems were destroyed. Not that it's a disaster. When the City men realize their situation, they'll be happy to trade anything they have for a packet of lammins, including their fems.

"It was my fault, in a way, though. The attention some of our 'Troi fems were getting in my experiments must have given the whole lot of them an inflated notion of their worth. I was working along several lines at once with the ones in my laboratories, not just on diet experiments."

He began to take up and devour, absent-mindedly and voraciously, morsels of food from Bek's plate, speaking rapidly as he ate.

"In the hospital I saw throwbacks killed as soon as they were born—cubs marred by oddities of feature, skin-color, hair type, all the peculiarities left over from the Dirties. A foolish waste; there's no reason why, with careful selective breeding over time, we shouldn't be able to obtain some very useful throwback strains. I foresee, for instance, a breed large enough and strong enough to bear a mounted man at a good pace—but too stupid to be dangerous. I had one very promising line started in the laboratory: two cubs with strong, hairy hides that might have been bred back to true fur-bearing form, given a few generations.

"The real problem is time. We have to work on ways of speeding up the maturing process. Breeding them younger helps, even if you lose the dam—after all, it's the cub's properties you want for the next generation."

"You sound as if you mean to resurrect the unmen!" Servan exclaimed. He was enthralled with all this, excited as a boy.

The fem sat composed and motionless, her head tensely lowered so that Bek couldn't see her expression. He studied the top of her head, willing her to look up at him. She must see that he repudiated all this. She must. His eyes burned with the effort to stare her into obedience to his mental urgency, as if he suddenly believed in witchery.

"Not exactly unmen," Maggomas was saying, thoughtfully, "but yes, they'll have to be called something, some word to clearly differentiate the males, in particular, from you and me. Fortunately you'll only need a very small population of throwback males for breeding purposes." He wiped his fingers on his apron bib and reached for another fragment of lammin. "When you get into this deeper, you may want to do some reading in my library to turn up a good label for them. And possibly I was too hasty in dismissing manna entirely just now. We should research the potential use of drugs for keeping throwbacks quiet and tractable. Later on, when you've separated the breeding lines you want, you may decide to release the hardier strains into the Wild to forage for themselves."

With a wrench, Bek thought of Kelmz, who would have gone into the Wild to search out non-human creatures had he been given time. For all of his brilliance, how small Maggomas stood next to the memory of the dead Rover officer!

Servan, still fascinated, asked what Maggomas would do with a fem like Alldera.

"She's cut out for breeding your sons and Eykar's, if she's smart enough to have intelligent offspring—as I assume she is, since she's in private service. Individual ownership of fems will be ended, of course; it's inefficient. Plans will be made for them on impersonal, rational grounds. Now, the smarter she is, the more careful you have to be that she stays out of mischief. You can't keep her pregnant all the time; it lowers the quality of the cubs. But between her gestation periods you can put her in charge of the working throwbacks."

"But didn't you say that you wanted the throwbacks drugged to keep them quiet?" Servan said. "How could they work, then?"

Patiently, the old man explained. "It's only your more dangerous types, the less controllable and less capable ones—near the beast level, you could say—that you'll want to sedate. The fems at higher stages will be a multipurpose resource. They won't be fit to breed men from, of course, only to mate and produce more of their own kind—like the Dirties, in fact. Well directed by your intelligent breeding-fems, these intermediate Dirty-types can replace most machines as we run short of metal for repairs. We'll have to feed them more grain so they can do heavy work, but they'll get exercise on the job, so it balances out: activity keeps up the muscle-tone, restricts the build-up of fat and improves the flavor at the same time."

"Flavor?" echoed Servan.

"Flavor, flavor," repeated Maggomas, impatiently, "of their meat. Haven't you been listening? I'm talking economy, total utilization of the few resources that are going to be left to us. You can't run a Reconquest on a bulk-food like grain, so you use throwback fems as meat, a food that young men can pack in quantity on long expeditions. We're going to rationalize society into a small group of superior men subsisting primarily on the meat, skins and muscle power of a mass of down-bred fems."

He jumped to his feet, leaning toward their stricken

faces. "Why else would I have had the 'Troi fems killed, if not for their meat? You didn't think I could pack 'Troi with enough lammins and lavers to feed my men for long—we would need a dozen 'Trois to hold that much seaweed!" In a conciliatory tone, he added, "Eating femflesh seems bizarre to you now, but believe me, you'll get used to it. You have no choice; you've already started.

"Ask your own fem, here, about it; she's a cannibal herself. What do you think is in that curdcake that they eat?"

At last, Alldera looked up, straight into Bek's eyes. She was smiling a fierce, wild smile.

Servan surged from his seat, stumbling backward a step so that his chair crashed over on the tiles.

"You don't think," Maggomas protested, "that we've been so crude as to feed you your own carry-fems! We recognize that there are claims, familiarities that men must be educated out of. In a way, though, it's too bad. You would feel differently if you'd begun your flesh-eating at its best—in fresh steaks, instead of the dried chips that were cooked up in your stew."

Servan doubled over and began to retch, gripping the edge of the table with both hands. It was at him that the Armicors were looking when the inner tide crested in Bek, lifting him effortlessly to his feet, his body pivoting for the blow, his spirit a storm. His right hand clenched like a hammerhead, and he whipped it in a tight arc to smash with all his power into Maggomas' face.

XXIV

Alldera crouched under the retaining wall near the top of the southern slope. The stones at her back were wet. In front of her, tall yellow bunch-grass formed a screen. The first light of morning was quenched to gray by the fine rain that had been falling for hours.

'Troi was taken. During the night, one of the great guns had blown itself apart, ripping up a section of the palisade. City men had poured, roaring, through the gap, and the explosions that followed in series had burst first the work-buildings along the river's course and then whole sections of the rest of the town. Mines must have been set off by the retreating 'Troimen, leaving the victorious Citymen with a handful of ashes. 'Troi's smoke rose this morning from hills of rubble.

She could see a few of the conquerors on the palisade. Two small City patrols were quartering the lower reaches of the valley for stray 'Troimen. The rest of the invaders were gathered on the docks, quarreling with one another as they stowed their meager loot in the barges. The dead lay pale and tumbled along the palisade; they had already been stripped of everything worth taking.

Alldera, watching, sat on a hip-pack she had stolen on her way out of the town and stuffed with provender salvaged from the kitchen of a deserted dormitory. She chewed a plug of lammin. Not that she was hungry—her belly felt bloated and cramped, either from the onset of menstruation or from the strange food she had eaten at Maggomas' table—but she had been running and hiding all night and knew she needed food. Through the unfamiliar covering of trousers, she rubbed the muscles of her legs.

Lethargy weighed her down. She felt no triumph yet at having slipped the leash of the men's authority.

She had not seen the blow that had smashed the bone of Raff Maggomas' nose deep into his brain. The vision she remembered was of his body, stretched out on the terrace between two parapet lamps. Their light had efficiently illuminated the dreamlike muscular flutterings into which he had subsided.

No one touched Bek. He stood gripping the back of Maggomas' chair with his dark-spattered hand, staring intently past the head and shoulders of the kneeling Second—the man who had been Maggomas' closest aide. The Armicors pointed their guns at Bek, and at d Layo who had sprung to his side, but all eyes were on the dying man; until the Second spread his jacket over Maggomas' face and looked up blankly from where he knelt.

They all started when Bek spoke in level tones to the Second:

"Arrest me, execute me if you dare—but you'll no longer be Second here when your negligence is recognized. Or you may continue as Second in 'Troi—Second to me, as Maggomas' heir, in which case I take the entire responsibility for his death.

"Did you think that he could hand over power to me like a fem offering cakes on a tray? I am his son and successor as he said, but in my own time and on my own terms." Composed and imperious, he stood among his speechless enemies, his face streaked with his father's blood.

The Second got shakily to his feet and rubbed his palm raspingly over his mouth. He could not seem to meet Bek's eyes. The other Armicors watched the officer for their cue.

Bek commanded, "Have my father's body taken into his rooms."

After a moment's hesitation, the Second made the cross-sign with an unsteady hand, and several of the others imitated him: accepting the crossed wills of fathers and sons. Averting their faces, the Armicors lifted Maggomas and carried him inside.

"Oh my soul," breathed d Layo. He looked dazzled, as though already living in the future which death and Bek's sudden reversal had unlocked for them both. Recovered from his nausea, the DarkDreamer would certainly manage his next meal of flesh with admirable nonchalance—he was such an adaptable fellow, Alldera thought dazedly, as are we all.

For here was Bek, buying life by seizing hold of the same future he had spat upon when his father had offered it—as if his refusal had been part of an ice-blooded plan to get his father's place immediately and without constraints on his use of the power it brought him. It was incredible.

Bek turned toward d Layo and said in the same clear, calm tone, "Second, arrest this man."

D Layo's face turned vacant with shock. "What," he began, and faltered. He looked down at the Second's gun, which was trained on his chest. "Why are you doing this? Eykar, I killed Bajerman with my own hands in front of you today!"

"Whatever that means to you, it means nothing to me," Bek said. He lowered himself into Maggomas' chair, easing his hurt leg out stiffly in front of him. "This is a matter of politics, Servan. I will start fresh here; my close companions will be men of 'Troi."

He was lying, for he did not drop his gaze in a traitor's shame, but watched d Layo as a man watches the receding shoreline of home from the ferry-rail.

D Layo turned away, his hands balled into tight fists at his sides. Perhaps he was decoyed by his liaison with Bajerman into seeing jealousy where none was. Perhaps he had always feared (and hoped) that Bek would turn out no different, no truer, than he was himself. Perhaps he saw deeper, caught the gist of Bek's intentions and instinctively played along in the direction of his own freedom and survival. He swung back again, crying,

"You can't steer these brutes to victory yourself, Eykar—you're no strategist! You throw me away too soon for your own good! And what if 'Troi falls?"

The Second, who had been looking uneasily from one of them to the other, interjected, "'Troi will not fall."

"Is that 'Troi realism?" d Layo jeered. "The Ancients fell, anything can fall! Eykar, you're green at the treachery game, I don't think you see it all yet. Are you sure you can take this smug idiot for your 'close companion'—until he turns on you? However tired of me you may be—and I trust the lesson of your fickleness isn't lost on this lucky fellow—can you actually put up with such drastic—"

The last words were drowned in a crashing from the plain that made the terrace shiver underfoot. The Second smiled: "That's why we're not going to lose 'Troi. Those are our big guns opening up all along the palisade."

"Heroes' weapons," d Layo snarled, "that kill anony-mously from a safe distance!"

The Second waved away the handpiece of the talk-box, which the box-bearer was holding urgently out to him. "Endtendant Bek, what's to be done with this man?"

"He's to be escorted to the gate and turned out," Bek said, his eyes still on d Layo, his voice rough with a tenderness that he made no effort to disguise. "And see that he's given a knife."

"He'll join the City men," the Second objected. "He knows a lot about our set-up here, and that we've lost—our original leadership. It's too dangerous just to let him go like that."

"I've given my orders, Second," Bek said.

"For our good or for our ruin?" the Second said, his hand hovering so that the gun he held covered Bek as well as d Layo. "You're very anxious to get him out of here—"

Bek looked at the Second at last. "I don't want him killed. I've loved him all my life."

"Eykar, you hypocrite!" d Layo burst out, his eyes glittering with tears. "Who paid your passage here, in sweat and submission to that old cunt Bajerman? Now that I've served your purposes, you order these yellow-guts to throw me out to starve, and you call that love?"

"I've outgrown you, Servan," the Endtendant replied. "Say goodbye like a man."

D Layo stood hunched toward him—silent, hating, hopeless—all his natural grace cramped and spoiled.

The Second's doubts were gone. He ran his eyes over the men at his disposal, nodded to one of them, and ordered the others back to their former stations along the parapet. The one he had singled out moved toward d Layo, gun drawn. The Second turned to the talk box, though he kept his eyes on the DarkDreamer while listening to the voice from the handpiece.

Suddenly d Layo strode forward, stooped and kissed Bek long and hard on the mouth, as if to draw the life's breath out of him.

Bek offered no resistance; but the Armicor stepped in behind d Layo and reached out to pull him away. D Layo rammed an elbow into the pit of the man's stomach, and the Armicor plunged backward into the talk box man and the Second.

The DarkDreamer sprang onto the tabletop amid a clatter of flying dishes. Not even pausing to look down at Bek's upturned face, he leaped onto the parapet and ran three steps along its length, then bent, pushed off with his spread fingers, and vaulted out into space.

Shouting, leaning out, they saw him turn like a tumbler so that he fell on his back—into the web of lines that linked buildings across the street below the level of the terrace. The cables snapped free of their fastenings, lashing upward so that the watchers flinched back. D Layo's fall was broken; he flipped again in the air, landed crouching in the empty street, and sprinted for shelter before the cursing Armicors had clawed their weapons out.

The Second, shouldering other men aside, leaned far out, squinting, and yelled into the handpiece. He shook it and wheeled furiously on the box-carrier, who cried,

"It's the wires! That fucking maniac ripped down the wires!"

The Second looked blackly at his handful of men, who would now have to carry messages on foot. He said, "I wouldn't mind having that punk's luck. By rights one of those cables should have fried him before he hit the ground."

"You misjudged your man," Bek said. But when the Second proferred his gun, butt-first, Bek shook his head. "You don't have to surrender your command because of this. I'm not sorry he got away from you, Second. I wouldn't want his blood on the hands of my friends."

Abashed, the Second backed off.

Bek got stiffly to his feet, motioning Alldera to attend him. He turned with her toward Maggomas' rooms, saying wearily to the Second, "I'm going in for a while. You're in command here, Second. Instruct your men as you see fit."

"Yes, sir," the Second said. He was Bek's man now.

Bek favored his burned leg heavily. In the privacy of the dark front room, he sagged so hard against Alldera that she was obliged to stop and steady herself.

"It's all right," he muttered, taking a long breath. He let it out in low laughter. "Well, that's Servan to the marrow! I tie myself in knots to arrange an escort out of here for him, and he turns around and improvises his own spectacular departure!

"You must leave more discreetly—"

"And you?" she asked, knowing the answer.

"Do you think I came here just to punch an old man in the face?" he retorted. "I have more to do."

Yes; but she felt bound to offer him such wisdom as her kind had so painfully won: "It would take a man like Raff Maggomas to undo Raff Maggomas' work," she said.

"It took a man like Raff Maggomas to kill him," he snapped. "Undoing his work is the job of his son, if anyone. I'm going to obliterate him and everything of his. You understand me, don't you? I think Servan did, too, to some degree. Everyone but that creature that called itself my father . . ."

On some dark level all this made sense to her. She could think of nothing she could say to alter his resolve, nor any reason why she should want to.

"Take the footbridge," he said. "After that, your best chance is to head out of 'Troi on the inland side where the fighting should be thinnest. That's the way Servan will go, for the same reason. Show yourself judiciously among the rocks on the high slopes, and he'll find you. You're more valuable than ever now."

She twisted violently free of his hand, so that he stumbled and swore, catching at the furniture in the dark for support. Harshly he said, "You must see that if anyone can survive this upheaval it's Servan and whomever he protects!"

"Survival," she retorted, "is an overrated achievement. Survival as what? For how long? For what purpose? I understand you, and you understand nothing. You give the same moldy advice I'd get now from the Matris; you, of all people. Do you think you're the only one with the right to say 'no?'"

"So." He sighed. "We seem to be kin of some sad and foolish kind, and in spite of everything. But surely you don't mean to put yourself into the hands of these—"

"No." She moved closer to the map, beyond which the shadowy figure of the Second could be seen watching the plain, alone, from the parapet. "I'll go inland."

Bek limped after her, speaking with sharp apprehension. "But how will you live? Winter's coming!"

"I expect I'll starve. Frankly, I'd rather do that alone in the mountains than down here in the company of men eager to gnaw my bones."

"You'll find no mercy in the Wild."

"Good!" she cried. "I've had enough of what passes for that quality. Plain indifference will be a mercy."

"Even if you're carrying a cub?"

"There are cures for that, and neither men nor Matris in the Wild to prevent me."

"And if the Wild isn't empty after all?" he persisted. "If there are monsters?"

"I am experienced," she snarled, "at handling monsters."

She stopped, surprised. It seemed she was one of the Pledged after all now, perhaps the only one—except for Bek, who was pledged in his own way.

On impulse, she added, "You asked me once what you said about Kelmz, that night at the Scrappers'. I never told you."

In his silence, she became aware of the distant concussion of the guns. The sound made her jump with nerves. She hurried on. "What you said was that you were sorry; that it was unfair—Kambl was after you, not after Kelmz; that there were things you wanted to talk about, but there was no one to talk with seriously or deeply; that it was your fault. You were ashamed to have left him. You wanted to know him better. Sometimes you blamed him for throwing himself away, but most of the time you blamed yourself for leading him to his death. You said you were sorry.

"None of it could have been taken for lust except by a jealous or mischievous listener. What you expressed was grief for a lost friend."

He lifted his head. "I've tried to keep Kelmz out of my thoughts," he said, bitterly, "because there seemed to be no way to think of him that didn't shame both him and me. But it seems the shame is all mine.

"I must be a mature man now. As a boy, I was reputed to have been a clever student, but I've been stupid lately."

The dark shape of his head moved over the glowing lines:
from Endpath to Lammintown, and on down the coast.
"Right from that grim ride south with those wretched
pilgrims, to the fierce young men on the ferry, and your
own people at Bayo—so alarmingly efficient and not
nearly alien enough—that tangle of passions in the City,
even Bajerman, even Servan, and you yourself. Everything has sharpened my eyes to know Maggomas for a
monster when I met him. And I still couldn't see
something as simple as Kelmz and myself until you
showed me just now."

The light glimmered on the gaunt planes of his face and
on the cords of his throat as he turned toward her. "Will
you come closer? I want to show you something. These
marks, see them, among the ones that stand for the
mountains?"

"I don't know how to read writing," she said.

He caught her hand, drawing her to the map. She was
startled by the warmth and strength of the contact. He
was vibrant with excitement, even laughing as he said, "It
says _Refuge!_ If you can reach it, and if no 'Troimen are
stationed there, you might find shelter, tools, even food,
who knows? Look closely; could you find the way?"

It seemed to be a matter of following the river for most
of the distance. She nodded, feeling suddenly buoyant
and powerful.

"Good." He let go of her hand, stepping a firm though
crooked pace back from her. "And there won't be any
master along to push you around—or to entertain you."

Angrily, she shrugged. "It's just as well that our ways
part here. My hope lies in speed, and you can barely
hobble."

He barked a laugh. "Then what are you waiting for?
The Second may eventually stumble on the notion of
locking up a scarce item like yourself."

"I'd swallow my tongue first," she muttered, glancing
out at the Second. Bek looked, too, and abruptly seized
her arm and thrust her two stumbling steps back into
shadow. Another 'Troiman had joined the Second at the

parapet. They both turned toward Maggomas' quarters as they talked together.

"Will you go!" Bek exclaimed. His fingers tightened on her arm. The old dislike of a man's touch stiffened her. He drew his hand away at once, and stood panicked and silent, an angular shadow against the glow of the map.

She said, with a kind of angry desperation, "Safe journey then!"

She could just make out the glint of his bared teeth, the brightness of his eye.

In the absurdity of this farewell she left him.

She sat on the hillside, not knowing whàt she could still be waiting for. The sun came out and dried her hair and clothing. Down below the boats of the City men departed, except for two hulls that had been smashed during the fighting. 'Troi seemed a deserted ruin.

There was no doubt in her mind that its fall was Bek's doing. After the breaching of the palisade, he must have used his authority to order the demolition of the town before it was actually lost. Endpath to Endpath, his journey was complete. It was not for him that she waited.

Near sundown, she caught the first flickers of movement among the rocks high on the western slopes. 'Troi fugitives were converging on the wreckage, to scavenge what they might and cut the throats of any City men who had been left behind. When the men had all filtered down to the valley floor, her way would be clear.

At last in the deceptive twilight she saw d Layo. He swept by her, far on the right; she heard the hissing of the grass past his striding legs as he ran down the slope, gracefully zig-zagging to control his speed. While she looked, frozen still, he dropped out of sight below the next retaining wall down.

It had been like the passage of some hungry beast, one of those amoral, instinctual creatures that had fascinated Captain Kelmz. So strong was her impression of a hunting predator that she pictured d Layo cutting down some less clever survivor and feeding on the flesh, rank or not; and so he would, if necessary, as innocently ruthless as any beast. The valley into which he had gone seemed very dark now; there was something primeval in the thought of the survivors stalking one another among the ruins—all hunters, all quarry.

To the west, dim with distance but still visible in the rain-cleansed air, the mountains measured the evening sky like waves of the sea. A dusky autumn moon was rising and would soon give enough light to run by, even over unknown terrain. She decided to strike straight up the rise behind her, traveling westward along the spine of the ridge.

The muscles of her legs were stiff from the hours perched here on watch. She rose slowly and stepped from one foot to the other while she adjusted the straps of the pack so that it would ride snugly and not slip or chafe. A tune began in her head, weaving itself into the beginnings of a step-song for the journey: "Unmen, the heroes are gone..."

Without another glance back she started uphill with the slow gait of a runner warming up for a long, hard run.